# Ghost Story

# Ghost Story

## TOBY LITT

HAMISH HAMILTON
*an imprint of*
PENGUIN BOOKS

HAMISH HAMILTON

Published by the Penguin Group

Penguin Books Ltd, 80 Strand, London WC2R ORL, England

Penguin Group (USA), Inc., 375 Hudson Street, New York, New York 10014, USA

Penguin Books Australia Ltd, 250 Camberwell Road, Camberwell, Victoria 3124, Australia

Penguin Books Canada Ltd, 10 Alcorn Avenue, Toronto, Ontario, Canada M4V 3B2

Penguin Books India (P) Ltd, 11 Community Centre, Panchsheel Park, New Delhi – 110 017, India

Penguin Group (NZ), cnr Airborne and Rosedale Roads, Albany, Auckland 1310, New Zealand

Penguin Books (South Africa) (Pty) Ltd, 24 Sturdee Avenue, Rosebank 2196, South Africa

Penguin Books Ltd, Registered Offices: 80 Strand, London WC2R ORL

www.penguin.com

First published 2004

1

'The Hare' has previously been published in *Granta Best of Young British Novelists 2003*
'Foxes' in *Heat* 3, New Series, 2002 and *Matter*, issue no. 3, 2003

Lines from 'The Watershed' from *Collected Poems* by W. H. Auden are reprinted
by permission of Faber and Faber Ltd and Random House Inc.

Set in 11.5/14.25 pt Monotype Janson
Typeset by Rowland Phototypesetting Ltd, Bury St Edmunds, Suffolk
Printed in Great Britain by Clays Ltd, St Ives plc

A CIP catalogue record for this book is available from the British Library

HB ISBN 0-241-14278-4
TPB ISBN 0-241-14279-2

For Leigh

BRING A LIFE TO BREATH;
GIVE A GIFT TO DEATH

# STORY

# THE HARE

For some little while now I have been chasing a hare – buck or doe, I do not know; never yet have I managed to come close enough to check. It is lanky, manky, and quite as rapid as its name. This past month I have pursued the hare through a gallery, my memory, some postcards, and a half-dozen books. In recent days, the hare has gone to earth in the British Library; and it is here – seated on this chair, at this desk – that I would like to re-commence the chase. (Please excuse the Victorianism of my voice, but I can at present see no way other to make the approach – this task being so obviously illegitimate. I intend, for once, as an improvised Victorian, to ignore the wraiths of contemporary thought; unobjectifiers, soul-suckers.) I will, in this great library – cavernous yet luminous – on this wooden chair, at this wooden desk, attempt to hunt the hare haphazard; to examine the quotidian grasses, to sniff the wind of correspondence, to trace the found tracks of the intentional, to crumble or squidge the meant droppings, and to come – eventually – into the real presence of a real living literary animal-idea, and not kill it.

## WALES

Allow me, immediately, to digress; I should like to recall my first encounter with a hare – whether or not it was this same hare I now chase I do not know: I will assume that it was. We were in Wales for our summer holiday: mother, father, myself, and my sisters, Georgina and Charlotte. I was at a guess eleven. The antiques trade (my father's) must have been down that year; we usually went to campsites in France, staying in tents that someone else erected – pitched at the start of the season and struck at the end; we never had to touch a belay. This year, it was Wales instead. We were, at the hour I am concerned with, visiting a farm just outside Cardiff, I think; picking up some keys, perhaps. I remember two sheepdogs, an old and a young, both of which we children were warned not to stroke; they worked, were not pets. Whilst whatever transaction it was was taking place, I took myself off for an explore. There was a barn, high-full of hay-bales; and, standing in the farmyard, in the thick of its smell, I looked (bored) across to an abruptly rising hillside opposite – where for the first time stood the live hare. It was long and potential-fast, sometimes upright, and here a later quotation intrudes: Auden's 'Near you, taller than grass,/ Ears poise before decision, scenting danger.' I realise now, in setting this down, that Auden may not have meant a hare at all; just as likely a rabbit or a man. But, more likely still, Auden was happy – in his early ambiguity – for the reader to infer whatever they wished. And here, the crux left of the watershed, I have from the first wished a hare. In all its liveness, I can't have watched the original Welsh hare for more than a half-minute. Something happened, perhaps it detected – so fine its tremulous senses – my watching, and at a slender lope it was off, up, over the hill, out of sight. It gave the odd baroque to its straight, but was going where it was going and that was for definite. There isn't much else to be remembered from the holiday. We immediately left Cardiff and drove to a farm where the farmer's wife fed us a roast every day: Saturday was beef, Sunday lamb,

Monday chicken, and so on through pork, duck, and goose (not hare); on the last of the seven days we all of us wondered what variety of animal she had left that she could *possibly* roast (we were sick of roast), and the farmer's wife treated us to an encore of beef. I remember the farmer and his farmhands harvesting with tractors the corn, and this later was the seed of 'Moriarty' – a story from my first book. I remember going up alone into the grain store, and this became the source of a cancelled section of *deadkidsongs*. A day or two before we left, the farm bull got loose, and was only a four-bar iron gate away from me – its erection pointing toward the plain cows in a nearby field; it had already broken through one dry-stone wall in its quest of lust. The following year the antiques trade revived, and we holidayed in Corsica.

## 3

I am certain the hare is somewhere here in this library, perhaps in many of its places at once – for hares, unlike rabbits and men, are not limited to a single, logical location. There are books through which I know, even before I order and open them, it will have passed. *Brewer's Phrase and Fable* – in which I learn 'It was once thought that hares were sexless, or that they changed their sex every year.' Buck or doe, even the hare does not know. Another book I consult contains the first literary hare I pursued: Kit Williams's *Masquerade* – which began and became a world-wide search for a buried leporine effigy, fashioned (by him) of gold and jewels. Kit himself, unkempt arts- and craftsman, lived a couple of villages along the ridge from Ampthill, 'where the Princess lay' (Shakespeare, *Henry VIII*, Act IV, Scene I, line 28);

Ampthill, where I grew up. He buried his golden hare in Ampthill Park, at the foot of Katharine's Cross, set there as memorial to the locally popular Queen, imprisoned in the castle pending divorce by her heir-hungry husband, Henry. Queen, not Princess.

## ENGLAND

My next encounter face-to-face with the hare – though there must have been many now-forgotten glimpses after Wales – was at University. Oxford, in this as in all things, was a perversion; the hare, here, was paraded in its most debased form: jugged. It was also undercooked, by the worst college kitchens in the city, and caused just by itself a small student revolt against the contempt with which our college (Worcester) treated us. The Food Rep, exploiting the jugged-hare incident, and bringing about a brief improvement in the quality of our meals, was the following term elected President of the Junior Common Room. Like all revolutions, ours met disillusion the moment it paused. During the former Food Rep's time and term in office, it was discovered the college had been surcharging all undergraduates on the electricity in their rooms, illegally, since the Second World War. With power of bankruptcy over Worcester College, the President, representative of our revolution, made not even a few polite requests.

### 5

Joseph Beuys, about whom I first read at University, performed *How to Explain Paintings to a Dead Hare* in 1965 at the Schmela Gallery, Düsseldorf. The gallery in which the hare made its most recent reappearance, late last year, was Tate Modern. In a room dedicated to Beuys, I came across a copy of his *Drawings for Leonardo's 'Madrid Codex'* – a woman-hare, my sketch of which I reproduce below.

A few weeks later, whilst we were visiting some friends of ours in Sheffield, my girlfriend suffered her second miscarriage. I attempted to distract myself, in a hiatus of respite, by glancing through John Lehmann's *The Craft of Letters in England* – a copy of which, for some reason, was kept on a shelf in the upstairs toilet. Here I found a reference to Jocelyn Brooke, author of 'two impressively morbid short novels'. On coming to the great library a short while afterward, I ordered up a book by Jocelyn (buck or doe?). It turned out not to be a morbid novel, but a morbid book of verse. The one decent poem was 'The Song of Isobell Gowdie's which contained the lines: 'I shall go into a hare,/ With sorrow and sighing and mickle care/ And I shall go in the Devil's name/ Till I come home again.'

The library at this moment resembles nothing so much as a forest – an enchanted forest. And as I notice this, the chairs of the reading room begin to push up in strange columns, and the desks to spread out and settle, as if through long decay. I stand up, step back. I am not as amazed as I feel I should be; transformations were only to be expected. When the trunks of the desks finally touch the whitewashed ceiling, it shows itself to be wrought out as a thick leaf-canopy. I know it is only at night that the library is this empty, and so it occurs to me that an amount of unconscious time has passed. I am awake, definitely, without the excuses of dreaming. The moonbeams are the only infrequent light here – prinking through the canopy, slicing down in crisp diagonals. The air is almost balmy, and as the beams wink out and zip back, I can tell that the moon is riding high in a cloud-chased, cloud-ragged sky. The library now resembles nothing so much as the cover of the copy of C. S. Lewis's *Prince Caspian* which I was given to read at Alameda School, Ampthill. The desks have now subsided entirely into the needle-thick forest floor – which, spongy and spicy, beds out a silence that makes steps sound as thuds and thuds as thrums. Although I have no reason to go in any direction, I decide to head toward where the Issue & Return counter once stood. As I walk, I remember and recite the words of the poem, the words taken from Isobell Gowdie's confession, her spell: 'I shall go into a hare,/ With sorrow and sighing and mickle care/ And I shall go in the Devil's name/ Till I come home again.' I myself do not turn into a hare, despite reciting them twice more – thrice in total. But I do sight a rapid-moving summat up ahead – a horizontal streak, appearing in front of and disappearing behind the vertical rhythm of the treetrunks; a real rubato, a pulse. It is the hare, I am sure: I decide not to sprint after it, that would for both of us mean humiliation. (The chase is waiting.) Instead, I call out to it; I call out a name I am far from sure it has or will answer to: 'Isobell!' A hiatus. It is as if there had been a spell and I have uttered the counterspell: the streak stops, in a sighted gap and also in the gaze of a moonbeam, becoming a haunch-supported tower of fur. Its ears are searching for the second sounding of its name, which I then make: 'Isobell!' The hare turns in my direction and hurls its senses toward the source of its loud denomination – all of them falling on me at once; I am savoured, and even also somehow caressed. A third time, in fairytale fashion, I call the hare to me ('Isobell!') – and in obedience to the law of three, she comes; not so close that I can touch her, but closer than ever – in a living, inedible form – before. How am I sure she is a she? Sure because confirmation confirms sureness, and because I can't be I if she isn't she. 'I want to speak to you,' I say. 'You can't,' she says, in a soft Scottish voice, 'without you put on the coat.' As she says it I see it: though I can't be completely sure but that it appears at that moment; hanging from a low, hooklike branch – a long coat fashioned from the pelt of surely the largest hare that ever lived. *Sans* hesitation, I step across to it, lift it heavily off the hook and punch my arms into its forelegs. As I do so, I notice that long ears dangle from the hood. No sooner is the coat upon me than it begins to shrink, until coat becomes pelt – and I feel my clothes dissolving beneath it, like meat in the spittle of a fly. I realise that as well as being on the cover of *Prince Caspian*, I have also come to where the Wild Things are. (If I am Max, I am relieved to know that I shall be getting home before my dinner grows cold: it was all a dream, while a cliché from outside, is a reassurance when within.) Something else is altering, too: I feel my internal organs lengthen and tumble into place, like grains of tobacco rolling in a cigarette paper. It is from inside out that I realise I am changing, going as Isobell Gowdie at her trial said she did, into a hare. The trunks of the trees give me some marker against which I can judge my height; the hare I am becoming is up high on its haunches, but still its eyes are only four feet off the ground. Sounds stumble toward me, from the deep darkness of the enchanted forest – it feels not as if my hearing is improving but as if the world is rearranging itself so that far is now near. I realise, too, that there are many more noises on the very cusp of audibility – ones I can sense, sense the danger of, but not clearly depict to myself. These almost-sounds are the most useful, as they are those made by predators aspiring to silence. I hope at this moment that I will be able to retain such a developed sense when eventually I return to my human form, though cities would be unbearable. But then I realise, and it is the first time I feel horror, that I may have become a permanent hare. The realignment of my muscles feels dreadfully like the relaxation that I have been my whole life yearning toward, as if my new body were a hot bath of fragrant water in which I had just lain myself down. Isobell, the hare, turns and runs away from me into the enchanted forest. Awkwardly, I follow her – finding my way down the tunnel of her fourfold footfalls; awkward, I am, because I neither know how to move this imposed body nor do I have any idea of hare etiquette. I am the buck, she the doe – should I follow or not follow? I do not know. Is there already romance between us, by mere meeting? And if so, what will it need to be – a courtship of ludicrous dance followed by long monogamy proven to science by grief and pining after death? I realise as I come within sight of her scut that with each step onward I feel less awkward and more afraid of the awkwardness I would feel if returned to human form. We run for a long time, downhill, through a hollow that never seems to find a further edge. A librarian carrying a book strolls along between the wide, wide trunks of the trees of the enchanted forest. He does not seem in any way lost, although as he goes he is gazing upward toward the canopy in wonderment. Wherever he is he is a long long way away from the Issue & Return counter. I have time, a little time, to think, and I realise that it is only now, transformed, that I know the forest as enchanted; though I should, of course, have known before. The library also, I sense, as if it were one of the almost-sounds, is or was an enchanted place. The recognition of enchantment comes, though, not because I myself have become an enchanted creature (which should be proof enough), but because I am now alive in a different version of the world – more alive, and the world in turn seems more of a world; more keenly etched, more exactly sounded, and above all more powerfully scented. This sense (twitching my new nose) only fades in slowly, as we descend, like walking into a mist, and I believe I can understand why: if the intensity of smell-upon-smell-upon-smell had overtaken me in one instant, it might have killed me, or rendered me – at the very least – inane with shock. It would have been like, I can only think to say, being transported, in one's sleep, into the tympani section of an orchestra halfway through the 'Ode to Joy'. Isobell has now become easily traceable through her scent, which I find the most delicious of all those attempting to impress themselves upon me. Symphonic music is the best analogy with which I can attempt description: a low bass hum of forestness, of accreted scent (there are many dead things buried here); fleeting piccolo notes that spatter me for a moment and then evaporate – like petals brushed across one's eyelids; and all the sounding tones in-between, the pungent dungs, ghostly fungi, motherly mosses, cinnamonesque barks. We have reached the bottom of the hollow, the size of which I can no longer estimate – I sense around me extents of forest that may be due to distance or merely to an almost overwhelming intensity of added sensual detail. 'Here we are not at home,' says Isobell. 'We would like it elsewhere more.' And I know where – exactly where she means, to the very hedge and angle and grass-blade; her longing has conveyed itself to me or, more likely, was in me already only waiting to be called forth. I remember that great receptacle and distillation of English nostalgias 'The Old Vicarage, Grantchester': 'Say, do the elm-clumps greatly stand/ Still guardians of that holy land?/ The chestnuts shade, in reverend dream,/ The yet unacademic stream?/ Is dawn a secret shy and cold/ Anadyomene, silver-gold?/ And sunset still a golden sea/ From Haslingfield to Madingley?/ And after, ere the night is born/ Do hares come out about the corn?' This, though, is not the summit of Brooke's past-love, that Everestine peak is crumpets for tea. But just before his death, young Rupert returned for a second and greater thrust at the same image: 'A wind of night, shy as the young hare/ That steals even now out of the corn to play,/ Stirs the pale river once, and creeps away.' Am I a young hare? I realise that I have no idea. And yet, I feel something more than nostalgia in Brooke's conjured corn: it is an intensified, sensualized homecoming – just as Isobell's spell promised: 'Till I come home again.' And I remember the miscarriage in Sheffield, the sorrow and sighing and mickle care. I grieve again, at great speed that is in no way cursory, for our two lost babies. 'Where is the Devil?' I wonder – if we are going in his name, why doesn't he show himself, or does he show himself only in my altered form? I think, for one awful instant, that I may be losing the instinct of language – for a memory of corn overwhelms me, and it is as if the susurrus of each stem rubbing against each sister stem – all stupendously audible to the long, leporine ears with which I seem to have heard it before – it is almost as if this breeze-borne, breeze-created sound were orgasm. 'We do not belong here,' I say back to Isobell, although I still have no proof or agreement from her that Isobell is who she is. Now that I am as she, her lankiness has become the shape of archetypal desire and the musk of her manky scut, catnip. As one, we move: her thoughts inhabiting my body, my will prompting her muscles; the ground begins to rise, the far side of the hollow finally reached.

7

All along I had been expecting this quest after an image or idea or ideal to end with a confrontation with myself – myself as a hare upon a steep Welsh hillside gazing toward myself as a boy, within a twenty years' vacated farmyard. I did not foresee this journeying as a hare toward a hare's longing; neither did I foresee companionship.

IRELAND

# OUR FATHER

## I

As I was walking back from the tube station I allowed myself for the first time to think, 'I'm going to be a father.' It was an experimental thought – like trying on a pair of silly sunglasses when one has a longer than expected wait at the airport. Just as, then, one would have no intention of buying the glasses and having to accommodate one's self-image to their silliness, so, now, I had no feeling of permanent personal investment in this sentence. I let it appear in my mind; I gave it a second in which to flash like a neon sign; I wanted to watch the afterimage gently fade: but I had chosen a wrong moment – I was halfway across the small side road that runs alongside the station, and although it would be making melodrama to write 'I staggered', I certainly felt a lurch inside of me – as if I were a small car and a suitcase full of gold bars (I was going to say bricks) had just been hefted into my boot. No-one looking on would have noticed anything in my walk more unusual than a slight extra give at the knees; the thighs and hips dropping an inch or two lower than one might have expected.

## 2

The weather the previous day, at almost exactly the same time, would have been more fitting for this burdensome moment: there had been an April shower, the sky looked orange, electric, as if shot through a filter for an apocalyptic

xxiii

car advertisement; the sun was low enough to shine out from beneath the cloud canopy, which was thick towards the West but thinned out to nothing and blueness towards the East – where Canary Wharf stood as a wedge of silver, looking its absolute, optimistic best. As I walked home, stopping briefly just past the chip shop to put my umbrella (my girlfriend Leigh's, borrowed) up, I had thought: 'There will be a rainbow here, somewhere.' But it was only when I had reached the fourth-floor walkway outside our flat that I spotted it, to the right of Canary Wharf – which already looked duller, pewtery. Leigh was on the sofa, reading, and I called her out to come and look at the left foot of the rainbow – which was all that could be seen of it before it disappeared behind the side of our building. I told her how I had predicted it, and I felt glad to be ratified by her believing me.

3

On this, the following day, when I thought I'm going to be a father, the weather-moment was quite different, was sun-go-downy in a nondescript, no-season way. As soon as I was over the side road, more words came into my head – and over these ones I had far less control, they were not a neon sign, they were stray reflections of already emitted light. I thought: 'Our father, who art . . .' Which was shocking enough in itself. But very quickly, in parallel almost, I had two further thoughts; one was, 'I'm thinking that I'm God,' although this had been by a few instants preceded by, 'I'm going to be God,' which I suppressed by conversion before I'd even voiced it. The next thought was that 'Our father' might make a good title for something, for a story or a book. But this thought, too, had its almost-instant dismissal: Andrew O'Hagan had already I knew written a book called *Our Fathers* – it was a great title; it was his. Good luck to him. Bastard. I forgot this very quickly, in the turbulence of my reaction to the God-sentence; the second version of it was disturbing enough, but something of the first still echoed around. I thought. 'Did I really think that?,' or some self-dismissive, self-comforting version of that sentence. At the same time, I was aware that I had walked past the off-licence. Earlier in the day, during a phone conversation, Leigh had suggested that for dinner we have a curry delivered. My first instinct, drinkwise, was wine – red wine – but beer came in heavily an instant later; beer with curry, cold & gingery with throatburn, and the anticipated sensation of how quite fantastic and proper that would be. Concentrating on this – going into the shop, saying hello to whomever was behind the counter – this, too, would give me some means by which to suppress the internal fact that, a few steps back, I had thought that becoming a father would make me become God. As I pushed open the off-licence door, a few dregs of this thought trickled away; they were disturbed recapitulations, intended to make it easier for me to believe my own accustomed version of myself. 'I meant God for someone: I didn't mean God – I meant, that position of power.' Behind the counter in the off-licence was a young black woman whom I'd dealt with only once before. My wonderings about how she found working there, racism in the area being fairly bad and the off-licence having been subject to armed-robbery a couple of weeks earlier – my wonderings effaced the God-sentence pretty well completely. I took the six cans of cold beer home to find Leigh sitting on the sofa, reading. 'I bought you some beer,' I said.

## 4

I should add something about the knee-dip in my walk as I had the God-thought crossing the road – that is how my father walks, though I only realised this fact in writing this. My father's walk is magnificently ornate, it comprises so many separate micro-movements into the simple accomplishment of forwards-going: up, down, left, right, strange, charmed; lifting, swaying, swinging, lurching – I can't possibly sort out the order in which these differences synthesize. I think my father is aware of the magnificence of his walk; I think this because sometimes, when we were children, he used to parody it for us – pretending to reel, drunk, or to be about to collapse under our huge weight whilst giving one of us a shoulder ride. It sounds ungenerous, but when you see my father walking away from you, he looks like an elephant doing a John Wayne impersonation. He looks, I'd say, like God must look, walking away from you.

# OUR TWO

## I

I expect the text COME HOME, expect it every moment; and I know exactly what it would mean for us, for the next month, for years. So far there have been two (miscarriages, not texts) – I have names for them, nicknames: number one, November last year, is the Coil Baby and number two, January this, is the Shed Baby. Don't worry, I will explain. But this is all they publicly qualify for – nicknames; and though it may seem an over-writery thing to say, there really is a problem expressing them – any part of them – when their existence is and was so much a matter of their failing to come to existence.

## 2

The Coil Baby we didn't know we were having until we had already lost it. We were, in other words, bereaved before we knew we were or had been potentially parents – if that makes grammatical sense; I suspect it doesn't, but it makes emotional sense. My girlfriend, Leigh, hadn't had a period for longer than normal, but had been experiencing intermittent spotting. She thought there was something going on, so went to see the doctor. The consultation was on Thursday, and as part of it a routine pregnancy test was taken. Leigh's doctor said that the non-occurrence of her period might have one of three explanations: the menopause, a pregnancy or an ectopic pregnancy. The reason for this latter was that Leigh had had a coil in for about three years. (Hence 'Coil Baby'.) Leigh came back from the doctor's relieved at having done something to lessen the anxiety she had been feeling. On Saturday, she began to bleed heavily: it didn't seem like a normal period; it was painful – and the blood was not merely thick, it was substantial, clotted. Leigh was relieved that her periods had started again, assuming that's what it was; she was also relieved that, if it had been an ectopic pregnancy, it wasn't going to take and, possibly, cost her a Fallopian tube.

## 3

The following Thursday, Leigh returned to the doctor and was told, 'You're pregnant.' 'I don't think so,' Leigh said, and started to cry – when she could, she explained why. She came home and very quietly took me aside and told me (the cleaner was dusting in the living room). We went straight to St Thomas's Hospital, and were seen by a gynaecologist within the hour. I went into the consulting room with them. Leigh answered ten or so questions, and an internal exam was performed. Leigh lay back on the examining table; I sat by her side. The gynaecologist advised that Leigh have the coil removed – a course of action which would increase the chances of miscarriage occurring with this pregnancy (though we were in little doubt that the loss had already occurred) but would reduce the chances of one at a much later stage (if, that is, it was still viable). I held Leigh's hand as she looked away and the gynaecologist sought inside her for the coil. Leigh had been told by a close female friend, Alex, that the removal of her coil had been the most physically painful experience of her life. Leigh had delayed having her own removed for fear this would be true in her case as well. In the event, it came out very easily and with relatively little pain. The gynaecologist placed it on a wodge of tissue paper, and placed this in turn upon an equipment trolley beside the examination table. I found myself able to look at it: 'coil' does not describe its appearance. Instead, it was like a stainless-steel version of some fairly elaborate bacterium: a long tight spiral for a body, a loop at one end and a spray of feelers at the other. I was reminded of the small metal whisk in our cutlery drawer; we use it mainly for vinaigrettes. Whilst the gynaecologist went off to do something, Leigh too had a close look at her coil; I didn't ask whether she'd ever seen it before. It was bloody and slightly gooed. The gynaecologist was away for five, then ten minutes; Leigh wondered whether she had been meant to put her trousers on again. She had been wearing jeans, and didn't want to be caught bum-naked. I locked the examining-room door while Leigh began to wiggle them on. When she was finished, I unlocked the door. Still the gynaecologist didn't return. We were bored, and started to say things to make one another laugh. I can't remember the jokes or even imagine what they might have been, they were I'm sure much more for the moment than the memory. I glanced round the room, fascinated as always by the Sharps' Bin – intended for used syringes, scalpels, etc. A few months later I did an interview at the BBC, and was puzzled to see a Sharps' Bin on the desk in the small, green cubby-hole of a studio – then I realised: some of the programme editing was still done by splicing tape, and all those razorblades had to be disposed of safely. At the time I did not, or did not allow myself to, remember the circumstances in which I'd last encountered Sharps'. The gynaecologist returned; we were free to go – Leigh would have to return to St Thomas's for another pregnancy test, a third, the following week: to check her hormone levels were decreasing, and that there was no ectopic pregnancy, no pregnancy of any sort. We walked out of the hospital, mid-afternoon, both hungry: Waterloo offered pizza, sushi, noodles or bagels. We ate sushi.

4

The Shed Baby we knew we were having and therefore knew we were losing. Medical advice, after Leigh's hormones had returned to normal, was that we should not try to conceive until a full menstrual cycle had come and gone. We waited the minimum time, having realised through our Coil Baby how much we both wanted a child. Her fertile period coincided with a holiday we had planned for a while: in Southwold, in an old fisherman's shed called The Shed. (Hence 'Shed Baby'.) It is a colourful place, decorated with jungle-print curtains and many many carved and painted wooden parrots and other birds of paradise. We came to conceive, and we did. When Leigh's next period was one day, two days, three days late, we became excited, and finally on the fourth day we did the pregnancy test together. Clearblue – a horizontal blue line in the large square window and it's a yes, nothing and it's a no. I sat on the edge of the bath whilst Leigh peed over the absorbent end of the white plastic dipper. It looked like a novelty pen, without a nib (but not, the hateful punner in me thought, without a point). I went off to get something to time it with – 60 seconds the instructions said – but as I was coming back into the bathroom Leigh said, 'It's already there.' We held it up to our eyes, disbelieving and overjoyed. Having not seen the square window in its blank state, I couldn't be sure absolutely sure that the blue line really had appeared, hadn't been there all along. We took photographs of ourselves gleefully holding up the white plastic stick of yes – photographs which, two months later, having forgotten they were on the start of that particular film in that particular camera, I had developed. Leigh has still to ask to see them, though I told her a few days after this that I'd got them back. Five days after the positive test, Leigh had confided in one good friend, Alex, and I'd inadvertently told the cleaner, by stupidly asking if she'd any experience of nannying.

## 5

That Friday we took the train to Sheffield, where we were to stay with some friends – M, D and their son, J. We didn't tell them we were pregnant. On the Saturday we drove up and across the moors. We went through a village called Hope; I remembered Bill Clinton: 'I still believe in a town called . . .' There was another village the name of which I could find out but don't want to with a castle above it. Leigh told me in the gift shop, which we had to pass through to get to the zigzag path leading up the steep grassy hillside to the castle. She was distraught but in control. 'I'm bleeding,' she said. Her voice thrilled with potential panic. She excused herself from the climb up to the castle, and went with M to a tea shoppe down in the village. I went through the stupidity of looking over ruined tower and walls and defences, of which I remember every detail. When I got to the tea shoppe, Leigh went again to the toilet, came back and confirmed to me what was happening. On the walk back to the car, I took M aside and explained. She phoned a doctor friend whilst Leigh and I, stepping out of the wind, did our best to comfort one another. The doctor recommended we go to the hospital, which we did. During the drive, the sun came out. This time we did not have an hour's wait and we saw a nurse – a non-specialist. A young man, he spent most of the consultation speaking directly to the electronic multiple choice form on his computer. He wasn't cruel or crass, merely unable to disguise how routine to him our little tragedy was. There was nothing to be done – nothing apart from 'take it easy' for a few days. Leigh and I went back to the house of our friends, and continued what had just become the worst, most embarrassing, most tender weekend. We had decided to stay, not take the train home. This time the pregnancy was more advanced, and the miscarriage was by that measure more physically extreme and emotionally distressing: we spent most of the afternoon in bed, and almost managed to sleep, then went out to dinner with M, D and J to celebrate D's birthday at the best restaurant in Sheffield.

# TELLING

Yesterday Alex guessed and Leigh confessed. It was a short-storyish detail which had given Alex her clue: at a friend's thirtieth birthday party, as Leigh and I were getting up to leave Alex saw me put my hand on her tummy. So it wasn't what we'd been worried about: that someone would notice Leigh wasn't drinking. This afternoon, we spoke on the phone; Leigh in her office at work, me working at home. Leigh is going out this evening with some of her other female friends; we have decided she can tell them, too. She is sure they will ask; she is fairly sure some of them have guessed already. 'I'm not very good at lying,' she said. 'How is it,' I asked, 'that other people are able to keep it secret until three months?' I had become superstitious about three months: conventionality was there for a reason, I illogically reasoned – if we followed it, it would keep us safe. 'I suppose,' said Leigh, 'because they haven't gone round telling everyone how much they want to get pregnant for a year beforehand.' I tell her that telling everybody is more her way of doing things than mine, and that she shouldn't blame me if I am slower in telling my friends than she in telling hers. When she asks me for a reason why she shouldn't, the only thing I can find – apart from superstition – is a wish that she keep as emotionally level as possible. 'What,' she said, 'do you think it's going to communicate to the baby?' 'It's just,' I said, 'I wouldn't want you going on a real trampoline – I'm not sure about you going on an emotional one, either.' What we have decided, in essence, is that this is going to be a public pregnancy (we are at seven weeks); if it is a miscarriage, too, it is going to be a public miscarriage. I put down the phone and went back to writing. We had also decided, whilst on the phone, not to tell our parents yet. It is the Antiques Fair at Battersea this week and weekend; we could go and tell my parents (who have a stall of French provincial furniture). But it was at the last fair that I told my father of our first miscarriage, even though we'd already done a test and knew Leigh was pregnant for a second time. Within a week she wasn't, and there was more telling to be done. A very small part of the time – or perhaps, put better, in a small sick part of me – I hope something does go wrong. Firstly, that appeals to the rational side of me: miscarriage is not treated as repeat miscarriage until the third occurrence. If this pregnancy terminated, there would be hospital visits, tests, explanations, recommendations – possibly, or possibly we would just be told to go away and try again in loving hope. My rôle in all this would be simple, definite. Instead it feels as if I have been asked to keep my fingers crossed for nine months. My fingers are already starting to hurt: I'm worried they won't ever go back into shape again. Secondly, it appeals to the irrational side of me: conforming to my worst fears. I think bad things, I write them, and sometimes after I've written them they happen. I am terrified not only of a baby carried to term but of a baby born deformed. During pregnancy, one attracts horror stories; tragedies seem to have occurred just to be brought to your attention. I heard recently of a woman who at six or seven months learnt that her foetus had died, and yet there was nothing for her to do at such a late stage but carry it dead to full term. This woman went to work, all her colleagues knew. How must it have been for her, chatting during coffee break? How must it have been for them, to share in a work situation something that tragic? Perhaps this didn't happen, was just an urban myth. I think about Down's Syndrome and about the character in *Finding Myself*, Fleur, who has a foetus aborted because the test for Down's comes up positive. What else am I left with but superstition? Which is why the protection of three months before telling has become so important: it's all that I could do.

Keep off the trampoline, my love.

## IT HAPPENED AND IT DIDN'T HAPPEN

'Toby,' Leigh's voice came to me, in my study, from where she stood, in the bathroom. Her tone was quite plain, although not neutral; it was transparent with urgency – and context, or lack of context, made it even more compelling: Leigh said nothing else, just my name. And yet I heard it as if it had been spoken by quite another person, by my daughter – by the possibility of her that it announced and at the same time, I was already beginning to sense as I pushed back my chair, threatened with denial. First, I replied, 'Yes?' Second, I ran: in the interim, I had decoded the lack of context because I had understood it could only mean one thing – the thing. (I expect a text: come home.) 'Toby,' meant come home. Leigh was standing up from the toilet, her jeans pushed halfway down her legs and her black panties stretched across between her thighs. I don't remember what she said: 'There was some blood,' or 'I'm bleeding.' My collapse was almost immediate, and hers followed as soon as she saw mine: we held one another, and I found nothing better to say than, 'God,' and 'I don't want this to happen.' The two sentences were not intended to be connected: 'God, I don't want this to happen,' or 'I don't want this to happen, God.' At first, they were the only things I found sayable. Then I asked questions – about the blood, its appearance. I went into the living room, found the book on pregnancy that Leigh had been browsing when I saw her last – in an entirely different version of the universe – kissing her and going into my study; from where, a quarter of an hour later, 'Toby.' The book was something to hold on to, a hope. In the index I found bleeding; I was looking for the possibility of any cause other than miscarriage. There was only one page reference, and it was in the section just before Miscarriages, but it gave me what I needed: a quarter of all women may experience some bleeding during pregnancy. I showed this to Leigh, she now standing in the hall with her jeans and panties still where they had been at the moment she cried out to me: we were already, even if only in imagination, one step away from the worst. But as Leigh put a pad into her panties and I sat on the sofa weeping into my hands, we were both thinking that step: the same thing, again, for the third time. Leigh sat down. We held one another. When we had stopped crying, so that we could talk, we tried to decide what we should do, GP, hospital or NHS Direct? Here we diverged: I thought that spotting might not be taken all that seriously, and that if we went to the hospital they might simply send us home again. I didn't want Leigh to have to make that journey unnecessarily. The GP was never that easy to get to see, so we decided I should call NHS Direct. It was Monday morning, and I spent several minutes on hold. I gave a telephonist some details. Plinky electronica played in my ear, making me think of all the people in even worse situations than our own who had had to listen to this; how some must have died, with this the last music they ever heard. Eventually I was told that all the nurses were busy, but that one would call us back, soon. She did; she asked if she could speak to Leigh. Leigh was too distressed, so the questions had to pass through me. Was there any abdominal pain? What was the appearance of the blood? As I asked Leigh, I put the receiver against my right shoulder – the place where one would hold a baby one was burping. The nurse suggested we go to a hospital in

Tooting. I said we'd been there before, though I was wrong: it was to St Thomas's, opposite the Houses of Parliament, that we had gone to on the previous occasion. Leigh reminded me of this once I was off the phone. The nurse, very sincerely, wished us well – and, to my surprise, her words made things slightly better; to have moved a professional dealer-with-pain, and over the telephone: we counted. We decided not to go to Tooting but to St Thomas's. Leigh found their number, and I called; they said we could come in, but they couldn't guarantee us a slot for a scan. Leigh said she wanted to go; we went. The taxi I'd ordered took about five minutes to come. The driver, luckily, didn't want to chat, even though it was a beautifully sunny morning, and perfect as a conversational opener. Perhaps Leigh's dark glasses informed him of our mood, or perhaps the mere fact we were going to the hospital. Dropped off, we found the ward, which had recently changed its name from 'Early Pregnancy Unit' to 'Emergency Gynaecology'. It had moved, too, since Leigh was last there – A4 photocopied sheets taped to the walls directed us once out of the lift to keep going down this corridor and this corridor. We came to a waiting room, like any waiting room, sufficient variety provided for us by the extremity of what we were awaiting. Afterwards Leigh remarked, 'No-one else there looked particularly upset.' One Australian girl who had experienced vaginal bleeding after sex seemed, in fact, quite bouncy about it. Leigh filled in a form, spoke to the receptionist (whilst other women stood beside the desk, able to overhear everything – as we had overheard about the Australian girl's vaginal bleeding). When she had told them all she needed, she came back to sit with me, read magazines and wait. In some ways, I think these cruel hospital rituals are wise and deliberate: having to speak about one's most intimate health details in the hearing of others prepares one for the internal examination by a stranger in white; waiting for an extended period helps one control one's emotions so that one can talk fairly rationally to the nurse. I read *Dombey and Son*, not realising the irony of the title until later. (An irony similar to having my broken-down hero reading *Bleak House* at the end of 'It Could Have Been Me and It Was', the first story in my first book.) A slot was found for Leigh, shortly before twelve. A doctor called out her name and, as she walked us to the examination room, tried to make us feel calm by saying, 'I'm Serena, and I'll be doing your scan today.' This, too, seemed wise: the Americanism of it distanced us from what was about to take place; the echo of 'I'm Chet, and I'll be your Cabin Assistant for today,' had us mentally fastening our seatbelts and putting our seatbacks in the upright position. In the small, dim room, Leigh was instructed to undress – bottom half only. There was a divan onto which Leigh climbed. The doctor explained she would be looking at the screen for a while herself, then she would explain what was going on to us. As she said this, she pulled a condom onto the plastic probe and lubricated it. Thank you, Serena, for in fact you turned the screen towards us almost as soon as the scan began – 'There,' you said, pointing to a white circle inside another white circle, 'there's the heart.' And, looking like an eye, blinking, blinking, there it was – beating.

# IT HAPPENED

At some point during the following events, the baby's heart may have stopped beating. After leaving the room in which the scan had taken place we went back into the waiting room, where we'd been sitting since a quarter to nine. The view from the window was of midday rain falling on the Thames, falling on the Houses of Parliament – though Big Ben was only visible from the office into which we were called a few minutes after the scan. The senior nurse, who I won't name, though I have no criticism of her treatment of us, was immensely reassuring: once a heartbeat was visible the chances of miscarriage decreased to around 4 per cent. Reassurance was just what we needed, even after seeing the scan – the bleeding might possibly continue for another seven months; we needed something to keep our morale up during that long time. The baby was 'fine': there was no necessary link between bleeding and miscarriage; the senior nurse had had bleeding throughout her own third (successful) pregnancy. In a couple of weeks Leigh could go along to what they actually called a 'Reassurance Clinic'. As we left she told us that this was all good practice for being a parent; when we were parents we wouldn't be without worry for eighteen years, or longer – for the rest of our lives. We walked out of the hospital, embracing in the corridor, in the lift, in the rain outside. I tried to allow myself to feel joy. Leigh said, when I asked, that she wanted coffee and a croissant. The nearest place was Starbucks, halfway between St Thomas's and the South Bank Centre. A voice from one of the darkest, unhappiest corners within me speaks up, saying: 'It's your fault. You made this happen. This was your punishment for lapsing into the corporate – which you normally manage to avoid: in terms of coffee, anyway. The baby died here, Starbucks.' Leigh ordered a decaf latte and an almond croissant; I had latte – heightening my high with unnecessary caffeine. We took our breakfast to a table, and talked in half-hushed voices, voices that couldn't believe their luck. We repeated to one another the nurse's reassurances, each saying what they said as much for themself as for the other. A minor television personality came in for a meeting; we heard her talking on her mobile. We discussed what to do with the unexpected rest of the day: both of us, earlier on, had thought mostly of a return home and to crying and the beginning of grief. Instead, we went to the Hayward Gallery, at which Sam Taylor-Wood's first major retrospective was in its opening week. Leigh said she would like to go there because she might not have the chance to visit galleries for too much longer. On the walk past the London Eye, we both of us called our parents to let them know the good news: I spoke to my father, Leigh to her mother. Outside the Hayward was a large poster for the show, 'Self-Portrait in Single-Breasted Suit with Hare'. As a review pinned to a corkboard in the foyer explained, the suit was a reference to Sam Taylor-Wood's cancer-caused mastectomy, the hare to the regrowth of her hare-coloured hair following chemotherapy. Hospitals. When we'd gone through the whole retrospective, Leigh said that this (the hare) was her favourite of all the works we'd seen that day – and I got the feeling she liked just as much the poster version we'd seen outside as the cibachrome in the first room we entered. Walking away from the Hayward, heading for the tube, we discussed video art – of which much of the retrospective was comprised. This, I don't have to remind myself, but I do have to remind you, could have been the point; halfway across the empty concrete behind the Royal Festival Hall – that may have been it. We will never know – a sentence I was to hear a great deal too much of in the following week. The work I liked best was 'Still Life', a time-lapse film of a bowl of ravishing fruit fulfilling their mouldy vocations. I had already seen this, and about half of the other pieces, in Sam Taylor-Wood's show at White Cube² (February). I told Leigh to wait with her eyes closed until the loop was right at the start, with the apricots and peaches at their most fragile/ impeccable. Now? The best of the works I hadn't seen before was '*Noli me tangere*', the meaning of which tag I'd forgotten but which, looking it up now in my *Dictionary of Foreign Words and Phrases*, is 'Do not touch me'. This, in the context of the other works in the room, one of which, a *pietà* with Sam Taylor-Wood cradling the act-dying body of reformed Hollywood reprobate/coke fuck-up Robert Downey Jr, this was a reference to paintings representing, so the *Dictionary* tells me, 'the reappearance of Jesus to Mary Magdalen at the sepulchre (John 20:17)'. I look up the biblical verse, and find it to be: 'Jesus saith unto her, Touch me not; for I am not yet ascended to my Father: but go to my brethren, and say unto them, I ascend unto my Father, and your Father: and to my God, and your God.' In ignorance of this, I saw a double-sided video projection – very tall, perhaps sixteen or seventeen feet tall – of a muscular man doing a handstand; however, he was projected upside down, so that it appeared he was not resting on the floor but, Atlas-like, holding the ceiling up. For just over three and a half minutes, slightly slowed down from real life, I think, the man tried to hold off his inevitable collapse, to hold himself at full ceiling-and-floor-touching extension. Looking at him, I thought there was a possibility I might start weeping – having made the direct analogy between his struggles of maintaining supportive form and my own; I didn't: the image moved me but also distanced me from myself. After exiting the show, we went and bought postcards – and I bought Leigh a copy of *High Art Lite* by Julian Stallabrass, which she said she wanted to read. I bought a couple of postcards of the 'Self-Portrait . . .' to go in my 'After the Hare' file. Then, quite possibly whilst our baby was dying inside her, Leigh talked to a market researcher with a clipboard and twenty questions. Yes, she was a member of the Tate and the Royal Academy; No, we didn't have a regular Sunday paper. Walking to the underground station we passed a busker playing a penny whistle, badly. Superstitious about such things, I forecast disaster to myself if I didn't give him some money: whenever I cross the Thames on foot, I give money to the first beggar or busker I see; this is my payment to Charon, who ferries souls across the river Styx. This time I was several steps past before I realised the doom, and by then – because Leigh was with me – I felt embarrassed about going all that way, that increasing way, back, to give money to a busker who wasn't even any good. We took the escalator down to the Jubilee Line, and I promised myself that I would give twice the amount of money to the very next busker I saw: I hoped for one in the station, but one wasn't there. Outside Borough Market, where we went next, there was a beggar beside the cash-point – but I realise now that I didn't fulfil my superstitious promise to myself, and didn't give him any money. We went into the market, perhaps doomed, our doom perhaps already having come, and went and bought bread. Then we went home.

# AFTERWARDS

I am going at points to allow myself to be angry, starting now.

Please come in. Did you find it alright? Let me give you the tour. This in here, to the left off the hall, is the bathroom, which is where Leigh had the miscarriage – on the toilet, into the toilet. After the first burst of our grief, which I'll describe in a little while, she picked the baby and its accoutrements out of the water and put it into a plastic freezer bag that I'd fetched at her request from the kitchen. I did not see this retrieval, she closed the bathroom door whilst I stood crying in the living room – through there. I also sat, I think, on the arm of the sofa – which is blue, cheap and which we have been meaning to get rid of for about a year. Leigh didn't want me to see what had come out of her. 'It won't help,' she said. I told her I wanted to see it. I said that I felt left out – I meant that *otherwise* I would feel left out. I didn't want that door closed upon me, too; I felt a need to see everything. She showed me, or rather let me look: the freezer bag was lying there, on the window sill. I picked it up, held it in my hands close to my face; I was wailing, not speaking, and my words were, 'I loved that.' I won't describe what I held, yet. Instead, I'll describe as promised our grief – but let's go through into the living room with the unlovely blue sofa. We came in here when it came time to decide what to do. Before then, we stood in the hall. I was behaving, with my voice and my body, as I'd only ever seen – and disbelieved – actors in Greek and Shakespearean tragedy. Extreme grief, perhaps, has brought me to a greater respect of bad acting, of truly full-hearted overacting. The tears went straight down my face, I could feel them; they only spread across my cheeks because I sometimes moved my head, shook it, violently, or crushed it onto Leigh's shoulder as she crushed hers onto mine. I tried to say things that would be of some comfort to her: that I loved her, and that I didn't regret a moment of the past eight weeks – that it had been a special time. In the bathroom, whilst kneeling in front of her, the first thing after she'd told me she was certain what had happened, I had said that I loved her, and that however terrible this was it was still part of my love for her. I'm not quite sure what I meant by this, perhaps something similar to what I said later, in the kitchen – that however painful this was, she had brought me so much joy that the pain didn't even compare. I thought of Dustin Hoffman's bouffant-haired Hollywood producer in the film *Wag the Dog* (which I'd watched on the TV in the corner over there a couple of days before). 'This?' says Hoffman, whenever disaster strikes. 'This?', whenever all seems absolutely lost. 'This is nothing ... This is a walk in the park.' This – for us – wasn't nothing, nor a walk in the park; but I wanted to say that, comparatively, it was nothing. I'm no longer sure if this was the right thing to say; at the time I felt it was and so I said it. (All through, I was less uncensored about what I said but, in trying to speak out of tenderness, I was aware of taking great care with my words.) Those flowers there, on the console table, are from my parents and were delivered this morning – making us cry. I was again sitting on the sofa, a while after the cry from the bathroom, perhaps an hour, when I phoned St Thomas's. I was, as usual, put on hold – more hospital wisdom, perhaps; calm them with delay. The tune that played, to placate me and

xlvi

others, was a tinny version of Bach's 'Air on a G String'. I was waiting to ask whether they wanted us to bring the embryo in, for them to do tests on it. Even in my distress, I was amused to be subjected to this supposedly bland piece of electronica. It reminded me inevitably of our American summer holiday the previous year. After checking with the company that our hire car would have a CD-player, I had selected about fifteen soundtracks for driving. California demanded the Beach Boys' *Greatest Hits*. Driving down to Venice Beach we had allowed ourselves the delightful obviousness of 'California Girls'; driving out of Yosemite National Park, I had been half-annoyed, half-amused by the nagging 'Lady Linda' – ripping the melody, as you probably know, off Bach's 'Air on a G String'. What different people we were then, I thought, as I waited for someone in Emergency Gynaecology to pick up. How changed by this we will be – have already been. When St Thomas's answered the phone, I explained our situation. They said to come in, but didn't require us to bring the embryo. Let me show you the kitchen. It's quite small, with yellow walls I now regret painting that colour. You may have noticed the bright violet-mauve of the bathroom – that was chosen by the girl I originally moved into this flat with. The yellow was, too; the living room used to be even worse – lime green and tangerine, the colour of lime- and tangerine-flavour Tic-Tacs. It's now, as you saw, a tasteful antique white. Here is the fridge, where I put the freezer bag and everything it contained, after we'd got back home from the hospital. Leigh cleaned out the bottom shelf in the door. We were already thinking of burying the baby, and Leigh had found something to act as a coffin – a baby-blue box with the words TIFFANY & CO. on the cover: it was oblong-shaped and very shallow. The allusion to diamonds, and what was sparkling, rare and precious seemed a good one. I folded the freezer bag carefully, ceremonially, and placed it inside the box – which I then placed in the cleared space in the fridge. Right there. If you turn round and come with me to the other end of the hall, we'll enter my study where I'm writing this now. To our right, halfway along, is Leigh's room. We won't go in there – but you see this postcard she has on the door, it's Freud's couch, bought at the Freud Museum. Here I am, at my desk. This is exactly where I was sitting when Leigh first called out my name. After that, I was involved with deciding whether or not we should go to the hospital. For some reason I took my mobile phone into our bedroom, which is just next door and we'll see in a minute. On the desk in front of me, resting on top of one of my black notebooks, is the stone Leigh picked from the beach in Southwold after we'd had our little burial service. Let's go into the bedroom – where, on the rich red bedspread, Leigh had her contractions. It was a particularly cruel parody of childbirth we had to experience: very short, very confusing. All through, I kept asking Leigh what kind of pains they were? Could it possibly be constipation? When was the last time she went to the toilet? (That morning.) This seems particularly absurd and grotesque, now – considering what was really going on. Absurd and grotesque were the words, was the phrase I later used to describe how I felt anything we did to dispose of the baby might be, if we were not careful. 'I don't want to flush it down the loo,' I said. 'I don't want to put it in the bin.' Initially (this was after we'd returned from the hospital), we decided to bury it in the park next to our house. I had some worries about this; us never being able to go in there without being confronted by our grief. Then Leigh said, when I asked her what she really wanted to do, 'I want to go to The Shed.' It was a fantastic idea, and first thing the following morning we hired a car, and after an excruciating wait for it to be delivered, we drove up to Southwold. I put the Tiffany's box in a black carry-all, about which I became very self-conscious, for I had offered the young man who brought our car a lift to the underground station. He might ask what was in it. I was equally self-conscious about the bag as we walked out onto the sand dunes at Southwold about three hours later. We had made good time, our speed increasing in direct proportion to our distance from London. In the car we played the Beach Boys' *Greatest Hits*, singing along to the bastardized Bach of 'Lady Linda'. Arriving in Southwold, we parked and walked back to a hardware store where we debated whether to buy a spade, a trowel or two trowels. I dreaded us being asked what we wanted them for – the young man delivering the car had already asked us where we were going, why we were going there. With disguised emotion we told him Southwold, and said we were just going to get out of town. 'It's good sometimes to just get out of London, isn't it?' he said. It was good; it was the best thing we could ever have done. We walked out with our black carry-all containing a baby-blue Tiffany's box containing a freezer bag containing what it contained. This was the second time in a week that I had felt like a funeral director. The first was whilst scattering my Uncle James's ashes – this we had done on the Wednesday, my mother (his sister), my father, me and Val (his last girlfriend). I said very little, not wanting to pretend to be a more important part of the occasion than I was. But a moment came when they had finished with the ashes (my mother and Val spread them widely, over the bluebells) and cried, and stood in a circle, and said a few private things; the two urns, one pottery and one plastic, were still in my mother and Val's hands. I was able to relieve them of the interference of carrying them, and put them carefully back in the cardboard box. I don't know why, but I felt it very important that I did this carefully – as if the urns were somehow sentient, and would know whether or not I was treating them with respect. This was odd, as I had been the one to carry the box – then containing two ash-ful urns – from the car up the hill to the chosen spot; and, at that time, I'd had no particular sense of James being in my hands. In fact, I tucked him under one arm; a position which seemed less solemn, less ceremonial and therefore more in keeping. I think that's what we all felt: we were doing this as if James were indeed present – ready to mock anything that was false or forced. When we stood together, in that circle, I think we were all aware that we were the most there would ever again be of James. I remembered this three days later, on the dunes at Southwold, when Leigh told me I can't, and I was left gently to tip the contents of the freezer bag into the small hole we'd dug into the grass-covered sand. As it was all we could do, we did it as well as we could.

# CALLING IT IT, CALLING IT A BABY

Or, in fact, writing about the subject, the incident, at all: isn't this merely grotesque and absurd? For *Corpsing* I did an amount of research into embryos and foetuses; one book mentioned in the Acknowledgements was particularly useful – Ulrich Drews's *Color Atlas of Embryology*. During this last pregnancy, Leigh and I got the *Atlas* down from the shelf to see what the baby would look like at seven and a half weeks. All the books I used in researching *Corpsing* had been kept together, and the *Color Atlas* had been sandwiched for over a year between *Gunshot Wounds* by Dr Vincent di Maio and Elizabeth Bronfen's *Over Her Dead Body*. I have forgotten most of the research I did; this, I think, is how it is with novelists – we are by nature generalists, able at very short notice to fake up expertise on almost anything. Looking at it again, now, I see and remember that the embryonic period lasts from the fourth to the eighth week; it is known as organogenesis. In pencil I had underlined the following: 'The embryo assumes a human shape and the large organ systems of the body – bones and muscle, gastrointestinal canal, liver, heart, and lungs, as well as kidneys – are established.' The embryonic period is followed by the foetal period, usually. After we had buried the baby and driven home, Leigh said, 'But it looked so perfect.' I was reminded, as so often in extreme situations connected with family, of *The Godfather: Part II* – the scene towards the end, during which Michael Corleone demands to know whether Kay's terminated pregnancy ('It was an abortion, Michael – it was an abortion!') was a daughter or a son. I have to admit that I am finding the idea of abortion particularly difficult to deal with. I realise that my principles haven't changed, and that I am still – as you'd put it briefly – in favour of a woman's right to choose. But as I looked around the waiting room of the Emergency Gynaecology Department on the day of the miscarriage, the thought that some of these women might decide to have abortions – or that, in another department of the same hospital, pregnancies were terminated as late as eighteen weeks – I found both these things very upsetting. I wanted to plead with these women to have the babies, if they had been lucky enough to carry them that far. Not particularly rational, although this feeling had a great emotional logic. What we lost was an embryo, whose sex will never now be determined. (Michael Corleone finds out that he has been denied a son.) And so, Leigh and I are left with genderless 'it' as all we can call it. A good friend of ours, Ian Sansom, recently wrote a book called *The Truth about Babies*, in which he collects together a vast number of infant-related quotes. When I was thinking the other day, at the local tube station, of writing something about calling it it, I remembered this one: Jerome K. Jerome, 'On Babies', from *Idle Thoughts of an Idle Fellow* (1886): 'If you desire to drain to the dregs the fullest cup of scorn and hatred that fellow human beings can pour out for you, let a young mother hear you call her dear baby "it".' Ian was the only close friend of mine that I told about the pregnancy *during* the pregnancy. In a way, Leigh and I do find ourselves, every time we hear ourselves referring to the baby as 'it', brewing cups of scorn and hatred that we ourselves – through no fault of our own – have to drink. We sometimes refer to it as 'the baby' but have not dared give it a proper name of either gender. Perhaps we should pick one that does for both: Alex, say. But Leigh's equivalent friend to

Ian is called that, so it won't do. I have told Leigh, once, that I thought of the second miscarried embryo as the Shed Baby; I could tell her that I called the third the Scan Baby, but it is far from tender.

# FOXES

When my wife gave birth to three foxcubs, I just couldn't take it any more; I took off – across country, hoping to find a sufficient difference in the wildwood. Within minutes of being born, the foxcubs had been tearing at the books on the lower shelves, some of them my own. I mean, written by me. It was a day of long wide high grey, not drizzle but as if the air were fuller of moisture even than during a downpour. The North Sea was on top of us; the month of March. The foxcubs had also been greatly attracted to toilet- and tissue paper; it was clear there could no longer be any place for me, in such a house. The three floors were two of them Elizabethan, one Georgian – you could tell by the size of the windows and the height of the ceilings. I would like to say I was sorry to leave but climbing through the fence at the sloping edge of a fallow field, just as the sun was being consumed by the horizon, I felt a sense of abysmal homecoming. The trees: their trunks were ivy-troubled and their upper boughs burdened with mistletoe. A few hundred yards in, I started while there was still enough light to construct a hide. I had not brought a billycan, though my penknife was in my inside jacket pocket along with a sprig of lavender, some folded paper and a very expensive pen. I had heard twelve very small feet, chasing me across the field, and ran like a maniac, but when I looked behind I saw only the opposite hedgerow. Unable to sleep, I was unable also to prevent myself from remembering the early days of the pregnancy – the first trimester during which my wife had become convinced there was a fishbowl in her belly – she even knew what kind of tropical fish it contained: Clown Fish. She developed the notion they were laughing at her. The salt water in which they had to be kept (inside her belly) made her feel nauseous from the moment she woke up to the moment she projectile-vomited, usually around fifteen minutes later. After that, she began to feel accustomed to it: 'We were sea creatures once, weren't we? I wonder what the pH of my amniotic fluid is. I imagine it to be like the vinegar in a jar of pickled eggs.' These conversations worried me; I was left no room within them but agreement, for how could I critique her sensations? In an attempt to distract her, I put posters of deserts from around the world on the walls of the kitchen – which was where we spent most of our waking time together. A man walked past, about ten feet away from my wildwood hide; he was accompanied by two cocker spaniels with whom he was engaged in very intense, though quite one-sided conversation. '. . . we shall do that, shan't we? And then afterwards we'll go back and we'll sort everything out. We'll leave the left side and the right side roughly as they are; but we'll move the middle up and darken in. There needs to be a smear, diagonally . . .' He was so enraptured by his words that I could probably have stood in the path blocking his way and he still wouldn't have seen me – unless one of the dogs had taken notice of my scent. But I worried that, on the way back from his walk, I might be discovered, asleep: I moved my hide further from the path. Night was now as dark as it was going to get; I had wanted to hear an owl, and I did a few moments later. It was at this point that I decided to think consecutively about the stages of the pregnancy, ticking off mental boxes. The first trimester ended with our visit to the nearest big hospital for a scan. The three foetuses were arranged head-to-toe-to-head, like slaves space-savingly arranged in a slave ship. This thought was interrupted by a splash of anxiety: How much was my house worth? How much had I lost by leaving it? How much would my wife be able to bank if she sold it and moved, with the three little foxcubs, into rented accommodation? The moon had come clear of the clouds it had been bathing in milk, and now shone a day or two off full, but most likely the brightest it would be all month. Another idea I tried to repress was of sending a postcard, a confessional postcard, to myself at home – containing in the text something so hurtful and hateful that I would have to return before it arrived, in order to be there to intercept it and prevent my wife from reading it. The dogwalking and dogtalking artist had not returned; perhaps his perambulations were circular – or perhaps I had caught him on the homeward leg – or perhaps he was in the pub. I felt a desire to see the painting he had been describing and this, in its weak way, reminded me of the second trimester and its black nightmares. My wife became convinced of a series of abominations, concerning myself and her and our children-to-be. Although the nurse present at the scan had assured us that the wombic arrangement of the foetuses was textbook, my wife had become convinced that they were trying to tell her something: as if – knowing they were being observed – they had arranged themselves into a letter: M or W, or a message: SOS or III. She was sure this letter or message meant either Yes or No: it tortured her that she could not, them being her intimate relations, decide which. Strangely, when they had been born as foxes at 3 a.m. – was it only that morning? – after an hour of painful labour, she evinced no surprise, only joy-times-joy. In the moments after the delivery (by me alone, at home), she wept and I could see her being invaded by religion – as if she were a nest that ants were entering, carrying lit matches between their front legs, ceremonially. Beneath the surface, she was being illuminated by a dangerous and itchy fire. I, at this juncture, was retching as if trying to dislodge a turd coated in stomach acid that had fought its way up into my oesophagus. The midwife arrived moments after the afterbirth, but I left it until evening before I left. During the slave-scan, my wife had convinced herself that she not only was able to distinguish the sex of each foetus but its future profession, cause of death and the number of children it itself would leave behind. I set myself to thinking of the weight and the wait of the third trimester . . . I couldn't. This was intolerable: I would have to return to the house and find out how my fox-children were faring; how many books had they destroyed? I was a bad father, to abandon them, thus, without giving them a chance to give me a good enough reason. Besides, it was a matter of no little curiosity to me that no attempt had been made to hunt me down in the wildwood. It was, after all, to the very same place I had escaped following the previous incident which there is no point describing here. As I emerged from the undergrowth, I felt a scrabbling at my leg and looked down fully expecting a weeping foxcub or three. It wasn't; it was a cocker spaniel – a second one followed, and then the owner, now no longer talking. I said hello in a high voice, before he could attack me. He did not immediately reply. I wanted to bring the conversation around as quickly as possible to painting, but could see no way to do this without revealing that I'd overheard him earlier – calling up the spectre of being accused of being a spy. An art-spy, if such creatures exist. I even had writing materials in my jacket pocket; a very expensive pen. 'My wife has had three foxcubs,' I said. 'They're a devil to keep,' the man replied. 'That's why I ran away,' I said. I noticed he was still walking. 'Are you a farmer?' I asked. 'No,' he replied, now over his shoulder. 'What do you do?' I called, realising I was only two questions away from painting. 'Mind your own bloody business,' he shouted back. I made all possible haste home, which was only two fields away. Once I hit the hardness of the road my footsteps echoed back off the hedges. There were no lights on in the front of the house, but that was nothing unusual – the kitchen was round the back. Quietly, so as to be able to escape if I saw anything disgusting, I crept through the gate and down the path at the side of the house. I was able to stare in through the window without attracting the attention of the corpse upon the kitchen table, feasted upon by three now full-grown foxes. It was not my wife, I would have recognised her; and besides, my wife wasn't a man. This was a man-corpse, cooked. For a very brief moment, I thought I might have got the wrong house, but I recognised the posters of the deserts of the world, left over from the first nauseous trimester. The foxes were talking as they ate, and this is what they said: 'One, two, three.' 'One.' 'One two three.' 'One-two.' 'Three. One.' 'One.' 'One!' 'One.' 'Two.' 'One.' 'One two three one two three one two three.' 'Two.' 'Three.'

# GHOST STORY

# CHAPTER I

'Y ou'll see,' says the young man probably an estate agent coming through the front door of the house.

'After you,' he says, and across the threshold step a woman and then a man, she is pregnant, he keeps close.

The man is about thirty-five years old, tall and slim, a little gangly, with sandy hair and grey-green eyes.

The woman, much shorter than the man, has long straight dyed-black hair, olive skin, bright brown eyes, and is dressed entirely in black.

'This is the hall,' says the young man, 'as you can see.' There is a short pause before the couple laugh. 'Original black and white floor tiles,' the estate agent says.

'Very nice,' says the pregnant woman.

'Mmm,' says the man.

'Shall we go through here?' asks the estate agent, and they turn left off the hall into the front room. 'As you can see, the vacating tenants did their best to take everything that wasn't nailed down – and quite a few things that were.'

The room is quite small. The floor is bare wooden boards, rough and dusty – a carpet has been removed. Wires branch out of the holes where light sockets and power points are meant to be.

'Been looking long?' the estate agent asks.

The woman is now walking over to the fireplace and the man is going to inspect the bay windows.

'Yes,' says the man, turning.

'Months,' says the woman, not turning.

'But in London,' says the man, 'not down here.'

'Really?' says the young man.

'Who *were* the vacating tenants?' asks the woman, then grimaces.

'Ah, well, there's a bit of a story there,' says the estate agent. The couple wait for it. 'You see, for a long time this place was unoccupied. Quite frankly, the owner couldn't be bothered with it – he lived in India, I think. Indonesia. And because it was empty, someone spotted this fact and moved swiftly in – started to squat it, if I'm perfectly honest with you. The area's come up a lot since then, but at one time it was pretty druggy. Anyway, that lot were in here about two years in total. They weren't too bad, I've heard, as far as druggies go – they had a little daughter, and she went to school and everything, was kept clean. But then the owner died. Food poisoning, I wouldn't be surprised – and his son took over the property. He had the squatters out within what? a month, then started to do the place up. He's the vendor, by the way. And he as you'll see got as far as the kitchen and a bit of the attic before, well, let's say he ran into some financial difficulties of his own – and now he's looking for a swift sale. You're not in a chain, are you?'

'We're moving out of a flat,' says the man. 'We've got a buyer already – and they haven't got anywhere to sell.'

'Lovely-jubbly,' says the estate agent. 'Like I say, the kitchen's been done up very nice.'

'Is that blood, do you think?' the woman says, pointing with the toe of her shoe to some dark red stains on the floorboard.

The estate agent comes across. 'Looks more like varnish to me,' he says. 'But I suppose you could be right. As far as I've been informed, they were crackheads not smackheads.'

As the estate agent goes back into the hall, the woman

whispers to the man, 'Looks like blood to me.' She smiles, and he smiles broadly back.

They follow the young man into the next room off the hall, also to the left. It has two narrow windows that look along the side of the house towards the green of the lawn.

'It's a good shape,' says the man.

'Not too small, either,' the woman says. 'I could fit a piano in here.'

They go back into the hall. A little further on, beneath the stairs on the right, is another door.

'Cellar,' says the estate agent, sliding back the small brass bolt. 'Quite a decent size one, too.'

'Spooky,' says the woman, which makes the estate agent laugh quietly.

The man opens the door and starts to descend.

'Paddy,' says the woman. 'It's dark.'

'I think there's a,' says the young man, and reaches round to try the switch. There is a dry click, but no light.

'I'm just going to see what I can see,' says Paddy.

'Bulb must be gone,' says the estate agent. 'You've got your fusebox down there. Electrics are all fine.'

'I wouldn't go down there,' says the woman.

'Why not?' asks the young man.

'It doesn't smell damp,' Paddy calls up.

'Why do you think?' the woman says.

'You don't like the dark?' the young man asks.

'Rats,' she says.

'Oh,' he says. 'You don't have to worry about those round here. It's very clean, like I said.'

Paddy re-emerges. 'Fine,' he says. 'Sure you don't want a look?'

'The kitchen is just through here,' says the young man,

walking further along the hall and opening the door. 'All very contemporary.' They follow him in. The kitchen cabinets are of pale maplewood. 'Do you know the area, at all?' he asks.

'No,' says Paddy, 'but we've got some friends who live just.' He is interrupted by the jingling of a mobile phone and kept from continuing by the estate agent answering it.

'Vince,' says the agent, then mouths the word sorry and holds up his palm. 'Yes, this is Vince,' he says.

The couple watch as the estate agent points towards the hall door and then goes through it. He goes out the front door, too. They are on their own in the house.

She looks at him and he looks at her, and they both smile, and then laugh.

'Why didn't you ask if we could look round by ourselves?' she says.

'I don't know,' he replies. Their voices are louder. 'We always have to go through this kind of thing, don't we? They won't let you alone.'

'Paddy,' she says.

'Are you alright?' he asks.

'I'm fine,' she says.

They look out through the French doors. The flowerbeds are overgrown: an appletree in the middle of the lawn has shed its fruit, which lies rotten on the long brown grass. It is a day with a white and dull sky.

'Plenty of work here,' she says, coming to stand beside him.

'Agatha,' he says, his voice lowered. 'Not for a while.'

'We'll have to make it safe,' says Agatha.

'It looks fine to me,' Paddy replies. They turn and look back through the house, towards the front door – where the frosty silhouette of the estate agent moves behind glass.

'Quick,' Agatha says, 'Let's see as much of the rest as we can before he comes back.'

'I like it so far,' says Paddy.

In a few moments they are up the stairs and onto the first-floor landing. Above the kitchen is a small bedroom, which they enter. It is painted pink. Glow-in-the-dark stars are stuck to the ceiling, lots of them, a whole glow-in-the-dark universe. There are stickers on the doors of the built-in cupboard, glossy pink. The bottom two panes of the window are crammed with transfers – of pastel ponies with flowing manes and tails, long-haired trolls with very dark eyes.

'This will have to be completely redone,' she says. 'The Monster wouldn't like it at all.'

'He might,' says Paddy.

Off the landing is the bathroom: modern, white-tiled, clean. 'Fine,' says Paddy.

The next bedroom along is slightly smaller, boxier. 'Yes,' says Agatha, her hands on the dome of her belly, 'it feels good in here.'

There is a large radiator beneath the window which has the same view, but elevated, as the rear living room downstairs. Paddy comes up behind Agatha and puts his hands around the top of hers; their fingers interlace. They sway from side to side. 'You like it, don't you?' he says.

'So far,' she replies. 'Let's see the rest before we get carried away.' She walks out the door.

'Who's getting carried away?' says Paddy. He follows her into the main bedroom. 'You were standing there deciding where the cot would go – I could tell.'

'So what if I was,' she says, looking round at the coving of the ceiling, 'it's only practical.'

Taking a few strides around the room, Paddy says, 'I like this.'

'It's big, isn't it?' says Agatha.

'We can get a wardrobe in,' says Paddy.

'Or two wardrobes.'

'Where are we meeting them?' Paddy asks.

'At their house,' she says, 'at twelve o'clock – or whenever we're finished at the next one.' They walk around the edge of the room.

'And we're going out for lunch?'

'You're not hungry already, are you?' she says.

'Well,' he says.

Downstairs, the front door opens. 'Hello?' calls the estate agent.

'Quick,' says Agatha, and grabs Paddy's hands. 'Before he finds us.' She pulls Paddy out into the upstairs landing and then up a narrow flight of stairs just to the left. Her feet make very little noise on the thick carpet.

'Ah,' she says, looking into the narrow attic with the ceiling sloped to either side. 'Our office,' she says, stepping forwards. 'The desk can go here.'

'Stop it,' says Paddy.

'Do you think I'll jinx it?'

'It's not that,' he says.

'Hello?' calls the estate agent, louder, from the upstairs landing.

'Agatha,' says Paddy, pulling open the velux window in the roof. 'Come here.'

Agatha goes to him. Paddy tips it up, and they step into the space created – heads and shoulders out the front of the house. 'I thought so,' he says, and points.

'Oh yes look the sea,' says Agatha, happily.

## CHAPTER 2

'COME in, come in,' says Agatha, standing proudly in the hall.

It is a month or so since anyone has been here. Agatha's belly has swelled so as to become unmissable.

Into the hall steps a large woman with bright auburn hair. Behind her, in a wheelchair pushed by Paddy, is a very thin man with thick gray hair.

'Welcome,' says Agatha, with a small fling of the hands, 'to our new home.'

'Wonderful, darling,' says the woman.

'That it is,' says the man, in a very rough voice. He coughs, and coughs again.

'Come on, Mummy,' Agatha says, taking her hand. 'I want to show you the kitchen.'

The two men watch them flitting down the passageway and through the door.

'Isn't it fantastic?' asks Agatha, her voice echoey.

'It's all just wonderful,' says her mother, and gives Agatha a hug.

As Paddy wheels him down the passage, the gray-haired man says, 'So you only saw it the once before you bought it?'

'Yes,' says Paddy, over the coughs. 'We felt very sure about it almost from the moment we stepped through the front door.' They enter the kitchen, with only a slight jolt. 'It had just the right feeling about it.'

'Donald, look at this,' says Agatha's mother, admiring the new kitchen. 'Isn't it lovely?'

'But how could you be certain?' says Donald. 'It's a big decision – lot of money.'

Agatha says, 'It was a bit of a bargain, actually.'

'It needs a bit of work,' says Paddy.

'Front certainly does,' says Donald, wheeling his way coughing to the back of the house. 'Completely repointing.'

'I'm afraid we can't offer you a cup of tea,' says Paddy, and then to Agatha, 'That's a point – we should get a kettle here before the builders come.'

'I'm sure they'll have one of their own.'

'Donald,' says Agatha's mother. 'Be a little more supportive, why don't you?' Then turning to Paddy, 'I think it's beautiful.'

'There are two sitting rooms,' says Agatha. 'But we're going to have them knocked through. Come and see.'

Paddy wheels Donald into the nearest one. 'This is the wall that's going to go,' says Paddy, putting his hand against it.

'Sure it's worth the bother?' says the old man. 'It'll make mess.'

'All houses need a lot of work when you first move in,' says Agatha's mother. 'What condition was your first house in, when you bought it?'

'Nothing like this bad,' says Donald, using one of his coughs to nod towards some exposed wiring.

'I'd like to show Mummy upstairs and around the rest of the house,' says Agatha. 'Is that okay?' Her eyes were still bright, not angry.

'Oh, don't mind me,' says Donald.

'Why don't you show your mum the cellar first?' asks Paddy.

Agatha gives him a brief look, then goes with her mother into the front room.

'Dad,' says Paddy.

'Yes,' his father replies.

'Don't you really like it at all?'

The old man coughs for a while. 'The thought of it' – he pauses, breathes – 'tires me out.' When he has finished coughing again, he listens for a moment to the women's high voices. 'Why does she have to call her Mummy?'

'It's what she's always called her.'

'It's embarrassing, that's what it is.'

Agatha and her mother come out into the hall and start up the stairs. Paddy watches their legs and feet, ascending diagonally.

'You can go too, if you like,' says his father.

'I don't mind.'

'Yes, you do,' Donald says. 'Go on. I'll stay here. Try not to electrocute myself.'

Paddy smiles his thanks down towards the old man, and takes off up the stairs. He joins Agatha and her mother in the back bedroom.

'– a little girl's. But we're going to decorate it for Max.'

'Do you really like it, Margaret?' asks Paddy.

'Are you trying to make me cry?' she asks back.

In a lowered voice, Paddy says, 'I'm sorry about my father. He's very difficult.'

'He's very ill,' Margaret says. 'I understand. I've lived with illness.' She ran her fingers into Agatha's hair. 'Your father was *not* a patient patient.'

'Oh, Mummy,' says Agatha.

'And now I am going to cry,' says Margaret, but she is smiling as her eyes go sparkly. 'Look at all the stars,' she says. 'So many stickers. What a sad, lonely little girl.' Paddy goes and opens one of the built-in cupboards.

'Don't be embarrassed,' says Agatha's mother. 'We're a very emotional lot, aren't we?'

Agatha's eyes too are bright.

'You mean the Welsh?' says Paddy, doing his best to joke.

'I mean the Williams clan.'

'The next room, my lovelies,' says Agatha, with a half-choke, 'is going to be the nursery.'

Out onto the landing they step. 'You forgot the bathroom,' says Paddy.

'We can look at that on the way back,' says Agatha.

Paddy allows the two women to spend a moment together in the nursery before he joins them.

'It's going to be such a wonderfully lovely room,' says Agatha. 'And it's all for you,' she says downwards, cradling her belly.

Paddy comes over to her and puts an arm around her shoulder.

'I wish I had my camera,' says Margaret. 'You two are a picture.'

'Oh, Mummy, you always forget to bring it, don't you?'

'You three,' says Paddy, to himself.

'I just never think.'

A more violent than usual series of coughs comes up the stairs.

'I'd better go and see how he is,' says Paddy. 'You can come and join us when you've completed the tour.'

As he goes down the stairs, Paddy hears Agatha saying, 'The next room, ladies and gentlemen, is the master bedroom.'

When he enters the back sitting room, his father looks up, takes a hard breath and says, 'I think you'll find those over there in that corner are mouse-droppings.'

# CHAPTER 3

THE builders come.

They shout back from the hall, throw dirty sheets on the floor, bring a cardboard box into the kitchen, pull out a kettle, fill the kettle, put the kettle on, look out through the French doors, make tea, unlock the French doors, go out into the garden, talk about yesterday (Ted is the gaffer, Charlie is his mate and Lee makes the tea), leave the mugs in the sink, carry in paint pots, buckets, brushes, stepladders, hammers, toolboxes, look over the living rooms, look over the rest of the house, read out the letter from Paddy saying what he wants done (Ted sends Lee to tell the neighbours there is going to be some noise and Lee comes back to say no-one is in), they put masks on, start at the wall with two big hammers, make jokes, cough, break through, shake hands through the hole, put the bricks in a wheelbarrow, enlarge the hole, step through, go for lunch, come back, hear knocking, answer the door, start wheeling bricks out to the just-delivered skip, finish enlarging the hole, finish taking out the bricks, sweep the floor clean, make tea, drink it, come inside, pull up old floorboards, cut to size and nail down new ones, wash the walls, reinforce the doorway with a support beam, knock off for the day, arrive early next morning, mix plaster, finish the doorway, make tea, drink it, play pop music on a radio, leave the front door half-open, bring in a sander and start on the floorboards, fix light switches and plugs and other small things, keep taking turns with the sanding, sit on the loo reading tabloid newspapers and smoking (Lee), stop for lunch, talk about television, international affairs, sport, money, crime, their girlfriends (Lee is hiding the fact he is secretly in love with Charlie's ex-wife – they have been seeing one another since before the divorce), do more sanding, make tea, drink it, sand, wash the walls, knock off for the day, arrive early, pour out paint, paint the living-room ceilings, wipe drops of paint off walls, paint walls, sing along to pop songs on the radio, whistle, make tea, drink it, stare out the windows at the rainy garden, think about men with whom they used to work and women for whom they used to work (Lee is worried that Charlie suspects something and Charlie, who has known for a long time, is secretly amused by this), put a second coat of paint on the walls, talk about television, death, hangovers, money, Paddy and Agatha, this house, children (Charlie has a child with behavioural problems), eat chocolate bars, stick masking tape along the edge of the window panes, fill the gaps in with putty, put a lightbulb in, turn the light on, go for lunch, paint the window frames with white gloss, tear off the masking tape, finish down-stairs, move upstairs, laugh, argue about who is going to make tea, make tea (Lee), drink it, steam and strip wall-paper in the front bedroom, talk to Paddy on the phone (Ted), swear (Charlie is very concerned about his son and the way the other kids at school bully him), whistle (Lee is very worried about his father who used to be an alcoholic and is now in a home and no longer knows his own name or recognizes anyone), fit anti-burglary devices to the downstairs windows, break for the day, arrive not so early, shout morning to the opposite neighbours, make tea, drink it, talk about hangovers, money, mathematics, astrology, homosexuality, tell the DJ on the radio to shut up, paper the bedroom (Charlie thinks it's time he told Lee he knows about him and his ex-wife), make tea, drink it (Lee thinks maybe it's time he broke it off with Charlie's ex-wife), talk about money, the lottery, answer the phone (Ted says *I'm sorry to hear that*, tells the others to pack up), they stop, pack up, tidy up, sweep up, check for anything they might have left behind, feel sad, laugh, lock the door.

The builders go.

# CHAPTER 4

S IX or seven weeks later, a key in the door.
It was Paddy, on his own. He was carrying a cardboard box full of tea things. He seemed a little nervous as he stepped into the hall around two o'clock. During the next four hours, he would become worse then better then worse again. He called Agatha to let her know he was safely here and that everything so far had gone well. 'When did they finish loading up?' he asked, then, 'So, when do you think they'll get here?' The removals lorry arrived about half an hour later. During this time, Paddy sat out in the garden and ate some sandwiches and then some biscuits. He had briefly examined the knocked-through living room but without a great deal of interest. 'Good lunch?' Paddy asked one of the removals men, the biggest.

'Alright,' he said. 'Fish and chips.'

'Good,' said Paddy, not asking a question.

'Not bad,' said the man.

'Would you like some more tea? Or coffee?'

'A bit later,' said the man. Paddy obviously wanted to be as welcoming as he could to these temporary guests. The removals men started to come through the front door with huge cardboard boxes; they wanted to know where to put them, and Paddy told them, saying *thank you* and *thanks* every time. 'Front bedroom,' he said, 'thanks.'

The men worked quickly and after an hour asked for tea. Paddy was glad of this, he felt like they hated him – for being middle class and for moving into this house, which was probably bigger than theirs. He had become very aware of their bodies, and how they were sweating and becoming tired and all because a few weeks ago he had given his credit card number down the phone. These were *men*, he couldn't but be conscious of the fact – and they made him feel boyish. Very often, whilst carrying the boxes in, they said, 'Books,' or 'More books,' or 'You've got a lot of books, haven't you?' And they did – book-boxes filled almost half the glow-in-the-dark room. There were more in the back-to-front room, which the men called the lounge – this name made it seem alien to Paddy. One wall in each room was now part-covered by a second wall of cardboard.

The men sat with their teas in the garden, quite as if it were their own – they seemed to Paddy more in possession than him. He said nothing as one of them stubbed a cigarette out on the concrete slabs, and left it there. 'Lovely,' said the tall one. 'Thank you,' said the black one, as they handed him the mugs. Paddy had insisted they lock the back of the removals van whilst they were away from it. He had closed the front door himself.

The rest of the stuff only took about half an hour to unload. Paddy became worried about whether the tip he intended to give was going to be the appropriate amount – whether the men would despise him if it were too small, and despise him almost as much if he made it too cravenly huge. He had had the notes ready in his back pocket since lunchtime, just in case one of the men asked for it.

The last box came through the door at three o'clock exactly – it was full of philosophy books. The black man, whose name Paddy now felt guilty about having once heard and then forgotten, put it on top of the cardboard wall in the back living room. 'That's it,' said the senior man. He got Paddy to sign a piece of paper, resting on top of one of the boxes. 'Thank you,' said Paddy, embarrassed. 'Great job.' The men had started for the door – demonstratively? contemptuously? – before Paddy remembered the tip. He gave it to the black man, asking him to share it with the others, then worrying (as he approached the door) that this had made him seem racist. The young black man smiled. 'Thanks, mate,' he said, and the mate made Paddy feel slightly better about the whole day. He, too, was a man – he had, in his own way, contributed to getting the job done.

They got in the van as he stood in the doorway to wave them off, unnecessarily. He looked for their faces in the mirrors – they went, with a couple of honks and some not, he thought, unfriendly waves.

Paddy went back inside a very unreal house – it seemed somehow to have lifted off the ground and was now setting itself down on his back, a responsibility. Already he had noticed things that would have to be done: nails to be banged in, paint to be retouched. He wanted to call Agatha but also wanted a few moments alone in the kitchen – he knew she was by now at her mother's and would come over as soon as he let her know the men were gone. He didn't want to lie. He didn't want another cup of tea, either – already he felt spinny with caffeine and unused adrenaline. Instead, he filled a glass with water (proprietorial: his water) and carried it, not drinking, from room to room. He tried not to pause longest in the glow-in-the-dark room, but this was where the bulk of the boxes had been placed. Everything here had been carried by somebody else – somebody who didn't care at all about what it meant. This made Paddy feel stupid towards his heavy possessions; perhaps he should get rid of some if not all of them – but most of them, the books, he needed for his work. Agatha, he remembered, had often tried to reassure him they didn't have an extravagant amount of stuff.

He went downstairs into the kitchen and picked up his mobile, hesitated for reasons he didn't care to analyse and then selected Agatha's mother's number.

'We're in,' he said, and there was the smallest possibility he might start crying with relief – he didn't, but he wanted Agatha to; she didn't. She said she'd be over soon; not, he noticed, as soon as she could get there, just soon.

After putting the phone down, he wished he'd called earlier, for now the time alone in the house seemed useless.

He ripped the tape off the top of the nearest cardboard box and began to unpack food packets and tins into cupboards that Agatha was sure to rearrange.

# CHAPTER 5

Agatha arrived around quarter past seven, alone.
'How was he?' Paddy asked.

'Thanks,' she said.

'How are you, I meant,' Paddy corrected himself, too
late.

'No, you didn't. He was asleep when I left. I didn't want
to wake him.' She walked through into the front room,
examined the new space. 'How was today?' she asked.

'It was fine,' said Paddy. 'I'm a bit knackered – trying to
keep control of everything; make sure it doesn't go in the
wrong place.'

'Nothing's broken that you saw.'

'Not that I noticed.' They talked about what they were
going to have for supper, with no possibility of cooking.
Paddy, who had been anticipating this conversation, suggested fish and chips; Agatha agreed.

He went down the road to get it, and she took a wander
around the house. In the bathroom she found a large
house-spider on the window-pane, beside the extractor
fan. She wasn't particularly scared of spiders – not more
than anything else – and she knew she was supposed to
think they were lucky in a house. One shouldn't kill them,
for they killed flies. She waited in the bathroom, watching
it, so that it wouldn't get away and be somewhere she didn't
know where it was. The spider didn't move, but when she
felt brave enough to look at it closely she could see it was
rocking slightly, as if on unsteady ground or slightly drunk.
When after ten minutes Paddy returned she called him
upstairs, and he reacted to her pointing as if she'd been

really afraid and he was her bold protector – went down into the kitchen and brought back a mug (the glasses still in boxes) and a tabloid newspaper left by one of the removals men. He reached out with the mug to trip the spider. 'Careful you don't kill it,' said Agatha, a tone moving towards pleading in her voice.

'Of course not,' said Paddy. 'Does it look like I'm trying to kill it?'

'It's unlucky if you do.'

'I won't.' Gently as he could, as if the action were towards Agatha and not the spider, Paddy slid the paper under the rim of the mug.

'I didn't know you were so superstitious,' he said.

'I'm not,' said Agatha, realising as she said it that she probably was, or was becoming so. Her reaction had surprised her, and this surprise upset her.

Paddy let the spider free on the sill, and Agatha slammed down the window so hard it almost cracked.

As they went back downstairs, she felt a disproportionate relief; she was familiar with her feelings, and what they now always referred to. This wasn't something, right this moment, she wanted to think about; she had made a very conscious decision, standing for five minutes on the doorstep before she rang the bell, that she was going to be as 'up' as she could. It was intended to be for Paddy, her attempted positive mood, and for her imagined future self, looking back on their first night in the house. She didn't want to remember an argument; they'd had an argument when Paddy left the old flat, and even though she knew it was a detail she would never forget, right now she couldn't remember what or who had started it.

They celebrated by opening the bottle of champagne which was the only thing in their fridge apart from milk, put there by Paddy earlier in the day. 'To the new house,' proposed Paddy.

'To the new life,' Agatha added, trumped. They did not make eye contact, even as they clinked mugs.

'It's funny, being here at this time of day,' said Agatha, 'in the evening, when it's dark.'

'I know what you mean,' Paddy replied, making the effort. 'It's almost as if we only own it at a certain time – at the time we first viewed it. Noon.'

'That wasn't really us, was it?' Agatha asked, and it seemed a genuine question, but not one Paddy was able to answer.

They sat in the kitchen, reflected back at themselves in the glass of the French doors. 'We'll only be camping out for a couple of days,' said Paddy. 'I'll put up shelves.'

'I don't mind,' Agatha said.

'I wish we could get rid of half of it.'

'No,' said Agatha, 'the house will be almost empty as it is – we'll need to buy things, not get rid of them.'

'Books – I mean books. When will I ever read them all?'

'On the train,' she said, using practicality as aggression. Against the light from the upstairs window of the house behind theirs, Agatha could make out part of the shape of the appletree. She had a moment of wanting, very brutally, to be alone, for Paddy to go out somewhere and leave her and the house together.

The fish and chips were very good. Whilst they ate, Agatha found herself able to ask Paddy more questions about the day and how it had gone, and to half-attend to his answers, whilst at the same time examining her sensations of being in the new house, an old house, a house they owned, that they were going to live in together, had already started – the moment she crossed the threshold (had she kissed him?) – living in. He was enjoying his food a little too loudly, as he always did – he chewed like his father. She thought she *had* kissed him; if she hadn't the omission would have been deliberate and she would have remembered it. One piece of cod tasted for some reason more strongly of the sea than those before, or perhaps she just for the moment became more aware of how it tasted. She wanted to say to Paddy, 'We're at the seaside,' and then to add, 'This is where we live.' She knew another Agatha, a previous one, wouldn't have hesitated to share her thoughts with Paddy. And she wondered why she was becoming so self-conscious now. It must have something to do with being in a new place; the build-up to the removal, as she remembered it, had been a mountain range of stress-peaks – phonecalls, arrangements, cancellations, rearrangements. Also, with Max not here, she was able to devote some of the attention she was always giving him towards herself – or the attention had decided that was where it wanted to spend its free time. She thought about the taxi ride over from her mother's – couldn't even remember if the driver had been black or white, couldn't remember how much she had paid for it. This worried her; not that she'd blacked out, but that she might not have given him a tip. Of course, she had no memory of the interior of the cab, either – she tried to remember the smell of it, couldn't. She had obviously been thinking very intensely as she was driven over, but about what? If she wanted to comfort herself, she believed it had been about Max and saying goodbye to sleeping-him – if only for a few nights, until they got themselves sorted. She knew that it was quite possible she'd been completely absent to herself, absent from herself, at least as a thinking person. This had happened so often, *since*, that she was aware of it as a habitual if not a usual state. What was different, now, was how terrified the idea of it was making her feel, looking back – almost as if she might as well have been dead. How long had it been since she had had a moment to take herself really seriously? She remembered hours in the maternity ward – several long days after the nurses had lost interest in her; she could not move, was being drained and lightly monitored and dosed and rehydrated. Her baby was not there to be brought or taken away, and she was determined not to break down completely, not till she was home – not to split into as many fragments as she felt she might; unfixable. This holding-together was impossible, the force of feeling was like a motorbike driven through her ribcage – or a golf swing through her head. Paddy had been there as often as he could manage, morning and evening, but that left her the afternoons and nights, the hours before the nurses came to give her drugs to make her sleep. She was all envy for the women she saw around her, those who had given birth, those who were pregnant, those just visiting who were only distantly concerned. How hard it had been and how sick, longing for lives that belonged to others – finding intricate explanations of herself, to herself; this was not her, she was quite unlike this. The biology of what would have been her soul had gone completely awry. Having split, doubled and grown her motherlove, all she had was one child to give it schizo-phrenically to – he would be approached by a hideous twin-headed mother who had not had time or chance to grow different, to customize herselves. What strange thoughts surrounded her then, and she was sure some of them were objective, waiting for her in the air, cobwebs to be walked through between far-apart forest trees. They couldn't actually, truly, come from inside her – they were too merciless. The gauze cloaked her face, dryly adhered, and before she even had a chance to try to pull it off had become a layer of her own dear skin. Paddy was asking her something, for a second time, she could tell. 'Yes?' she said.

'I said, Shall we go for a walk?' Paddy said, for the third time. 'Along the beach,' he added nervously.

'I'm very tired,' said Agatha, 'and though I'm hiding it very well, very upset.'

'Tomorrow, then.'

# CHAPTER 6

A LL Saturday Paddy put up shelves. In the afternoon
Agatha's mother called and held Max close up to the
phone so they could speak to him and he could say words
back. Again that evening Paddy asked Agatha whether she
would like to go for a walk on the beach; she said no. And
so he went on his own.

Sunday they spent taking books out of boxes and putting
them, alphabetized, on new shelves.

'What time shall we go?' asked Paddy when they had
finished and were having tea.

Agatha understood what he meant but pretended not
to – she didn't have a reason for this; she knew it would
annoy him, and that they were going to have an argument
anyway: one he would lose but she would feel worse about.
'Go where?' she said.

'To fetch Max.'

'Paddy,' she said, 'I'm going to ask my mother if she can
keep him for a while.'

'What's a while?'

'I don't know yet – I haven't thought about it properly.'

'But the house is ready.'

'Not really. There are still dangerous things around. We
need to make it completely safe.'

Paddy looked carefully at Agatha. She was giving him
false reasons, and he wanted to know why. 'Tell me,' he
said, letting his tone explain.

'I just,' said Agatha, 'I just want a little more time.'

'Time for what?' said Paddy, thinking *time and space*;
end-of-relationship clichés.

'Time for, I don't know. Time for time. My mother enjoys having Max, and he enjoys being there. I need longer than I've had.'

Her voice was hardening with each further word, and Paddy could tell how many words more, exactly, would have her shouting.

'Alright,' he said. 'I'm missing him.

'Do you think I think you're not?'

'No. I was just saying,'

'I want him here more than almost anything.' Paddy knew she meant than him himself – that she might have been content to have Max back and him not here. He didn't want to think too much about that as a possibility. 'In a while – he can come in a while.'

Paddy refused to let himself ask again how long she meant by that. It disturbed him that Aggie, which was how he thought of her, could be satisfied to be separate from Max without some terrible reason. From the way they had been *since*, he expected this minor estrangement of theirs to last until the following morning. Once or twice in the flat, he remembered, there had been two-day silences between them. Of course, they had spoken to and through Max; he must notice as little as possible. The house, though, made their silences seem more expansive, more adult.

Although he felt it might be seen as continuing the argument by other means, Paddy fixed a few of what Agatha might have perceived as dangers. He was wrong, however, about them not talking. In bed at the end of the day Agatha said to him, 'I feel as if someone's going to come along and steal the house from us.' She spoke quite lightly, as if they hadn't been not speaking.

'You mean a burglar?'

'No, I mean really *steal* the house – right from under us, so it's just not there any more.'

'That would be clever,' said Paddy, for the lack of anything more penetrating.

'In fact, they're not exactly going to steal it, they're just not going to let us have it to begin with. This is somebody else's house – I feel it – and it's never going to be ours; it's always going to be somebody else's.'

'Whose?'

'I don't know. I don't think I'll ever find out.'

'You're being silly,' Paddy said, before realising he should be encouraging all Agatha's sillinesses, so as to help her ditch them.

'Silly is what a house is – it's too big. Politically, I can't agree with it. It's obscene.'

'You should have said this before; we could have given all our money away and found a commune to join.'

'What money?' she said.

'Exactly.'

'Oh, Paddy, don't you feel what I mean?'

'I feel we don't *deserve* it. I feel more middle class and excluded from everything, as if I've moved up a demographic – from C3 to A1.'

'E1 to B2, actually. We have. We'll get more junk mail here, more offers – though not as many as if we were living in London, Chelsea.'

They slept.

# CHAPTER 7

U P, coffee on, shower, shave, clothes on, coffee – and Paddy was out the door.

Agatha said goodbye in the hall then went back to bed.

She came down again around ten o'clock, made herself a cup of tea and then went back to bed, again.

Alone in the house, properly, felt from the first very different to alone with Paddy around. Although Agatha had not had recourse to his comfort, the protection of its possibility had always been there – had always been present with her. She sat on the bed, cross-legged, a book in her lap. After half an hour, she put the book aside and listened to the house; she listened as hard as she was able, stilling her breathing – although this caused her blood to boom in her ears. And the house felt wonderfully alive, populated with movements and noises which Agatha could not yet identify – there were too many of them, their rhythms overlapped and syncopated. It wasn't because the place – the building in the street – was loud; compared with London, the implied movements and the noises were for the most part microsounds (no jets overhead, or very few): tickings, creakings, crackings. The only drama came from the juddercrash of the pilot light catching, or the yawp of the central heating waking up and that was long past, now. Agatha enjoyed listening – doing nothing but listening; she took possession of the house first of all through her ears.

In the late morning, she went with her book and sat in the front sitting room. The air there smelled empty; very old, behind-things dust had been lifted and moved around.

It was extraordinarily odd to look out the window, when she saw movement, and see people. In the flat, four flights up, the things glimpsed moving had always been the branches of trees. So far, they had no curtains downstairs, and she had prevailed against nets; Paddy, disturbingly, had thought they would make a nice suburban irony. People passing along the pavement could, she was aware, look in, but surprisingly few of them did. After a while, she turned the sofa through ninety degrees: she would sit with her back to the window, not minding if what they saw of her was her hair and an ear on either side; they couldn't see the most important thing, the page of the book she was reading.

It started to rain around two, whilst Agatha was making lunch – she hadn't been hungry until then. She made herself boiled eggs and toast with Marmite. This weather sounded different than in the flat. The windows there were double-glazed, but here the drops really blattered against the French doors. Agatha for a while watched the tips of the leafless branches of the appletree nodding in after-acknowledgement of being struck. The area beneath the tree was a circle of mud. Apart from this, which took up most of the space, the garden was sick-looking grass and weedy flowerbeds. She sat at the table, food finished, and considered what she could see. She had no idea about gardening, apart from that she might one day like to do some.

During the afternoon, Agatha was distracted from her book. Another noise, or set of noises, had added themselves to those of the front room. They were sometimes like paper being scrunched and sometimes like fingernails being tapped on wood. After a couple of occurrences, she set out to find where they were coming from. She didn't feel scared; from the sounds, she could tell that whatever was making them wasn't dangerous. They seemed to be coming from the back room – the wall there to the right of the fireplace. She stepped through the new wide doorway from one room to the other, through the wall that was no longer there. Perhaps it was the neighbours. She assumed they had neighbours, though she hadn't seen any yet. With her ear against the wall for a couple of minutes, aware that she could probably still be seen from the street, of course the noises stopped. And when she went back to her book, a page and a half in, just getting absorbed, they started again. She put her foot on the boards and walked across, aware the scrunching which was perhaps more a scrabbling had already ceased. This time, she stood still – any shift of balance caused a slight high groaning in the floor; she breathed herself towards stillness. The scrabbling definitely scrabbling took a minute to start up again. It was over by the wall, where it met the floor. Agatha looked, and noticed for the first time a long triangular gap between one floorboard and the broken-off end of another. She stepped towards it, the quiet coming immediately; the noise-maker was alive, definitely. A couple of steps away, at the thought of a rat, Agatha stopped; it could be a rat; there was no reason it wasn't a rat. They didn't know this house at all well. Agatha's small terror felt exactly like Max's hand reaching up and grabbing her windpipe; she could even feel his elbow nudging her breastbone. If it was a rat, she might have to go out for the afternoon and wait for Paddy that evening on the doorstep. This thought, she realised, scared her almost as much as that of a rat. And because it was raining, she would be wet as well as ridiculous in his eyes. Another brave step towards the hole, as she tried to convince herself that a rat was quite a big animal and would make bigger, deeper scrabbles. Another step, and she was almost there. She leaned forward, a loud creak coming from the board beneath her heel; the hole was too dark, nothing could be seen in it but black. What if the cellar light still didn't work? Agatha thought of the torch, then where Paddy had told her he'd put it: the shelf at the top of the cellar stairs. What a stupid place, Agatha now said to herself. Why not the miscellaneous drawer in the kitchen, along with the back-door keys and the clothespegs? She walked stealthily out of the back sitting room and into the hall. It was best if she didn't pause before opening the cellar door. The dark in the triangular hole was merely the little brother of the dark down at the bottom of these stairs. She tried the lightswitch; it gave a loud click and nothing happened. Up and down she flicked it, but the cellar light stayed off. A pause for thought and breath and a little fear – this was not good. Agatha reached for the torch on the shelf and clumsily knocked it with her fingertips. It rebounded from the wood behind it, fell over and rolled towards the edge of the shelf. Agatha reached to save it but succeeded only in touching one end and making it spin off into the air. The torch descended the stairs, loudly, end over end. Agatha could just about see it, the light catching its black rubber ridging. Bump on one step, bump on the next – and then it seemed to catch. There was a moment's pause and then bump-bump-bump-tink-clunk. The torch had reached the bottom, and it sounded as if the bulb might have shattered. Damn. Agatha moved to go and fetch a candle from the kitchen but then remembered with a sniff they still hadn't bought any, though intending to for months. She considered giving the whole expedition up, but didn't want to think of herself as silly – or approach the word 'cowardly'. Immediately, she set off down the steps – not hurried, she didn't want to fall; she held on to the bannister and was aware how tightly she did this. With every step, it got darker. Agatha reminded herself not to think of rats, and the fact that if there were rats under the floorboards there would certainly be rats down here. She stopped, listened; she could hear a slight whining, which was the gas in the pipes beside the meter. She tried sniffing the air; dusty, not damp – and not putrid or urine-smelling. She sniffed again, more deeply now she knew it wouldn't be horrible; a cool, long, chalky, plastery smell, but nothing to hint at animal occupation. She continued down, her pupils having dilated, the dark not seeming so dark. Perhaps, she thought, she should leave this for now – wait for Paddy to get back and tell him what had happened. But she hated to think of his gained superiority. The torch at the bottom of the cellar stairs would be taken, by him, as yet another minor proof that she couldn't *do* things any more – that she botched them. It seemed, to her, as if by giving this up she would be passing over a proportion of the house to him. Two more steps down, the air was cooler but not in any way unpleasant. She waited for her eyes to do their work of adjusting; they did, but she still couldn't see the bottom step. Looking behind her, she guessed it would be the next or the next but one. She listened again and realised that the main sound was the blood in her ears – a waterfall in a forest, heard but not seen. Her right foot reached down and patted the next, wooden step; she shifted her weight and followed it. Her left foot wouldn't move, so she used her right again – it made a harder sound: the bottom. She could smell dust, thought about getting dirt under her nails. The dirt frightened her almost as much as the dark. But she had to do it – bend down and start feeling about with her hands. What if one of them touched hair? Not even a living rat with teeth but a dead one with scrapy clawed feet. Her hands moved in small arcs, Agatha following them forwards as little as she could. If the doorbell rang, she thought, she might pee herself; if Paddy decided to phone. One of the fingernails of her left hand touched something, something which seemed soft. She pulled back, not sure if she was judging herself correctly – whether she was really the kind of woman who could do this. Run! Both hands out, to refute this thought, and they closed around the shaft of the torch. Slowly, Agatha stood up. She didn't want to switch the torch on. Not seeing was bad but seeing might be a lot worse. She turned and now ran, almost tripping, up the stairs and out into the light-filled kitchen. The torch was dusty, and a long blond hair was caught between it and her fingers. Agatha pulled this off, though it seemed determined to cling to her, and let it fall into the bin.

After a glass of water, she walked silently as she could into the back sitting room. She had confidence: this little hole couldn't be as bad as the dark cellar; she had been braver than the cellar. She turned the torch on – it worked! – the bulb hadn't smashed – and pointed it down at the tip of a tail disappearing. The shriek she gave surprised and then embarrassed her. Her hands jumped to her face and the torch was now shining in a pale circle on the ceiling, but in the instant before this she had seen something other than the tail. She wasn't sure she could bear to look into the hole again, although she was almost certain she wouldn't see eyes looking back. It had been little black dots, probably droppings. 'Oh my God,' she said, and was glad to hear herself speak. She let her hands cascade down her sides, flop. The torch shone into the hole, and there the droppings were. They looked small – too small to be ratshit. And the tail, she talked convincingly to herself, the tail had been too thin for a rat.

When she took a step backwards, she could feel blood sloshing around in her feet, like water in Wellington boots. A bit dizzy, she helped herself over to the sofa – touching one of the cardboard boxes they were using until they bought a coffee table. Once she had sat down, Agatha realised she was immensely happy; she had been, for a little while, so completely, fantastically distracted. She hadn't thought about, and here she started to cry; she hadn't thought about it at all.

When she had recovered, she made a conscious decision to spend the rest of the afternoon in bed. It wasn't that she was scared of hearing the scrabbling again; she just didn't particularly *want* to.

When Paddy got home, she hugged him harder than she had been planning to. 'Come here,' she said, taking his non-umbrella-holding hand. A definite march across to the hole in the floor, picking up the torch from the arm of the sofa. Click and shining it down into. 'What are those?'

'Those things –'

'I saw it.'

'Hang on. I think they're droppings.'

'Do you think it's a mouse?'

'You saw what?'

'I think it's a mouse. I think we've got mice.'

'What did you see?'

'I saw its tail.'

'They look like mice droppings to me, yes.'

'Mice, that means we've probably got rats too, doesn't it?'

'No, it doesn't.'

'It means we've got an infestation – a nest.'

'Calm down. We'll just have to buy some traps, or borrow Henry and May's cat for a few days. They're easily got rid of – no problem at all.'

'It was a bit of a shock.'

'I'll buy a trap or two tomorrow,' said Paddy, amused at the idea, 'easy – we'll put some cheese in it, or whatever fashionable mice are eating these days: bang, problem solved.'

'I don't like to think of them being in the house, not when Max is back.'

'I promise we'll get rid of them by then.' Paddy was glad this little crisis had brought the subject up easily. He wanted to ask when that was likely to be – the weekend? Surely Aggie had missed Max terribly today, and wouldn't want to be without him much longer. He looked at her in the hope that he would be able to see this in her.

'Tomorrow – you'll do something tomorrow.'

'As soon as I can. Don't worry about it. Were you scared?'

'No,' said Agatha. 'But the bulb in the cellar has gone.'

'You went down there?'

'No,' she said.'I just know the bulb has gone.'

# CHAPTER 8

Paddy brought home a trap the following evening; an old-fashioned one of the sort that Agatha, when he presented it to her, remembered from childhood – a balsa-wood base with a spike for the temptation, a spring-loaded bar coming straight down on the mouse's spine. 'I'll set it before I leave tomorrow,' said Paddy.

'I didn't see the mouse today,' said Agatha, who had spent most of her time reading in the bedroom. 'I think perhaps it might have left. Perhaps I scared it off.'

'I bought some cheese, too,' said Paddy, producing a comically large slice of Gouda.

Agatha felt distressed, and all the following morning sat in the armchair opposite the hole, waiting and watching and wondering. Her answer came when the pinky brown nose of the mouse shivered its way, tentative-tentative, out of the floorhole. Mice, she knew, usually move very fast – she had seen them on the tracks of the underground, zooming out from under rapidly bearing down trains. They were escapologists extraordinaire, but this little one, with its forward-asking nose, was heading trapwards. She could see it dying and see it dead. With this knowledge, she watched herself, unsure what her reaction was going to be. The mouse was out on the floor now, moving in zigzags, faster and more definite than before. It stayed within a foot of the skirting board, which was where Paddy – advisedly, after phone consultation with his farmer uncle – had placed the trap. On getting off the phone he had mentioned that mice have no bladder control, leaving a slight smear of urine behind them wherever they go. Agatha remembered girls at school in black acrylic uniforms with pink tails twitching delicately in-out of their top pockets. Mice had been a craze, shortly before and for some girls overlapping with and facilitating introduction to boys; some rebels dyed their mice pink or orange, or even stripy, if they could be bothered. The nose of the mouse, which Agatha was now feeling through as if it were one of her own fingertips, touched the cheap balsa wood of the trap's base. 'No!' Agatha screamed. 'Don't!' The mouse zapped down the hole, unharmed, quicker almost than she could see. She lurched out of the armchair and towards the trap – off-balancedly reaching her hand down to pick it up; she misjudged, put her fingers wrong, and snap was in bad and immediate pain. Laughter was her first reaction, then the thought that if the trap left any mark on her fingers she would have to tell Paddy what had happened – and Paddy would mock her for being soft, and she would have to say, 'But I couldn't just sit there and watch it be killed,' and Paddy would say something like, 'You didn't have to just sit there and do anything at all.' He would put her down, again, for a sentimentalist – all this she thought, whilst in pain. Then, left-handed, she forced back the jaws of the trap and was able to slide out her fingers – one of which was bleeding, having been punctured by the little spike-of-a-nail Paddy had pushed the cheese down onto; the cheese that had now fallen onto the floor and which, with the last of her laughter, Agatha pushed with a bare foot into the mouse hole. 'You deserve it,' she said, 'after that shock I gave you.' The fingers of her right hand, when she came to look at them, were pale with a pink line diagonally across the knuckles – there was a spit of red where her blood had seeped into the balsa wood. 'I saved the mouse,' she thought, 'I saved the mouse's life.' She started to weep, aware that she could be seen through the front window – about to put her bleeding finger in her mouth, she thought better of it. Crying harder, she took herself through into the kitchen where she turned on the cold tap and put the hurt hand into the flow. Agatha was by now quite used to rationing and delimiting her crying; this time, she thought, I'll cry until I've finished washing my hand. She was still sobbing, however, when she reached for the kitchen roll and wrapped her finger in a temporary bandage of softish, roughish paper. 'I'm a fool,' she said, out loud, 'a bit of a bloody loon.' Paddy will laugh at me, she thought, hearing his expostulations – perhaps she could delay it until he'd been in the house an hour, or until after they'd eaten. But he was observant, he would soon notice. And what had happened with the mousetrap was their little cliffhanger, their tiny narrative hook of the day; it gave them both a way of avoiding, 'Did you go out?' 'No.' This already was becoming a question between them. If Paddy got bored enough at work, it was possible that he might even call during lunchtime to ask if anything had happened, mousewise. Agatha unpeeled the paper, which had formed itself around the ridgy contours of her finger. The bleeding had stopped; there was a little v-shaped flap of skin, stuck down by a sliver of congealed blood. She had, she realised, stopped crying; the best way out of the evening's awkwardness, at her expense, was to kill a mouse – or to let Paddy know, the moment he came through the door, that joking would be absolutely the wrong tone. But, she thought, she had discovered something about herself: she couldn't bear the idea of being a deathbringer, not to anything. She kissed the finger better – those maternal reflexes, she thought – then opened the fridge door to find the cheese. I must learn, she thought, I must remember what I was before; we can't have Max with mice running up his trouser-legs and biting him, or trailing pee across his plate before dinner. She pulled the metal spring back and pressed a crumb of cheese down onto the spike. I am brutal, Agatha thought as she carried the trap through into the sitting room and replaced it exactly where it had been before. Back to the armchair she went, a self-conscious warrior-woman, tasting the soap on her finger. She sat there another hour, and the mouse did not return; from the kitchen, that afternoon, through the smell of coffee, she heard a sound she had forgotten the meaning of – and it was Paddy, not having phoned during the day, who found the brokeback mouse that evening, pink nose a dead millimetre from the cheese. He didn't notice the finger, but Agatha told him everything anyway, with a laugh and a wail he was quite used to, even in this odd combination. They hugged, briefly. 'Perhaps it was a different mouse,' he said down her back. No, she had looked, as Paddy dropped it into the bin; she had seen the mouse she had seen before – and had saved. 'Why did I do it?' she said, and Paddy didn't feel like asking what she meant.

When Agatha got up the next morning, she saw the deathtrap remained unsprung on the top of the microwave; she didn't set it, though she thought about it; more drop-pings appeared, the mice unseen; that evening Paddy came home with a different design of trap under his arm in a box – one that didn't kill.

'Thank you,' said Agatha.

Paddy felt angered. He wanted to tell Aggie about the surprise he was planning for her – he couldn't, and it seemed to him that she was controlling every aspect of their lives. This she did by making her mood the mood of the house; so, *she* decided who would come to their house, and when. Agatha, for instance, that afternoon, had phoned and arranged for her mother to bring Max round at the weekend, probably Saturday for tea. Of course, Paddy, when told, was delighted at the chance to see his son but, emotionally, annoyed that he hadn't been consulted. The argument was obvious, and not worth having: Agatha would say, why ask when the answer couldn't be anything but yes? Paddy's only response pushed him into pettiness: You should because you just should. He meant it as something more: You should because this is a bloody marriage. To this, Agatha could reply: Exactly, that's why I didn't ask. He objected most of all to the coming normality of noncommunication. More and more was passing unspoken – their present understanding, though, was based entirely upon past sympathy, and the further they left this behind, the less chance they had of returning to it. Paddy intended his surprise to change things, slightly, slyly.

On Friday, Paddy arrived home late – and called out from the hall, when usually before he had come to find Agatha wherever she was. (She had not, since they moved into the house, ever run to him returning – in the flat, Max had always directed her attention towards Daddy's arrival: wanting to see his father as soon as possible, wanting and wailing. When she had been going to work, it was Paddy who was usually waiting at home for her.) Agatha was in the kitchen, making macaroni cheese with the rest of the mouse-Gouda. She stayed where she was. Paddy called again. 'I'm here,' Agatha called back. Paddy gave in, walking disappointedly down the hall and into the kitchen. Without speaking, Paddy produced from behind his back a plastic box with a grille across the front. 'She might be a little terrified,' he said, crouching down to the floor with it. 'She didn't enjoy the journey much at all.'

'You got a cat,' said Agatha, startled.

'It's a kitten,' Paddy said, unlatching the grille.

'Did we agree to get one? I don't remember agreeing to get one.'

'I mentioned it to Peter,' who, as Agatha knew, was another philosopher in the department, 'and his sister's cat had just had a litter.' Paddy put his hand inside the box, elbow jutting, which reminded Agatha of too many visits to the gynaecologist – of too many other things. '*There* you are,' he said.

'You'll have to take it back,' said Agatha, as Paddy drew the kitten from its dark den, detaching its soft claws one by one from the blanket. 'Don't get it out, you'll just have to put it back.'

Paddy was patient (nothing if not); he had the kitten comfortably draped over his hand, its belly in his palm; he could feel each of its tender ribs and, behind them, the thrill of its heart, beating fast but not panic-fast; there was no smell of urine from the carry-case.

'Oh, it's tiny,' said Agatha.

'Yes,' said Paddy, 'only a few weeks.'

'Is it old enough to be away from –'

'Peter's sister seemed to think so, and she's been giving away kittens for as long as he can remember. It was either this or a bag and a bucket in the yard.'

'Paddy,' said Agatha, saddened by his attempt at cruelty. He was bringing the big-eyed fluffy thing towards her. It was aggressively sweet, that was what she felt: merciless in its undislikeability; a weapon of endearment, a cute-bomb. The kitten's survival mechanism was hooks in human hearts; Agatha felt them sliding itchily in. 'No,' she said, shifting herself sideways away from the thing.

'At least it can have a little runaround. It can't just go straight back in the box.'

'It can,' said Agatha. The thing was tortoiseshell with six parallel lines of black furrow down its forehead. Its paws were too big for it, some growing would have to be done before they ceased to look ridiculous. Paddy paused for a moment, holding it. If he had been kitten-confident, he would have transferred it to a pinch between his fingers, dangling it from its scruff like a mothercat would – moving it with her mouth from place to place, out of danger. Paddy made a decision, one he *was* brave enough for, and gently put the kitten down on the floor. 'No,' he said, 'it's been in that little box for most of the afternoon – it would be cruel to put it back straight away.'

The kitten stood shakily, looking around with its topaz eyes – where, it was feeling, were the soft shapes (with occasional claws) of its brothers and sisters? The tiles were cold beneath its pads, and the kitchen was a vast open expanse. Agatha looked at Paddy, the tears distorting him. 'Why did you do this?' she asked. 'It's so cruel.'

'I saved it,' he said.

'Bringing it here, letting me see it.'

'It will help with our mouse problem.' Paddy seemed to shrink. This had been an inspiration, and he'd been hoping Aggie would recognise it as such. They were always wondering what to do; well, this was something he had done. 'You're determined I should take it back?' Paddy asked.

'Of course I'm not,' said Agatha. 'It's like showing me an orphan. It's unbearable.' She stood up and went towards the door. The kitten was investigating the bottom of the oven, throwing tentative little sniffs in its direction. Paddy stood aside to let Aggie leave. He was no longer hugely upset, apart from sympathetically, by her tears; he did not immediately take their blame upon himself – although in this case he gave a moment's thought as to whether he should. Footsteps along the landing; into the bedroom directly above his head; the door did not slam, he didn't even hear it shut. 'Behave yourself,' he said to the kitten. 'Don't disgrace me – or I'll never forgive you.' He opened a bottle of red wine and poured out two generous glasses. (He had thought Aggie might start drinking during the day; that was a possibility – it hadn't yet happened but it still might.) One in either hand, he went steadily up the stairs and through the open bedroom door. Agatha was not going to be easily persuaded. He would refuse to take the kitten back that night – he couldn't take it back. Where to? Peter's sister's farm? He didn't know where it was. Peter had gone away for the weekend (he hadn't, but Paddy would say he had). Agatha, for her part, was thinking the kitten should spend the night in its box. 'Where is it?' she asked.

'It's where I left it – in the kitchen.'

'Loose?' asked Agatha.

'On the prowl,' said Paddy.

'We had a tortoiseshell when I was nine or ten,' said Aggie, a while later, the wine finished. 'Did I ever tell you that?'

'I've seen the photograph with you in the garden.'

'I'm holding it like a mink stole, aren't I? My arms right round the middle. It doesn't look like it's got any bones in it at all.'

'And you've got glasses on.'

'Thank you,' said Agatha.

'And an eye-patch.'

'I had a squint – it was to correct it.'

'Where is that album?'

'In a box, in the sticker room, I think,' said Agatha.

'Shall I get it?' asked Paddy, already sensing he was being too keen.

'No,' said Aggie, and the moment was ended – but Paddy felt it had been a good one; rare.

When they went downstairs ten minutes later they found two small craplets alongside a tight circle of piss. Beneath the kitchen table, a few moments after this, thanks to the smell, they discovered an equal-sized splat of puke.

'It's disgraced itself,' said Paddy. He looked the long, long way down to the kitten. 'You've disgraced yourself.'

'It can stay,' said Agatha.

'Really?' said Paddy, who had been doing his best to let neither his happiness nor his disappointment show.

'Is it a boy-cat or a girl-cat?' Agatha asked.

'Girl-cat,' said Paddy.

'Let's not give it a name just yet,' said Agatha. 'Let's wait and see what it's like before we give it a name.'

They cleared up the messes, which smelt sweet but were very disgusting – even compared to baby-shit; then Agatha put the fluffy little thing in the corner and poured out some milk for it. The kitten's tongue was, like all cats' tasting tongues, a miracle of fast appearing and fast disappearing pink. 'I still have reservations, though,' said Agatha.

'I know you do.'

'I'm not sure how I feel about having it around Max.'

'Max isn't here.'

'You know what I mean – when he is here.'

'Max will love it – it will save him having to nag us for a pet when he's eight and a half.'

Agatha turned to Paddy. 'Thank you,' she said. 'I know what you're attempting to do with this' – a gesture towards the kitten – 'and I appreciate it – I really appreciate it, but I don't know how I'm going to be able to respond.'

'You don't have to respond.'

'If we run out of milk, you would expect me to go and buy some. There are practical problems.'

Paddy let his voice darken. 'We won't run out of milk,' he said. Agatha's confession that going outside the house was no longer something of which she felt capable shocked at the same time as it gladdened: he had been right – and this was a serious problem to be dealt with. To do so now, though, to make of this mentioning a beginning, would be crass. The kitten represented progress, though from a point far back from where he'd hoped Agatha was. He looked at her, very conscious of their marriage, and felt an extreme vertiginous distance. His next thought was of Max – postponing the idea of bringing him to the house; their restitution as a no longer normal but at least attempting-it family. Paddy just then hoped Agatha would be momentarily distracted by something, that the kitten would amuse, because he was terrified by what she might see if she looked at him – what that glance might tell her, and what damage it might do.

The kitten obliged, but only by continuing what it had been doing. It was almost finished now, its tiny perform-ance of need-satisfied in great contrast to the thoughts and discussion going on at cloud-height above its head. 'It brings up the problem,' said Agatha, repeating her confession. 'And I don't know how I'm going to be able to cope with that.'

'I'm sure you'll cope beautifully.'

'Coping is never beautiful,' said Agatha. 'My coping is angry and botched and unsatisfying . . .'

'Coping is all we can do,' said Paddy, 'at the moment.'

'No,' said Agatha, 'I've changed my mind – you'll have to take it back tomorrow.' When she said this she had been looking at Paddy, not the kitten.

'But you just said –'

'Exactly: look how unreliable and flighty I am.' Agatha started to cry. 'Why do you make me make decisions?' she said, now looking at the kitten – who was sitting in the saucer, mopping up the last of the dampness with her tail.

'At some point,' said Paddy, 'you will have to make decisions again – in fact, that's wrong: I'm sure you make decisions all day long, you just don't think of them as such.'

'I don't,' said Agatha. 'I drift and I follow my appetite. I limit my world; I'm getting into a routine.'

'I spoke to Henry today. I invited them round for lunch this Sunday.'

'Why?'

'They're going to bring Hope, too.'

Agatha might once have used this moment to begin sulking. Paddy said, 'You want to see May, too, don't you?'

'Some time. Not right now.'

'They only live ten minutes away, and that's walking, with a pram. We moved down here, partly at least, so we could be near them – and we haven't seen them at all. You might not want to see Hope right now, but you'll regret it in future.'

'Of course I will, I'll regret lots of things – some of them I do exactly because I know that I'll regret them.'

'This involves them, too,' Paddy said. 'It was Henry who called me; they want to see you – they want to do what they can to see that you're alright.'

Bored with the emptied bowl, the kitten now had her nose up against the French doors.

'Tomorrow it goes,' said Agatha. 'Before Max gets here. We can't have him falling in love with it.'

'I can't take it back – Peter lives in Hertfordshire. I'll take it back on Monday.'

'I won't change my mind.'

'I know you won't; do you think I don't?'

'We can't let Max see it.'

# CHAPTER 9

APART from the mouse incident and the kitten evening, their routine had developed smoothly during the first week. When Paddy got up in the morning, Agatha shifted to the centre of the bed; her arms and legs reaching towards its four corners, hands beneath the heavy pillows. She fell asleep again as soon as she had heard the front door shut behind him, and it was a better, less exhausting sleep. This she was grateful for: her nights during the months *since* had been full of difficulty. There were hours of blackout, welcomed in retrospect; then more often there were nights whole long nights of struggle. She kicked Paddy, hard – and he never got used to it, always woke in an outrage. She babbled words, wardings off; there were witches flying through branches over her head, and now moonlight on the back of a fat rat. Sometimes she was in the forest and sometimes she went everywhere: directed the orgy alongside the obese emperor, hid in a cellar from the SS, escaped from the harem, was buried beneath an avalanche, felt the desert sun burn her face into a permanent smile, forded rivers – or failed halfway across to ford them, was swept over Niagara Falls, Victoria Falls, drowned, sat in the café beside the suitcase containing the bomb, bought sweets in an Arab bazaar which turned out to be seeds for poisonous plants, ate them, turned into a monster, burnt to death in skyscrapers and tenements and crashed cars, went zombie in Haiti after marrying her sweetheart's brother out of spite, took tea with a murderous imposter Queen, fired a rocket launcher at a Zeppelin which then crash-landed on her, lost jewels down a sewer because her hands were slippy with frog-slime, failed to recognise her father in a crowd, found a book of miraculous answers on a scrapheap but had it stolen before daylight by a gang of naked children, sat beside mothers-to-be on the bus with knitting needles in her fists, underwent spinal surgery which was botched, gave birth to porcupines, bats, rats, all possible deformities, gave birth to Paddy, to herself. In the forest, she was a frog gooed with fecundity at the time of spawning, a wolf in the pack, a tree struck by lightning, an ant milking the Queen, a mushroom knocked off a branch by a bear, a cuckoo in a sparrow's nest, a lost child. When she was not alone, Max was there, in danger – or was the object of some quest. There were conspiracies against them; he was perpetually being abducted. More often than not, she failed him and he died. She was always late for meetings to arrange his safe passage to a neutral country, or stop the damaged cable-car leaving with him (a young man now) on the roof, or prevent him signing up for the army of an indistinct military. She failed him, and the guilt, which remained with her all day, was never remembered as dream-caused but attached itself to the idea of Max – Max without her. Sometimes, and this was worst, it was all reunion, embrace, safety; her body would remember its feelings of fullness, of sweet invasion. 'Empty my head,' she wanted to tell Paddy, 'flush it like a toilet.' She was surprised, and proud of herself, for never having wet the bed; she had come, soft orgasms, once or twice, in the middle of some grotesque pulsing image. She wasn't, as people sometimes said, afraid of the fear, so much as the fear of the fear – or the fear of the fear of the fear. But the dull, unmemorable slumber after Paddy had left for work was quite different: she enjoyed it extraordinarily, waking as the week went on later and later in the morning.

Once up and out of bed, she was hardly less pleased with the state of things. The house during the day was exquisite pleasure – she drank in the undisturbed-but-by-herself air: to be able to *choose* which room to spend time in, not constantly to be called, required, needed. If the sun was out, she sat with a coffee and looked out through the French doors. This, for reasons of her own, reasons secret even from herself, was as near as she was prepared to go. She looked into the appletree and watched the smoke from her imaginary cigarette blow through it, emphasizing the spaces between its green leaves. All that she worried about, at such moments, in that spot, was being spied upon by one of the three house-windows with a view down into the garden. The reason this occurred to her was that she had herself started to become a little obsessed with watching the houses – the ones on the other side of the road. During the day, with most adults at work and most children at nursery or school, the houses opposite did almost nothing – which was one of the main reasons she watched; of course, and this was another big reason for her fascination, whatever did happen was completely spontaneous and unpredictable, unlike television: curtains could be drawn at any moment across an ambiguous encounter. Agatha, though, could see only a short distance into the rooms – those with windows clear of curtains, blinds or nets. The rest of her penetrations were made up. One house, the most fascinating to her, had a window with a model sailing ship in it – a clipper. There was often movement behind the ship, movement she suspected was male, old. Agatha had yet to see anyone leaving or entering the ship house. Mostly, she stood back and watched, stepping side to side, through a small gap calculatedly left between the main bedroom curtains. So far, she had learnt very little about the lives of the people across the street. But her observations of them made her suspect that, quite probably, one of their windows was hiding behind it a watcher-back – although as the newcomer to the street, and the beginning spy, it was Agatha, strictly, who should have been regarding herself as secondary.

When she was not watching, or drifting, she cleaned – dusted, vacuumed, polished, ironed, read recipes, made shopping lists for Paddy, made to-do lists for herself. Most of all, though, she read books. She was, she realised, quite consciously, almost systematically, living out her own mother-with-toddler fantasies of uninterrupted time. *If only* – she had thought, in the months after Max was born, in the months during which he wailed into life – *if only he* – taking instants to dream long days – *if only he wasn't*; but this had been another guilt, one which she tricked, for her own self-facing, into *if only he wasn't so*. The *so* was false, she knew now; how could she not? She had wished him away, and he had gone – and *if only he wasn't* had become *and now that he isn't*. One new-mother fantasy had been of reading a whodunnit cover-to-cover in a morning, and this she had done – twice; another, achieved only the once, had been a mid-afternoon bath, long enough to read a couple of chapters. But she did not particularly like to be alone with her unclothed body, and soaping between her legs brought the sorbet texture of remorse into her mouth.

Agatha's body had gone wild: her legs were as hairy as they could get – as hairy as Paddy's: black hairs, animal; she hadn't shaved under her arms or waxed her lip *since*; her hair was a shapeless, more-than-shoulder-length thing which she often put up with a couple of pencils. The fingernails were bitten away, although she could never remember biting them (she did it when she watched television). She had a small cyst in her vagina, about which she hadn't told Paddy – he might make a fuss and start insisting she went to the hospital. She had had enough of hospitals, she felt, for the rest of her life: if it was a choice between dying and going to hospital again, dying looked – she flippantly thought – the more attractive option. Most of the time, she didn't put in contact lenses and forgot or couldn't be bothered to wear her glasses. She turned the world deliberately into a blur, so that whatever came out of it to hurt her would be softer and she wouldn't see it until it was already upon her. Television was better, she found, indistinct; the objects that appeared on it were far more intriguing when improperly seen, and the people more mysterious and charismatic. What were they doing? The music usually explained, narrating and moralizing the action. Why were they bothering doing what they were doing, with the world as terrible as it was? Cooking? Gardening? Decorating? Perhaps, she thought, they did these things *because* the world was as it was. Agatha at least in the first few days regularly watched advertisements she had helped devise; she recognized her own slogans, though not the intonation with which the actors mispronounced them. She felt sorry for the actors in advertisements; they were so obviously dying, on screen – their souls desiccating from having to do something so unShakespeare. They didn't deserve it. She wore her glasses only for looking at the appletree in the garden; cooking she made more interesting, and a little more dangerous, by doing it short-sightedly.

When the house was very quiet, she closed her eyes and listened to the waves. It had been one of her great discoveries about the house – that they were audible all the way up here. The house was four streets away from the beach – opening the windows in the bedroom did not seem to make the sound any louder, or bring the beach any closer; the smell did that, the wet-sweater smell of seaweed. Standing in the front porch, something she had never yet done, might have given her a better idea of how loud the waves really were. Other sounds interrupted: cars drove past, seagulls made their uncanny noises – as if they had a baby stuck in their throats. Her dislike of seagulls had become a major part of their deliberations as to whether to move to the seaside; just as her fear of heights affected their choice of holiday destinations – no clifftop drives for her, no thank you. Now she heard the gulls every day, she did not hate them any the less. Once, she had surprised one on the ledge of the bedroom window, and the bang of its taking-off wings against the glass had made her squeal and then giggle with fear.

She felt lonely, on her own, and doubly childless, but, if asked, would have denied feeling lonely – would have said, instead, she felt 'lonesome' or 'just alone'. The quiet of the house, its small noises, microsounds, were something that gave her extraordinary pleasure; she listened to them actively and intensely, just as she would have listened to a song recital by someone she loved. She was not a long listener, she gave it three or four total minutes, standing on the spot or looking up from a book, but they stood in for the hours of Max's wail, whimper, burble and prattle – which was what she missed about him most of all; his needs, his need, she could do without, but the reminders of his continued life – they, she felt, were her need.

Always around teatime she called her mother and got her to hold the phone up to Max's mouth; she had to hear his breathing – after that, she could try to appreciate his efforts with two or three sentence-making words. He probably knew who he was speaking to, just about. She had reconciled herself to missing out on some of the more important (and memorable) stages of his linguistic development. At least she would be seeing him on Saturday – this she and her mother had confirmed towards the end of the week.

When Paddy returned, around seven usually, she had dinner ready. They sat down together at the kitchen table, and ate with great care. He tried to tell her about his day; she tried to listen. On the one evening Paddy was late, Agatha had begun to fantasize he was dead. She made guilty plans for herself, Max and the house: they would stay inside, ordering food deliveries from the local supermarket, and clothes and everything else from catalogues; or they would go to a Scottish island and work towards being accepted in their tenth year there by the locals; or they would disappear hand-in-hand into the great and easy mall of America, become thoughtless. This kind of morbidity had become common with Agatha, *since*. She had become used to staying at home in the company of her death-fantasies. Her assumption was always that when Paddy was late he was dead. In some ways, he *was* dead for her all day long – dead, routinely, from the moment he left in the morning: killed by a pavement-climbing car or a brain haemorrhage or a fallen piece of space-debris. If she spoke to him during the morning or afternoon, she was convinced he'd be killed the second he put the phone down – by a freak electrocution, by another brain haemorrhage, by the murderer looming up behind him with a knife even as they'd been talking to one another for the last time, again, final, repeatedly. Unexpected callers during the day –

meter-readers and evangelists – were always, though she never answered the door, sombre policemen with their hats tucked under their arms. 'Mrs –?' 'Yes. It's Paddy, isn't it?' 'I'm very sorry to have to inform you –' Eventually, she had begun to acknowledge the comedy aspect of the morbidity. 'Don't cross any roads,' she'd said, as he left for work. (This had started, she remembered, about a month ago.) 'I won't,' he would say – before he caught on to her anxiety-expressed-as-mock-anxiety, and started to reply, 'Nor you neither.' Then she would close the door on his back, certainly for the last and final time: never that smile, never those eyes again. Much had changed since they moved into the house, not least that his death seemed to have its liberating aspects, too. She did not see him off at the door; she stayed in bed.

# CHAPTER 10

I T was clear the moment Max came carried through the door that he was delighted with the house, and that getting him to leave would be difficult – almost as difficult as separating him from Agatha. Some form of trick would in all probability have to be used. They might have to wait until he was asleep, then carry him out stealthily to the car. For now, though, Agatha took him from her mother's arms and carried him into the kitchen. She and Paddy had decided not to take him upstairs: the kitten, in its travel basket, in the attic, was still clearly audible from the upstairs landing – a ludicrous but still affecting helium meow: aeiou! They didn't want to risk Max hearing this; both remembered *meow*, learnt from picture books, had been one of his earliest words: after *moo* and *woof* but before *no* and *dad*. As she set him down on the kitchen floor, Agatha tried not to let her tearfulness show. Agatha's mother was glad to see this, the mothering, the tears and the attempt to hide them; she believed that guilt had a necessary part to play in bringing her daughter back to her senses. (This alone shows how unaware Agatha's mother was of the extent of Agatha's already existing guilt.) 'I'm exhausted,' she said, after Paddy had offered her a cup of tea. Paddy took this to mean yes, and filled the kettle. He, too, was aware of Agatha's emotion. Max was only interested in the garden. He kept crawling towards the French doors and leaving smears of fascination on their bottom halves. After a couple of minutes, Agatha said, 'I'll make the tea – why don't you take him outside?' Paddy knew immediately that this meant Agatha wasn't allowing herself the garden, either. He became very angry but mutated this into swift action: the doors were opened, Max was lifted shoulder-high and held up to touch the small new leaves of the appletree. Agatha's mother followed them out, as if she too wanted to embarrass her daughter, eventually, into crossing this threshold. 'It'll be lovely when you've done it, won't it?' she said, to Paddy but loud enough for Agatha to know she wasn't excluded.

'It's the time,' said Paddy, then saw his mistake, and tried to cover it. 'I think I'm much more into gardening than Agatha.' Max was grabbing his ear with both hands; it felt wonderful. He realised he'd failed – had only emphasized who wasn't gardening, who had all the time.

'Tea,' said Agatha, laying the things on the table. With an instinct for the difficult, her mother said, 'Why don't we sit out here?' The day was sunny if not comfortably warm.

'It's still a bit muddy,' Paddy said. 'Let's try and keep Max fairly clean.' He carried his son back inside. Agatha's mother followed and closed the doors, for the time being, behind them.

This visit of Max's was fast becoming atrocious for Paddy. He had to restrain himself from thinking and doing so many things. His instinct was to encourage Max's desire to be here; he wanted his son to associate the spaces of the new rooms, from the first, with happiness, fun, security. But he could do none of this, not without the certainty that any attachment of love towards the house that he caused Max to feel would be wrenched when, after tea, after more treacherous talk, his grandmother tore him away. Paddy thought of divorce – how divorce wasn't a singular event; divorce was perpetual, for its children. They were regularly wrenched, to a legally established timetable. He hoped he was underestimating the damage done to Max

– if he had it right, they were in for a lifetime of behavioural problems. Paddy had, already, many times, lived through Max's first fight at school, his first caution by the police, his first overdose. He wished, as a father, that he had lost his capacity for imagination, since it did nothing but present him with horror after horror of dramatized guilt. While Aggie was pregnant for the second time, they had been smug – that was what Paddy now believed; they had reached a high-point of conceit. Two children, they would have – two not perfect but intelligent, happy, growing children. And now, he hoped for one young man who wouldn't, whilst his mother was still alive, jump under a train. Max, pressed up against the exciting doors to out-side, must sense this change – he had become a surlier child, quicker to anger and slower to calm. His grand-mother, Paddy knew, used sweet things all the time as a control device. Aggie had told him about her own confec-tionary childhood. It had always been her mother's way. When Max arrived, Paddy had noticed, he was already half-frantic from the sugary treats that had kept him quiet during the drive over. He was not hungry now, and Paddy was concerned about the bad habits and tastes he was developing. A grandparent, particularly one on their own, could be expected to spoil their grandchild – but that was meant to be during, at most, weekly visits; Max was in danger of being spoiled full stop. And of course there was nothing Paddy could say about this, for Agatha's mother would quite happily have removed Max's seat from her car, brought it inside and driven off without him. Perhaps, he thought, this was something – not knowing her daugh-ter as well as he did – something she genuinely expected. But it wasn't to happen. Agatha did not ask whether her mother was happy taking Max back for another week, and so made it clear that she didn't consider it in question. This angered Agatha's mother. She had a life of her own, too, didn't they know that? There were things she was missing out on, important occasions the like of which would not come again. This she would say on the phone, that evening, after Max had been successfully (for the moment) put to bed. She promised herself the pleasure of the unadulterated truth, and the longer satisfaction of knowing Agatha would have to ask *then*.

Agatha felt her mother's growing annoyance and, to some extent, went along with it. The presence of Max made her feel her own almost-evil. She, too, wanted to do something *against* herself – but what was there? To take Max back, for a night or two, then force him out again, would be worse even than this few hours' visit (which, anyway, she'd arranged).

A certain exhaustion had overtaken Agatha, a certain apathy creeping up from the ground, through the soles of her feet (bare) – she could no longer impose her will upon any part of the world. By refusing to leave the house, she called many many things down upon herself: her mother was not the least of them. There was no emotional logic to this visit, it could only do Max harm – the idea that anyone else, that Paddy, was looking at Max as she looked and mentally calculating how much harm, every day, every hour, he could safely be expected to take – that notion was unbearable to her. Yet she, guilty herself, could find no argument against it: *you mustn't because I do* did not work; nor *no-one should*; nor *this is unbearable*. She bore it, she did it, she had given them their example.

Max and Agatha's mother stayed another couple of hours. She went out, at one point, to do a little shopping by herself. Paddy took Max out into the garden again, and Agatha — full of self-hate and tenderness — watched the normality of this. As they had anticipated, it was easier to smuggle Max out of the house whilst asleep. Goodbye, like this, wasn't really goodbye, but at least it avoided being the end of the world.

After Max had gone, they didn't talk about him — not more than to say he had looked well and hadn't seemed unhappy. They didn't speak again, really, until they were in bed, when the conversation was on another subject. Agatha was calmer, seeming to want to be in contact with Paddy about what they were experiencing together; he improvised as best a reaction as he could.

'I haven't lived in a house since — since I was a child,' she said. 'You forget what they're like, don't you? You forget how many different noises they make: a flat is chamber music, a house is a symphony orchestra — or a big band, I suppose, if it has real structural problems.'

'Hmm,' said Paddy. 'God, I hope not.'

'I don't mean it like that,' she said.

'No, it's safe — I think.'

'It is full of character.'

Paddy hesitated, then, 'Character.' He found the word difficult to accept, though Agatha was clearly using it with some care.

'Yes, and one that's so distinct,' said Agatha, jealous of her relationship with the house — she knew it better, and she wanted to prove this to Paddy, 'it almost feels alive.'

They weren't going to sleep for a while; that — lights out — had been a sham.

'How would you describe its character?' asked Paddy. 'Is it a male house or a female house?'

'I don't think it has — houses don't have to be either: some people would say they are all female, like ships are all women, or anything that you put other things inside . . .'

'Comfort, safety . . .'

'But this feels both: masculine in a feminine way, feminine in a masculine — it has dignity.' Paddy after hearing this was silent, a little disturbingly — to himself as well as Agatha. 'You don't agree?' she asked.

'Of course I do.'

'It's not at all *of course* — dignity is an insight, I'm sharing it.'

'You are. Thank you. I'm thinking that it's not the first thing I'd have said.' And this was, indeed, what he had been thinking; as well as how glad he was they were having this conversation. He remembered that, at work during the week, he had been afraid of the return home, of how Agatha might be.

'You didn't say anything.'

'So I can still say the first thing, which is that I think humility is a more important part of its character than dignity. It is showing itself to be a place that is happy for us to live in it, and change it, and it isn't trying to impose itself upon us.'

'That's its dignity — it is slightly withdrawn: you have to go to it if you want to find something out. It doesn't advertise.'

Paddy snorted slightly, recognizing Agatha's autobiographical irony.

'You call that dignity, I call it humility; isn't it the same thing?'

'No, because dignity is more public — I don't think the house's humility is just for us; it feels directed outwards.

That's what's so odd – living here makes me feel I should behave better than I do anywhere else. It moralizes me.'

'Then why . . .' he hesitated.

'I know what you're going to say. As soon as I feel I can fit Max in with that, I will take him back. I won't waste a night – I'll go in the middle of the night. At the moment I know I can't live up to either of them, not the house and not him.'

'That's your new reason for –'

'It's not a new reason, it's the same reason as before, only better expressed.'

'So, your behaviour isn't to do with you in yourself, any more – it's to do with this house?'

'To do with what this house makes me feel about me in myself. Anyway, there isn't a me-in-myself, there's me in this house, and me in the street –'

'Not since we moved, there hasn't been.'

'Because I'm trying to simplify things, so that I can deal with them: me-in-this-house limits the input – it heals me – allows me to heal – by not lacerating me all the time with new this and new that.'

'You mean seeing mothers with their babies?'

'I mean all the possibilities that exist outside but which I'm protected from here.'

'Nowhere is exempt from anything that can happen in the world – that sort of safety is an illusion. If this house looks kindly, it's because we paid for it to suit us.'

'It felt kindly the moment we walked in, that very first day. Anyway, this humility you're talking about is something we've paid for, too.'

'The humility is the way I feel the world behaving towards us, in this house, for the time being. That could change at any moment.'

'Oh, nothing is certain, I agree,' said Agatha.

'You can't keep things out by staying inside.'

'Do we always have to end up talking about this?' said Agatha, which stopped the conversation altogether.

This was the issue between them; how could it not be. Paddy found himself fussing, and saying the wrong thing – out of love, out of disconnection, like a parent dealing with an adolescent. There was nothing he could say which didn't sound interfering, patronizing. He knew this, hated it. Agatha was telling him, indirectly, about her life whilst he wasn't present. He should have accepted what she said with a bit more graciousness. He should try to listen harder, at the moment when the listening might make a difference, which was usually when it might also cause him most pain.

# CHAPTER II

Henry and May came round the following morning, bringing Hope along with them; Hope, who was about the same age Agatha and Paddy's second child would have been. 'This is lovely,' May said to the hall. Paddy had opened the door to them: they had driven round, for May's sake, not Hope's. It wasn't raining and didn't look like it would. Henry carried his daughter in a plastic basket, the handle kinked in the middle for comfort. Paddy shook his free hand. Hope was wearing a dress of pale background with tiny blue flowers on; her chin glistened with drool, slightly milky; her head lifted and lolled. Agatha was waiting in the front room, feeling awkward. 'Oh, she's very lovely,' said Paddy. Then said, 'Sorry, this is very difficult.'

'Oh, Paddy,' said May.

Agatha could tell that the others were hugging, probably awkwardly – the front door still open to the street, and passers-by able to look in. 'Yes,' she heard Paddy say, answering some unheard question. She moved from the front to the back sitting room and stood beside the door – quite calmly, it seemed to herself. 'How's Agatha?' she heard Henry ask.

'She's in here,' said Paddy. 'You can ask her yourself.'

Agatha heard movements, feet on the tiles of the hall, and then Paddy saying, 'Aggie?', as he came into the empty front room. She was hidden by what was left of the dividing wall, as it jutted out. Choosing her moment, fairly sure the others had followed Paddy in, Agatha stepped into the – yes, empty – hall, and quietly as possible ('Aggie?' shouted Paddy) made her way up the stairs. It was only when she'd reached the first-floor landing that she realised exactly what she was doing: hiding. Paddy came out of the back-to-front room, directly below her feet – and strode wordlessly towards the kitchen. Agatha could imagine May and Henry in the front room, looking intelligently at one another, across the head of their beautiful and healthy baby. She had a choice: she could slip into the bathroom, lock the door, flush the loo, wash her face and come out completely excused. 'Aggs?' Paddy had turned round. Hide and seek, now, they were playing. Or she could go into one of the bedrooms and really hide – being a little genuinely strange. She wanted to get into bed and have May and Henry go away. Their growing baby she was quite keen to see, but would have done so, given the choice, without coming near them – or so she felt right now. Paddy was on the stairs; a few steps higher and he'd be able to see her feet. Knowing he would hear her, Agatha walked with as much dignity as she could into the main bedroom – and sat down on the edge of the bed, looking up to where Paddy's head would be after he came through the door. She didn't want to have to explain; she wanted the sight of her, the sight of her eyes, to be enough for Paddy to know immediately the right thing to do – even though she didn't know herself. But Paddy took longer than she expected to come; he had been checking the other bedrooms and the bathroom. Agatha thought she had heard him trying the built-in cupboards – which distressed and angered her, even though she had fleetingly wanted to climb inside the biggest of them. It showed that Paddy, infuriatingly, understood quite how mad she was being. He was a step or two outside the big bedroom when she said, quite quietly, 'I'm in here.' She knew this wouldn't mean she hadn't been hiding, but it at least showed her proved to her that she was capable of speech. Paddy, not annoyed, concerned, came in. 'I can't,' said Agatha, and it was the last thing she was able to say for five minutes at least. Paddy could only sit down beside her and put his arms around her, rub his hands up and down her back; he knew this was behaviour he could only call silly after Aggie herself had – a joke wasn't the way out of this, he had to enter her tragedy. 'It's difficult, isn't it?' She nodded into his shoulder, her nose fitting the fissure between arm and chest. 'They're our friends,' Paddy said, looking over Agatha's head towards the handles on the wardrobe – from which dangled a knitted glittery heart. Agatha made a half-suffocated rising umphle-mumble-grumfle of assent meaning *yes*. 'They want to see you,' said Paddy. Agatha thought, another sentence and he will be patronizing me – treating me like a child (which, she inwardly laughed, wasn't at *all* how she was behaving). 'They love you,' said Paddy, starting to cry. It was, she felt, the worst thing he could say and the best – completely unpatronizing, and for himself as much as for her.

A couple of minutes later, Paddy hugged her hard and then went downstairs. Henry had unhooked Hope from her carry-seat and was sitting in the armchair with her on his lap. Paddy looked at May, who understood immediately. She stood up, then took Hope from Henry who was only a moment puzzled. Paddy quickly told May where she would find Agatha. Another look was good luck.

Carefully supporting the baby's head and watching her own feet, May carried her up the stairs. Creeping along the landing, very unsure of what she'd find, May was nakedly terrified (what if Agatha attacked Hope?) – but at the door, she made her face into her bravest smile-face (smile back along the hospital ward, smile in the rain outside the crematorium). Agatha was on her feet, having heard May coming, and standing awkwardly, adolescently, with one knee resting on the corner of the bed. She had made herself stop crying, but when May wordlessly lifted Hope off her shoulder and turned her round to face Agatha, held her out and said, 'Take her,' she began to cry in a completely different way – her chest was uncaged, bars had been drawn back. She came away from the bed, and May brought Hope a couple of steps towards her – and next, they were lightly hugging with the baby's face a third, smaller, between and to the side of theirs. 'This must be so hard for you,' said May.

'She's gorgeous,' said Agatha.

Downstairs, Paddy was saying almost the same thing. He and Henry had been trying to find something to talk about that wasn't Agatha or Agatha's behaviour. They were aware of themselves as two men, and that a gender separation had just occurred for which, politically, they could find no real defence – but which, quite deeply, they believed in. There was no such thing as women's business, officially; privately, they were glad not to have to go through the scene as a coupled quartet. Women on their own were better at dealing with something – an occasion like this. Of course there was secret women's business, and of course, and rightly, it was something from which they were to be excluded. Henry sat down on one of the armchairs, although he kept the plastic basket close – rocking it by wedging his toes beneath its end and flexing them. 'How's it been?' asked Paddy.

'We're coping,' said Henry, 'just about – it is, I'm sure you remember, quite a shock. I don't think, to start with, you can do much more than cope.'

'Yes,' said Paddy, thinking of Agatha.

'I'm always a little suspicious of people who seem to be getting through it completely unscathed. It's usually to do with money – there are couples in our antenatal class . . .' Henry stopped speaking, stopped rocking the basket. Beginning again, what he hoped was more honestly, he said, 'It must have been terrible. We were very upset to hear.'

'Thank you,' said Paddy.

'Agatha's due date was so close to May's – even though we hadn't seen you all that much, we were very aware that we were going through similar stages at roughly the same time. And then – the worst thing, really.'

'Aggie's been amazing. I think I would have gone mad.' They looked at one another, and Paddy smiled to assure Henry that Agatha hadn't, really.

'I remember them talking on the phone – roundabout five months. May was so excited when she got off. They'd been talking about the babies being friends, when they grew up. I hope you don't mind me talking about this . . .'

'No,' said Paddy. 'Being pregnant was a lovely time, until it wasn't any more. We were so full of expectation.'

'And May was full of Hope.' They laughed at the feebleness of the pun. 'By the end,' said Henry, 'when she was six days overdue, she was very very full of Hope. I thought her stomach might just split, it was so tight.'

Again, they stopped talking, but this time they both tried to hear what was going on upstairs. The floorboards directly above their heads hadn't creaked in a while. They both imagined some fairly static scene of consolation – which wasn't far off what Agatha and May were performing.

'If you do want to meet up, talk about it, give me a call,' said Henry, who had a powerful curiosity – driven, at least in part, by the terror of hearing (during the latter part of May's pregnancy) Paddy and Agatha's news.

Lunch was cooking and, eventually, after about ten minutes, Agatha had to come down and check on it. May, bringing Hope, accompanied her – but the men sensed as their partners were coming down the stairs that, if they had been wanted, either Agatha or May would have let them know – raising her voice slightly, perhaps, whilst saying something about them. Paddy had a thought, 'Shall I show you the rest of the house?'

'I'm happy here,' replied Henry.

'I'd get you a drink . . .' said Paddy.

'I understand,' said Henry.

When the food was ready, Agatha sent May to call them through. Henry took the basket, and Hope was placed in it where she could watch them eat. 'They've got a kitten,' said May. 'But they don't want it.'

Henry was a little confused by this, but May pointed out the bowl on the floor. 'Where is it?' Henry asked.

'I'm not sure,' said Agatha. 'It was in here, the last time I saw it . . .'

Agatha, who was a good cook when she wanted, had made roast chicken – its crispy skin was covered in salt crystals. They sat down to eat, and began to talk about food. There were carrots, parsnips, roast potatoes and gravy but no bread sauce. Henry, especially, was full of compliments. Hope behaved herself, and for pudding they had ice-cream and biscotti, for which Agatha apologised. They talked about London – how they hardly missed it at all; how much more relaxed they felt living here. Paddy made coffee. Agatha asked Henry about his parents, who were both in a nursing home. When May asked Paddy, he said that his father was getting slowly worse. 'He needs the

oxygen almost all the time,' he said. Agatha brought a box
of chocolates out from a cupboard; Henry accepted – May
refused, refused, and then accepted. Then Hope began to
wail; she needed to be changed: Henry offered but it was
May who went upstairs to do it. Agatha stayed at the table,
thinking of varieties of nappy-contents. They talked about
Christmas, what they'd done. Henry asked about the kitten, which had reappeared from under one of the units –
what were they going to do with it?

'I'm taking it back tomorrow,' said Paddy.

'You really don't want it?' Henry asked.

'No,' said Agatha. 'Definitely.'

'I think we might,' said Henry.

When May came down, Hope was still crying. 'She's very
tired,' May said. 'She didn't sleep much at all last night.'

'Is it colic?' asked Paddy.

'I think it might be,' said May.

'We're not sure if that's started yet,' added Henry. They
decided, with a look, it would be best to leave.

Agatha was feeling rent by their visit. She had enjoyed
parts of it, but did not – despite what she now said – want
it repeated very soon; and she certainly didn't want to
have to repay it. This was the awkwardness when they
were saying goodbye: and of course Henry and May several times said, 'You'll have to come round' and 'Soon' and
'Yes, very soon.'

'That would be lovely,' said Agatha, thinking the
absolute-abysmal opposite; not only would it be horrendous, it would have difficulty being anything at all. It was
outside the house and therefore, for her, outside the realm
of possibility. They stepped over the threshold; Agatha
and Paddy allowed themselves to be for a moment framed
in the doorway – watching and giving small waves, hands

not raised above shoulder level, towards a fairly impassive Hope. Henry and May took an embarrassing amount of time to install their new daughter in the back seat with a safety-belt wrapped around her carry-basket. They were having a discussion about something. Henry then came back to the front door. 'I think we would like the kitten, after all.'

'I'll get the basket,' said Paddy, and went inside. A few minutes later he came back, and handed it over to Henry.

'Look after it,' said Agatha, almost involuntarily.

'We will,' Henry said.

He got in the car, handing the basket to May in the passenger seat. Then they drove off, with Henry giving a very delicate pip on the horn. Paddy closed the door behind them, expecting a complete collapse from Agatha – but it did not come, not until they had walked back into the kitchen to begin clearing and washing up. 'I feel so wrong,' said Agatha, her voice becoming a liquid wail. 'I feel so evil – I thought –'

'You're not evil,' said Paddy. 'You're hurt, we're terribly . . . it's natural.'

'It's not natural,' snapped Agatha, 'nothing's natural.'

'I'm sorry,' said Paddy.

'Don't be intellectually lazy,' said Agatha, a little ridiculously, with a thick voice. Paddy, too, began to cry. His head was full of memories, his body ached as if he'd swum a hundred lengths the day before.

# CHAPTER 12

AGATHA continued to get up later and later every morning until, after a while, she was getting up in the afternoon. At first she tried to go to bed the same time as Paddy, but there was no chance of her falling asleep such a short time after she'd woken up. She began to wait until he had started to breathe sleepbreaths, then took herself downstairs for another hour or two, three and four. She found she loved the nighthouse even more than she loved the dayhouse, despite the fright of the darkness. She left her glasses off – and everything appeared to her through a vague mist; she much preferred it that way. The hours of light were becoming too explicit for her – too hardcore in the rawness of what they exposed; she wanted a veil between herself and the seen world. Daylight wasn't poignant enough to assist in the wanted pathos of her vision; things she had hoped by now would have become scrubbed or invisible weren't. She needed all the human cavities, including her own, to remain enticing shadows, not red-gleaming orifices of failed defence. One night, towards the end of the first week, she turned off all the electric lights and lit a candle instead. She felt Victorian, in the pallid flicker of it – participant in a less light-loving age. Candle-light, she found, calmed her raging insides, head and otherwhere, was what they used to call bromide. A few days later it passed through her mind that what she really wanted were servants to light and raise a candelabra – then the front room would all be visible but would still glow with the gentle shine of candles. This was not some-thing to which she gave a great amount of thought – it was an image; one that, if it came too close to being conscious, she rejected. Her job had caused her to develop a reflex against the past: she could never allow herself, during brainstorming sessions, during client meetings, to be seen going or looking backwards; not unless it was to some retro-futuristic vision of how ironically to sell, say, yellow fat – agency slang for all the various fake butters. But she had a deep reactionary seam, a conservatism that made her detest parts of what she was and feel disgusted with the whole of what she might, if she wasn't careful, vigilant, become. If this happened, she knew, if she turned Tory, friends and colleagues of hers would say – fashionably, knowingly – that it had always been inevitable. Yet she knew that her politics were changing, aging, just as surely and in many of the same ways as her body: they were both becoming saggier, baggier, more porous and less forgiving. What had given her physical confidence after the birth of Max – the feeling of being a woman (not girlish), unapologetically, unmistakably – was now, since, the cause of its almost complete destruction. Paddy, she knew, felt it was horrendous that his own body remained unchanged, even with the ravage of her second pregnancy. He had done his best to allow himself as much as possible to age: he had neglected his skin, and it had gone dry and acquired some apologetic (to Agatha, and through her to all mothers) wrinkles. This wasn't enough, he knew, but it was all he could do – and Agatha pitied him both for his efforts and his failure. In the same arabesque of mind, though, Agatha could curl around to a guilt that Paddy's politics too seemed unaging; he was watching her drift rightwards. Her age, her aging bothered her less at night and far less than, on occasion, it had done recently. Most of all, for this was already firmly in the past, and distanced as much as anything by their distance from London, Agatha had felt her agingness whilst shopping for clothes. Then, if she found herself reaching towards any hangered thing with the merest hint of mutton, she felt nauseous; sometimes, when trying to look in a mirror at the sight of herself from behind, or assessing the effect of the length of a skirt, she had felt herself to be on the very very edge of old: even if this piece of clothing, this top or skirt usually top, were all right now, in six months' time it would be quite unfeasible for her, for a woman her then-age (luckily, fashion and the change of season would already have rendered it ungenerallywearable by then). Even before she had had Max, winter had been welcome to her – for the relief it brought from exposing areas of no longer impeccable flesh (not that, when it had been impeccable, she had ever believed it so). Agatha realised how imposed and unfair her increasing belief in her own physical shitness was. She read fashion magazines before she went shopping, to see what she might want to buy, and then after she came back from shopping, to see what she could no longer wear without looking mutton. The purpose of fashion magazines, of all magazines, was to make one feel lack; Agatha had long ago made this fact out. It was one of the reasons she was, or perhaps now *had been*, so good at her job: she had great clarity of vision as to the viciousness, essentially, of what they at the agency were doing. The rhetoric of products was, these days, fairly undisguised, even when in the presence of the client; 'advances in technology' were discussed in terms of sexiness, not utility. There was, in it all, a strong ironic element of 'Okay, girls, here comes the science' with the coded message, 'This is nonsense, switch off your brain for a bit.' Agatha had been particularly good on haircare products, shampoos, conditioners, dyes – it was a specialisation that being a redhead, if only a dark and reasonably unginger one, had prepared her for from the first time she walked onto a screaming playground. Here, on her head, and in her head, she knew where the reservoirs of fear could be located – and she knew how to tap them, control the flow, and use them to irrigate with anxiety the ever-refilled fields of shelves with their irresistible products. Just as she knew this, she knew that her ideas of a pristine, pre-advertising past (the world's, not her own) were sentimental: if her history-student friends had taught her anything in the college bar, it was that everything happened at least a hundred years before you think it happened (and that included the things that happened a hundred years before they did). There *had* been a human privacy and intimacy once, though; *that* Agatha refused not to believe in: the Victorians, some of them anyway, had been made of different stuff to us – of the Bible, John Bunyan, folksong, Dickens, George Eliot, scandal sheets. They were made more of the cold of fireless hearths, the dark-darkness of midnight houses and the frail light of carried-upstairs candles. She read Victorian poetry, remembering that once upon a time, before university, she had thought that poetry, writing it, might be something she would have something to do with. In this, she had become a disappointment to herself. An English degree, a first-class one, had taken away from her, or forced her to suppress and disguise, any language of passion – which meant any passion in the language read and any passion in the language she was allowed to use to discuss it. *We care about this*, the students' constructed attitude was, *because it is formally intriguing, sociologically revealing, not because it rips our heart out with the wild claws of a bear and reinserts it with the gleaming tools of a surgeon.* It was this, however, the wild surgery to which her earliest literary readings had subjected her that she now wished to re-know, re-live. At fifteen, once or twice, she had read by candlelight, having realised that was what the first naughty or merely nightly readers of these books must have done. Now she tried to resurrect this, as if it had been a whole important long period of her life; it hadn't, but also it had – an hour, the right hour, was an epoch; not just in youth, at any age of life. She was chasing, or beckoning, her own new epoch. It was important that she survive this one: in the flat she had done this in one way, by overcaring for Max and preparing for their move to the house; in the house, devoid of Max, she had to adapt. Night helped her think. Agatha knew her feelings towards suicide were not genuine and could be a little indulged – mainly she knew this because they expressed themselves within her as a misty nostalgia for the two or three periods in her life when she had been, truly, on the point of killing herself. Agatha was cute to herself (cute and deep) in her remembered past-self: she could not believe that a being so undamaged could have felt itself so wretched-wrecked. Nothing really bad had happened to her before she was, what, thirty? thirty-two? Her father's death. She knew this mood was a glimpse ahead, to looking back once more, as an old woman, if she ever made it, upon herself as she was today: deep, cute. The thought that she might in future have the capacity to have endured worse worsts, and be able to think with coolness and yet with life of all of it, that was of all possibilities the most terrifying. Not suicide, but survival – what if she had to suffer being stronger than herself, than her own heart? If only I'd done it then, her reasoning, had she attempted to reason herself through to clarity, would have followed – if only I'd attempted it, and succeeded, then I wouldn't have had to go through any of this. That, she felt, though she did not think it, was a lovely notion, so gently beautiful: to pause her life as it had been. Exactly because Agatha had in the past known genuinely suicidal moments, she now knew exactly why her nostalgia was completely other. Her present feelings were a retrospective imposition of a desire to avoid the future that had not then happened but which now had. There were definite events which the imaginary death of her younger self would have forestalled. When she had truly felt suicidal, about a year before meeting Paddy, there had been no gentle feelings, no haze, only a clear gesture – a grab – towards the knife, and of the knife – a lunge – towards her. Some of the attractions and aversions, however, did remain the same. Just as before, the abdication of responsibility, the number of things death would save her from having to do or face or negotiate – that was the motive; or rather, that was what she, in her thought-movements, was fleeing. But she would, she knew, be making no positive decision towards death: now, the world was different, now there was Max, and also Paddy, but mainly Max, though Paddy wasn't completely unimportant. Max if she had died would have been left with Paddy, and no memories of the mother who wasn't even able to live long enough to reject him for who he really was.

Agatha sat straight-backed in the middle of the sofa, affirming her enthronedness within her own life. She queened it over the world for whole half-hours at a time: it was a good feeling, regality, almost unique, *since*, and what was most marvellous – though she did not marvel, because that would have ended the effect – was that she did not instinctively interrupt herself with guilt.

It was during one of the nights early in this week that Agatha first noticed something unusual about the sound of the waves. When she had been trying to go to sleep at the same time as Paddy, Agatha had often used to lull herself by listening to the very quiet and very distant sound of the soft waves on the pebbly beach. She longed – part of her longed – to go down to the sea itself, but she remembered that even when she had been at its edge in times before, had sat for an hour and stared out across it, or dipped her hand in up to the wrist, or – in summer – swum out beyond the breakers (she was a strong swimmer), even then she had not felt intimate enough with the differing element. There was always a preventative quality about the sea; her first sight of it forestalled any real understanding – which had, originally, been one of her reasons for being very keen to live within an intimate distance of it. Her childhood had been for the most part landlocked, but she remembered her eight or ten weeks at the seaside (in Devon and Cornwall, over the course of several summer holidays) as more lingering than the interior rest. Her seawards impulse was one of the most powerful she could recently remember herself having – apart from, perhaps, her griefwards one. In her mind, the two began to assimilate one another, and she became afraid that a visit to the sea would inevitably (like a visit to a patient in a mental hospital) be a courting of glamorous distress, at some level. As she listened now, seated on the sofa, the two rhythms ran over and across each other: her breathing and the hushing of the waves. At times, the two synchronized – she allowed them to synchronize; keeping her breath regular but at a different, slightly slower pulse than the sea. In this way, like two clocks with minutely different tick-tocks, there was an eventual coming-into-sync; at which point, Agatha matched her breathing exactly to that of the sea. It was a great relief and comfort; one of her most basic decisions being made for her – how to breathe and when. She had, ever since her first pregnancy, been very aware of the difficulties of breathing when it becomes self-conscious – and now she was self-conscious about almost everything almost all the time. (One day, not far off, she felt convinced, she would no longer be able to undress in front of herself – already she hid herself, when she could, from Paddy.) There was a definite danger that she would soon be taking every aspect of herself far too seriously – in a childlike way, believing that decisions she made about whether or not to breathe now, now, now or *now* were world-changers. She was particularly worried that she might find a way of becoming superstitious about her breathing patterns. (The remembered childself on the car journey, promising herself a present from her parents if only she could hold her breath until the next but one bridge across the motorway.) She was capable of it, and she feared these capacities – they seemed to operate for their own delight, these days. Enamoured of havoc, and with an almost homicidal curiosity – the smallest change, like the change which had already begun between her and Paddy, was enough to reduce her to her alone – Paddy gone, taking Max with him. Nothing comforted her but things which ran parallel; the sea-breathing – this she was able to bring to the point of ignorance: stripes lined up over stripes, when moved causing backwards ripples – like two fences seen, one in front of the other, whilst riding on a train.

This night, she wasn't satisfied with the volume of the waves – she kept missing her rhythm. Perhaps the sea was too calm; she should check, by a proper listen. The obvious place was out of the attic window. But Paddy's unspoken attitude to this was clear to her, as clear as if he had been whispering it into her ear: *be brave*. And perhaps, she felt, she could and should be. Night might make it easier. She went to the front door and began slowly to open it – an act which, in itself, did not yet terrify her, as she knew the act was in no way promissory. Paddy, asleep, definitely asleep (she had quickly checked), would never know of it. Her achievement, opening the door, would give him no increased hope, and her failure to follow it by a step into the street would cause him no dismay. As she opened the door, its heaviness and greater legality compared to the doors within the house struck her. The outside that she was becoming afraid of was not one of actual man-made or man-incarnated threat; what she feared was not the specific but the vague – not what it might do to her but the totality of the almost infinite vicious possibilities it contained. The air in front of her did not contain the simple blade of a knife, it was entirely blade and entirely, in every direction and encountered with every movement, edge. A single step forwards, she felt, and she would be cut to steak tartare – a smear of grey and red – meat-mist. Agatha stood and looked out through the knife-air, the edge-air, feeling the impossibility of it – it wasn't a medium, it was a billion-billion tragedies. But she got as close to it as she could without getting cut. A young man walked past, head down, not seeing her, and it was like watching a shark in an aquarium or a tiger in slow motion – how did he not die? How did he make this his element? Agatha closed her eyes when she was sure he, still unharmed, was gone. She listened to the sea – and was amazed to hear that, since the last time she listened to it, a few moments before at the top of the stairs, after checking on Paddy, its pulse seemed to have slowed down. It sounded different, of course, she had expected that: louder, larger, deeper, but the pulse . . . She counted the seconds in between the waves, making it five. Inside, she heard every wave, she believed, not just every loud one or every seventh. A deep breath, and now she concentrated instead on what she could smell. Strongest was not the sea itself but the bittersweet of the seaside town, burnt sugar and bitumen. She could easily have told, blindfold, driven there by terrorists, that there was dense human occupation around her: toxins were upon many levels of the air. At this hour, she smelled no specific smells – no cooking, not even a car gone by with a broken exhaust. Agatha heard a seagull nearby make its plaint, she couldn't tell whether or not it was overhead. There was something unnerving, now, about the sound of the waves. Inside, she had to listen but not very carefully in order to hear them. Here, they seemed hardly audible at all – how was that possible? The house wasn't capable of focusing the sound, making it louder – the soft crash, the crumple of wet momentary cliffs. She listened and was disconcerted by the illusion that the sound was coming from behind her, from inside the house. She suddenly became aware of her pyjamas, blue and white vertical stripes; old, soft, many-times-worn cotton. Embarrassed, though no-one was there, the young man gone, she needed to concentrate properly on the sounds. She could hear cars, and knew them to be – together with lorries – those on the main road, the one that ran along the seafront. The yawl and cark of seagulls was punctuation to this, as their shit was punctuation to the slate roofs and the concrete pavements. They were a fact to be accommodated, somehow – it wasn't good to admit, even to oneself, that one would prefer them not to be there (despite this being the seaside, and them being a requirement). Acknowledging their presence didn't make them any less aggressive; they had been known to steal food out of people's mouths and in some ways it made the whole town seem more hostile. Not liking that thought, or its suggestion of an even longer self-containment, Agatha took a step back and closed the door. It was a couple of minutes before her breathing had slowed and calmed enough for her to listen again to what sea-sounds made it into the house. She heard them differently now: they seemed more human, more raggedy. That was what she thought initially. This time, she didn't want to listen to them long, just hear they were still there. But it wasn't possible for her to ignore the fact that the waves were louder in the house than outside. She walked to the back of the hall and listened; they didn't seem quieter the further away from the door she got. To test again, she took herself into the back bedroom; they were the same. And again, she found, the same in the attic. Here, she opened the window in the roof – for only the second time since they had viewed the house; this, surely, should be the best and loudest place for hearing the sea. But it was quieter. Perhaps, she now worried, it wasn't even the sea she heard outside, just cars going by on the London road. It was also, as she heard it, slower in pulse. Bringing herself inside, closing the double glazing, the waves were audible. But Agatha knew they couldn't be what she heard them as being. Scientific and decided, she tiptoed downstairs and into the main bedroom; here, she listened to Paddy's breathing. It wasn't the same as in the attic or the hall – slower still, and more rasping. (Her heart was knocking her around, putting shaking blood in her hands.) She went into the nursery, and a memory engulfed her: standing over Max's cot in the weeks and months after he had been born; each of Max's breaths had had the emotional impact of a small loaf of bread being baked: the weighing, kneading, covering, leaving, returning, repeating, greasing, ovening, smelling. To lean over his cot as he slept small and growing was, for Agatha, richly to be fed. There had been no opposite to this, it was everything; she had hated herself for the essentialism of it, but there – that baking – was a hook on which she'd happily hang the coat of her soul: a moment of permanence. She had been greedy, she knew, asking for another little bakery-baby; after all, she only had one soul to hang – as long as it did not slip off, let it grow dusty where it was, for as long as it lasted there. The bread-thought left her when she stepped out onto the upstairs hall, making a deliberate break of the doorway. But it had left a suspicion with her; that the regular whooshing-swooshing sound that she could hear wasn't the sea, or her breathing, or Paddy's, but was coming from the house – was the house's breathing. She didn't believe this, and nor did she want to believe herself capable of believing it. Madness was, right now, something best not thought about. If the house could breathe, what if it started talking? (Her blood flipped from head to toe, and she shivered in response.) Only very rarely during her nights had she put music on – now she needed some. It wouldn't matter if it woke Paddy up; that might force her to tell him what was happening. The stereo was in the front room, and Paddy's old LPs were on a single shelf above it. She chose Billie Holiday – a singer who she felt sang what she (Agatha) was like: she wasn't unaware that this, too, was how millions of other women, and men, felt. At this moment, 'I Cover the Waterfront' was Agatha's lifesong, and she listened to it closely four times – ear up against the speaker cabinet. This, she was sure, wasn't the recording she had first heard; that had been on a very cheap tape bought in a charity shop, subsequently (university) lent and never returned. That version had been frailer, even more moving in its loneliness and mistily hopeful despair than this one. Agatha knew herself to be in danger of sentimentality, didn't mind. What did she have in common with a long-dead black American drug-addict ex-prostitute genius jazz singer? Except everything ever. Surely, she thought, that's what Billie would have wanted? In the recording she could hear the desire to communicate – and possibly, too, the knowledge that this communication could be disembodied: the ghost of Billie coming out of radios whilst she herself was on a tour coach with the boys, or on an airplane, or in Europe, or dead. Agatha decided that, best as she could, she would forget the breathing. It wasn't the fast-breathing of a baby – that she at least was sure of; it wasn't, she hoped, the coming-to-life of a madness. When Billie Holiday stopped singing, Agatha remembered the moment she had left Max with her mother; through the just-closed front door, before she had even had time to turn away, hands still in the air from waving, Max's small voice, 'Where mummy?' She had stopped to listen. Her mother, in the hallway, had said to Max, 'She's gone to get your new home lovely and ready for you,' and Max had said, 'Wheremummy?' three times before starting to cry. The music was beautiful.

# CHAPTER 13

A GATHA was immediately aware, as she woke up the
next morning just before noon, of the breathing of
the house. Although she could not remember her dreams,
she knew that in them every rhythmic thing – her breathing, Paddy's, Max's, Rose's, the alarm clock's tick, the
crump of the waves – had become one and the same thing.
She didn't want to think about this, so got up and made a
noisy breakfast. Without Max, though, there was only
herself around to make noise, and she was nowhere near
as good at that as him: she put the radio on then turned it
off, annoyed. The appletree in the garden was just beginning to show its buds – it distracted her for a couple of
minutes before she realised she was listening, again, to the
breathing. Perhaps, she thought, she should have told
Paddy, woken him up when she got into bed with him. She
wondered how he would have reacted, and was dismayed
to think he would probably *emotionally* have taken it very
well, whilst in the same gesture rejecting it intellectually.
But with every moment that passed, now and now and
now, and with every breath she heard uneventfully, she
became less scared and more comforted. She went through
into the front room and sat for a while with her book; she
didn't read it, she wasn't yet sure if she could, and yet the
sounds from the house were definitely unaggressive. If it
had to be anything, she thought, then breathing was probably best. Finally, she began to read. Her new favourite
spot for this was the back-to-front room. Every day, she
would drag the armchair (heavy, leather) across the
wooden floor to its perfect position – beside and back to

the long windows: it was important, somehow, that Paddy not know this detail of her routine; she had always needed there to be something secret, something furtive about her reading for its fullest pleasure to make itself available to her. As a child she had always taken a book with her when playing sardines or hide-and-seek; and some of her hours of deepest immersion and greatest rapture had come from ignoring the bumps of those helplessly looking for her – and then having given up looking for her, their shouts telling her she'd won, adult voices joining in to threaten her with missed birthday cake or worse. There were a number of small deceptions like this which she found it necessary, or comforting, to practise upon Paddy. Drinking tea, she used Paddy's exclusively-for-coffee mug – then washed it quickly, as if he were just about to come back, which she supposed wasn't impossible. One day when he had left for work, definitely, she turned round in bed so that her feet rested upon his pillow – she had no idea why she was doing this, it wasn't intended, she didn't think, as a sign of contempt. Again, she would have liked smoking to be one of her daily secrets, but there was the impossibility of a regular supply of cigarettes. She thought about opening the door to the postman and asking if he could bring her some tomorrow – for a fiver; but that suggested an image of herself as a mad old lady or as a lascivious housewife, neither of which she could accommodate. She never masturbated, though she thought about it; she was waiting for something to happen before she did that – she had no idea what that something was or would be. This day, she read in the back-to-front room until she became hungry, by which time she realised that the breathing house scared her far less than she had been capable of scaring herself. Making and eating a very late lunch, she thought this thoroughly through. There were moments of watching, hearing and internally reading herself which Aggie had made special efforts to forget – even as they were happening. Sometimes, she now recalled, she had found herself parodying her own morbid thoughts – grotesquely imagining hacking Paddy's killed body to bits on the kitchen floor; and at other times she ran through her least usually approachable nightmares at double-speed, turning them slapstick. These recognitions made Agatha, briefly, feel as if she were not a properly serious person, one whose sincerest feelings were only and always sincere. Alongside her guilt at moments of half-happiness, or simple self-absence, came these moments of self-parody and self-torture. She was, she knew, different now in many ways to what she had been when first visiting the house: a less confident person – a person less confident about being a person; it seemed a far more troubling, challenging thing to be. Previously, she had hardly been aware of how many machines inside her had worked since her birth without her having ever to tinker with them or even remove their covers; they had hummed, given off warmth, *functioned* in a way she now found astonishing – astonishing from the sad point of view of the mechanic, wandering around a vast floor covered with the parts of a machine, several machines, she had only now discovered she had the skill to take apart but not to reassemble. Agatha no longer felt convinced of her own persona: Agatha, Aggie, Mummy. The house, she realised, was full and had been for days, nights, of different versions of her; sometimes she walked in upon herself at her absolute worst, keening almost inhumanly on the bathroom floor – and would either run really run away or would collapse and join in; at other times she glimpsed herself going out through the front door not only as if none of it had ever happened but as if none of it ever stood a chance of happening (when she saw herself in ignorance, like this, she was disgusted by how much envy she felt); and again, she barged in upon herself on the sofa, breastfeeding three-month-old baby Rose. They had made the mistake of naming the unborn 'Rose', after a good friend who could now only be retained as a friend with a greatness more of grief – for they had also, mistakenly she now knew, told everyone, especially the named-after Rose, that this what what Baby Two was going to be called. During these awful moments, Aggie stood and watched as baby Rose struggled to focus her small brown eyes on her happy mother's face. Another version of herself which she met, sometimes, was round-bellied and smiling and smug – seven-and-a-half-months gone, the pain just about to tap her on the shoulder. Before all this, Agatha had felt indivisible, now she felt, almost, plural – as if there were no longer an Agatha but merely a different Agatha and Agatha and Agatha and again Agatha every time she entered a different room. In comparison to this, the breathing was wonderful: if she had to choose a variety of madness, she would have no hesitation – to be in the bosom of an imagined giant was far better than splintered into a hundred confused and conflicting selves. Agatha felt strangely convinced of her sanity, though – glad that she was finding some unclichéd way to think of herself and act her thoughts out. By the time Paddy was due back that evening, Agatha was quite at ease with the idea of the house being, for her at least, in her need, alive: she would not tell him about it, if he needed to know about it then she trusted it would let him know.

When Paddy did finally arrive home, an hour late because of the train, he sensed almost immediately that something in Aggie had changed. He knew that, according to what she would tell him if he asked, she had done little more since last he saw her than read, watch television, clean, cook. He suspected that she had been visited during the day, that she had had company. (Normally, he might have thought someone had telephoned, but he knew that Aggie had stopped answering – knew because of all the messages left, all the calling-back and lying he had to do.) It wasn't anything definite about her, nor any clues around the house; although he did begin to look for them – was this hair stuck in the bathroom soap hers or his or someone else's? could he smell cigarette smoke in the kitchen or was it burnt toast? It was not leavings; it was that Agatha seemed changed by what he could only depict to himself as intervention, human intervention. Yet there had been nobody, as far as he could make out, to intervene. There was something new and definitely a little strange about her; decisiveness, decidedness – he feared that he knew too well what it was, and that it was an end to him together with her and Max. Some event, some realisation had occurred to her, he was becoming sure, but what could it possibly have been?

No, she hadn't gone out; he could have told, from how she looked, acted and smelled if it had been that – Aggie would have looked windblown, just slightly. Instead, she had about her the atmosphere of some object brought out after years lost at the back of a wardrobe: a mustiness that could get inside even a marble. Paddy didn't believe she was deceiving him in this, only in almost everything else. He pushed his senses closer to her, and felt sure, again, that no-one had visited – a visitor, too, would have blown at the mustiness.

Facing her over dinner, he went through the thoughts

that followed on from her deciding to leave him. As they weren't talking, he had the time to argue it through semi-philosophically with himself. He regretted, in parallel, he couldn't appreciate the rich food more: meatballs with mashed and butter-run potatoes. This decision of hers might show itself in opposite ways: either she would be in greater tension with him, until she found her moment for the announcement, or she would be more relaxed towards him, more caring because it meant so much less – care would have become finite, almost nostalgic. *It is over*, he thought, hating the pure audibility of the words in his head – *a marriage, a good one; my marriage.* Paddy was extremely lonely, and the thing in front of him, Aggie, which made him feel that was the thing which should have stopped him feeling that: her absent presence saddened and infuriated him. The house was a changed place, submerged; he felt a suffocation, and a huge weight pressing upon him from above – a weight like water. He was, if anywhere, at the very bottom of the sea. The light which entered his eyes was all ripples; looking at Aggie, he could see nothing without a shoal-like shimmer of possible tears.

Later in the evening, Paddy on the sofa, Agatha in the armchair, they began talking about the house, and whether they could afford it; both of them knew they couldn't, not the way things were going, but talking about it at least showed they were making the effort. Suddenly, or at least suddenly to Paddy, Agatha broke out: 'I need this!' Paddy knew he'd heard her shout like this before – *stop!* – *no!* *don't!* – to warn Max off dangerous things; never exactly in this way, though. 'I need this house – I need the feeling it gives me,' Agatha said, her voice no quieter. And now she diminished: 'It makes me feel safe, loved. Right this moment, it's the only thing that's keeping me going.'

Paddy let this honesty thud, then said, 'Thanks.'

Agatha resented his implied flirt; it made her hate him, a little – a tiny puff of poison, as from the spine of a tropical fish: 'You know what I mean,' she said.

'What do you mean?' Paddy could still feel her shout, zinging in his skull – it had with a snap changed his mood: he knew he could, feeling as he now did, tell Agatha exactly what he thought of her selfish behaviour. This wouldn't be, of course, what he thought; it would be a summation of the anger her perfectly understandable selfish behaviour created in him. Above everything else at this moment, Paddy did not want to say what he was thinking: It's not me, it's you; it's your fault. He felt Agatha was forcing it out of him, and he didn't know whether this was to make things between them better or to bring the whole of them closer to an end. He didn't want to risk that; and he had already sat there without speaking for several pulses too long. 'I do know what you mean, and I'm prepared to do everything I can to help keep us here – but I can only do so much.' And Paddy realised he'd ended up, unwittingly, unwillingly, saying exactly what he most wanted to avoid saying.

He found Agatha's reply shocking – she laughed. 'This is being middle-aged,' she said. 'We're here – we're in the middle of all the things we hoped we'd somehow manage to avoid.'

*If anything's middle-aged*, Paddy thought of replying, *it's your unnatural attachment to this house – your clinging bloody* . . . This first reaction wasn't sayable, and he had none ready with which to replace it. A pulse later and still all he could manage was, 'Is that how you see it?'

'I wouldn't mind going to live somewhere different, if I knew I would feel the same about it and that –' She seemed ashamed of what she was going to say, 'it would feel the same about us.' Paddy knew Agatha had been going to say not us but me, the sentence otherwise was unbalanced and inelegant. Her small self-correction, at least, was a sign of attempted reconciliation. 'I'd live in a tiny one-bedroom flat with you and Max, on the top floor, if only I could be certain that I wouldn't feel abandoned there.'

'This isn't rational,' said Paddy.

'No,' said Agatha, 'I'm not rational right now; I'm emotional – I'm desperate. I'll take anything I can get – and right now that's the feeling, which might be an illusion,' delusion, thought Paddy, 'that the place I live in isn't entirely indifferent to what happens to me. I don't want a moon – I don't want to live on the moon.' Agatha had embarrassed herself; still, she went on with what she most darkly meant, 'I want to live inside a heart.'

'What?' said Paddy.

'I'm fed up of not saying what I mean, what I really feel: I want to live somewhere that's warm and liquid and pulses and is full of life – and that's a heart. I'm inside it now; it's like being with you.'

'You mean like being with me used to be.'

'Yes, I probably do,' said Agatha, being at least consistent in her recklessness. 'This house is a heart, and I'm not leaving it just because money tells me to; I'm not listening to money.'

'I have to assume,' said Paddy, 'that you're not deliberately trying to break us up.'

'Not at all,' said Agatha. 'But I can't go on lying. I'm not living in the same – I don't know – universe as you any more: I disagree with your physics. We have to find some way of dealing with that.'

'You're admitting the chance we might split up.'

'There's always a chance of that; we've just pretended there wasn't. For us to go on, we have to want it. Do you still want it?'

Paddy's reply wasn't instant. 'Of course,' he said, a pulse too late.

'You want it enough to say that,' said Agatha. 'But you think about outside this relationship, don't you? You imagine being with someone easier, someone younger.'

'I want to be with you,' said Paddy. 'Difficult as you are.'

'No. Don't answer by rote – let's try to say new things. I want to live in a heart – that's my ideal home; I haven't said that before. It feels,' she reached for, 'released. Now you say something.' Agatha was in a particular, peculiar state; for Paddy it was like watching something fragile, a vase, bouncing on a hard surface, marble, having survived the first impact of fall.

'I want to live with *you*,' said Paddy, deliberately failing to make an effort of imagination. He wanted to annoy Agatha out of this distressing-for-him mood.

'You do live with me,' said Agatha, 'that's not exactly visionary.'

Paddy was shamed into something closer to what he wanted to say: 'I want to live with you as you were before this happened.'

Agatha was shocked. 'You want to live in the past?' she said.

'I want to live – I want not to have to live with so much damage,' said Paddy, attempting eloquence. 'I want a life that isn't almost unbearable every day.'

'Is it?' said Agatha. 'Am I? Is that how you see me?' She didn't seem bitterly angry, as he'd expected her to be; so divorced was she from normal feeling and conversation, her reaction now was curiosity.

'I don't think I see you any more,' Paddy said. 'I don't think I know you, or understand *me*.'

'Then how can you love me?'

'Oh,' said Paddy, 'much much too easily.'

'But do you know what you're loving me for?' Agatha was mischievous and also emotionally vicious; playing with multiple griefs. 'Is it for who I am and for the future or for what you remember me being, and the past?'

'At the moment, it's for the past and what I hope you'll be again.'

'I won't,' she said, as abruptly as she could. 'No-one is ever anything again – it may seem like they are, but they're in actual fact always moving forwards, away from what they've been. How can I pretend that what happened didn't?'

'I don't want that,' said Paddy.

'It changed me more than anything has ever changed me.'

'Of course I know that,' said Paddy.

'To pretend to be the same would be perverse – I wouldn't be worth living with any more; I'd be a robot doll acting myself out.'

'You asked me what I wanted,' said Paddy, believing they were on the point of a permanent break. 'I told you.'

'You did,' said Agatha, 'thank you. Now I know you a little better. I thought you wanted something like that, and I was becoming annoyed at you because you wouldn't admit it. Now you have, now that your me-nostalgia is out in the open, I feel better; do you feel better?'

'I feel humiliated.'

Agatha looked at Paddy with more eye-adhesion than before. Inside, she had been juggling selves – she had been acting out a scene she really wanted to go through with but couldn't do so entirely as herself. She asked: 'Humili-ated by me or by what you want?'

'I can be clever,' said Paddy, 'and paradoxical, and say that I'm humiliated because what I want is a you who isn't you. But I just feel confused: you're deliberately being elusive, and I feel flatfooted, slow – and I'm afraid I'm never going to be able to catch up with you again. Where are you getting this energy from? I'm exhausted.' He had a pulse or two's pause. 'I want to give up, that's what I want to do. I don't want to have to make the effort of going on, being with you, being alive, any more. It doesn't seem worth it – not without some help or encouragement. I need a sign from you; that it's going to be worth it.'

'I am helping you,' said Agatha, becoming with every moment more compassionate. 'This is helping you.'

'It isn't,' said Paddy.

'It's a sign,' said Agatha, snapped straight back at him, lovingly. 'If I didn't think it worth it, I wouldn't be bother-ing with this, would I?'

'Why are you so impish? I can't see anything to be energetic about.'

'I'm being energetic *against* – that's where my energy comes from. It's a fight; I'm thinking and hating my way out of where I was a few seconds ago.'

'I'm surprised you're not more exhausted than me.'

'I probably am,' said Agatha, 'inside.'

It was the glimpse of a gap-of-need Paddy had been wishing. 'Come here,' he said. Agatha moved matter-of-factly across from the armchair to the sofa. She sat down within hugging distance, and Paddy brought her into his shoulder – but felt more vulnerable, perhaps, than he had since the first time he ever tried to embrace her, not knowing if he'd be rejected or not. He still often felt doubt with regard to her affection for him; there was this degree of thought-formality about it: affection, regard. Agatha in his arms felt like a benediction from a far authority, although he knew it was, in fact, she who had granted herself. He wanted to feel she was in need of something from him – in need of him. He felt she was but feared she wasn't. He couldn't see how she could leave him, not if she weren't prepared to leave the house. But she could ask him to leave, and he would have to go; he would take it seriously, realising she had never asked him anything similar before, and he would have to accept it would be up to her to decide whether or not she had been wrong. This wouldn't, he felt, happen; the end, with Aggie, would be a true, clear finality. Still, for this moment at least she was in his arms – where she felt a huge desire that Paddy, in some way she couldn't at all see, some fatherly way, could prove himself adequate to the situation. Agatha was judging him against criteria she could only establish once he'd failed to meet them; the game wasn't invented yet, it was improvised.

# CHAPTER 14

ONCE during this week Paddy woke around half-past three in the morning, felt Agatha wasn't there, waited for the loo to flush and for her to come back to bed.

When she didn't, he went downstairs to find out what she was doing – which, on this occasion, was lying across the sofa with hands behind her head and eyes closed. A cup emptied of what had been coffee was beside her, on the floorboards.

Paddy didn't wake her, and went back upstairs thinking that it wasn't because she couldn't sleep that Aggie was getting out of bed, it was that she didn't want to sleep in their bed – didn't want to sleep with him, perhaps couldn't.

In this, Paddy was doubly wrong; Agatha hadn't been asleep or dozing even – she had been very awake, thinking of her life and how the various bits of it had ceased to fit together, of the breathing and what it might mean. If Paddy had 'woken' her, if he had just said hello rather than tiptoeing in and out again (he, father of a two-year-old, was a world-class tiptoer), the misunderstanding would have been exploded. (She would have been annoyed but he wouldn't have been deceived.)

Instead, he began from this time onwards to resent Agatha's laziness in the morning, and to suspect that she didn't sleep in, as she said she did, until the afternoon; she was up almost as soon as he was out the door (he believed) – she wasn't having fun, but she *was* having breakfast.

Within a few days, Paddy would come strongly to resent Agatha's being asleep when he left in the morning and even more her avoidance of their bed at night. He could think of no other reason for her behaviour than that she wished as far as possible to avoid his company, even when unconscious.

It was hard for him to understand how this aversion had so quickly developed – immediately after Agatha came out of hospital they had slept violently in one another's arms, legs stepping, as if each were a doorway the other was trying and trying to walk or climb through. They woke one another up, constantly, but their definite presence – even as disturber – was enough to reassure the waker back to sleep. If they were not limb-entangled, there had always been some flesh-contact between them: the back of a hand against a buttock, an ankle against the sole of a foot. Now a physical estrangement, a divorce, which was how Paddy began to think of it, was beginning.

The following morning, when Paddy woke, he did not immediately remember the reason why he felt upset. Agatha, beside him, was fully asleep, and it was the sound of her breathing that reminded him of what he'd seen and learnt.

The bedroom was very dark, their curtains were very thick which meant that, now, Paddy couldn't see Aggie's face; but he lay there and looked across into the warm dark place where he knew she was.

He was angry at her, and partly wanted to wake her and tell her why; however, he also had become aware, uncannily, of what her being there meant – what it meant about her as a person.

He could tell that her head was more intensely *her* than her feet: he would have hated to say, or even to think, that it gave off 'vibes' – yet when he was directing his feelings, mainly his love but also his annoyance, towards her through the darkness, he did so towards her head – he was angry at her head – because he knew it was her head in which her Agatha-ness was most powerfully vested.

It did, in a way, reassure him: this unconscious Agatha was Agatha set apart from the stage of grief she was in. She wasn't some eternal Agatha but was one he knew – the earlier Agatha, sleeping on the sofa, had been different. Not a stranger: an Agatha glimpsed as if single, separated from him and from Max – a possible future Agatha. Paddy's dark gaze at her now was partly an attempt to kill this image and partly a simple enjoyment of the calm of her, that she could still be calm.

Recently she had had terrible nightmares, which made her shake, shout, kick and wake both of them up.

It felt, this early situation, more communicative, more fructifying, more blood-enriching than most of their conversations.

Paddy's alarm clock clicked, and he got to it before it went off; it was large, brass and extremely militant, but Agatha was learning to sleep through it. He lay there for another few minutes, projecting his day upon the ceiling: sometimes, at this hour, he thought in a philosophical way, more often of students and admin, plagiarism and pastoral care. His life, last week, had begun to feel pointless: he wanted to have Max there with them, in order to remind himself why he was doing what he did. The argument didn't hold: he had done the exact same job before they'd had Max – but after Max was born it had been easy to make him the universal motive; and the job, with the commute added on top, felt different. There was something humiliating about being so exactly in sync with the major-ity of the working population. Being a commuter was a constant exercise in received contempt. To begin with, Paddy had come back with traveller's tales he wanted to tell Aggie but did not – stories of people's unbelievable selfishness on the London train: of a pregnant woman, obviously exhausted, left standing by six young men comfortable on their seats; of elbows, knees, toecaps and their various aggressive uses; of the annoyances (for him) of the people-in-the-way, the people-who-stop-and-gawp. The irony of this, with regard to his subject, was a very old and dull one for Paddy: he had been working for several years on a book about scepticism – the difficulty of proving that other people, or more specifically that other people's minds, exist. A common-sense philosopher of the sort Paddy definitely was not might have argued that a single journey on the 7.15 to Charing Cross was all that was required to settle this question for ever.

Paddy did not believe, particularly lying in bed in the morning, that he had proved anything much of anything – perhaps what he had written would, one day, help someone, someone more brilliant, to construct a brilliant proof; he had, like so many thousands in departments around the world, been attempting to clarify as close to absolutely as possible the language in which the question was framed. Scepticism did not excite his students very much, and Paddy often worried that he was boring them; then he remembered his own boredom at university, and how grateful he now felt towards it, how necessary it had been for his intellectual development.

He had been teaching the same courses for several years, and the amount of preparation he these days had to do for each class was minimal. He would leave the house with a plastic wallet of typed-up notes in his bag, and the train journey up to London gave him enough time to hold them up to his face and review them. As long as he took the correct plastic wallet, he was fine. (He did not always take the correct plastic wallet.) Occasionally, when he felt like putting in the extra effort, which his students didn't really deserve, he would reread one of the books or papers around which their course had been structured. This, for his pride, was always a difficult toad to swallow: these arguments seemed so flawed, and yet the papers that contained them had such a monumental presence in his mental life – and had done now for almost half that life. He was a philosopher, he sometimes said, in order to disagree – and not just with others but with himself, and with himself about the idea of 'others'.

He swung himself out of bed; Agatha did not wake, and he felt his anger towards her rise and then subside – let her sleep, let her sleep for as long as it took. He showered and shaved then got dressed in the back bedroom, having left his clothes and shoes there the previous evening. This morning he wouldn't have breakfast. Before leaving, he went and gently kissed Agatha goodbye. It was a conscious attempt at forgiveness, his gesture, but it was never likely to work. She shrugged, not wanting to wake more than she had to. Then Paddy went quietly down the stairs and out the front door. He was far from understanding the truth of everything, though – most of what he was thinking was wrong. For in fact, Agatha *did* superstitiously touch Paddy whenever she got back in bed with him, eventually, at three or four in the morning. The touch had to be very light, the caress of an earlobe or the stroke of an exposed shoulder blade (Paddy slept nude; Agatha in her stripy pyjamas), but she could not sleep until she had assured herself that he was warm and real and alive – and also separate from her, in his dreams (whatever they were; however similar to hers). Before touching him she listened hard to his breathing, her own breath held until she was sure it was Paddy and not just the sound of the waves she was hearing. (This was before the realisation they weren't waves; afterwards, she just listened to confirm his sleep.) She had to get very close, careful not to make too big a dip in the bed – she listened with her head above his; his breath had a very slight rasp on the intake, which reassured her now, where before it had worried her (lung disease, his father), and once upon a time when they first went to bed together had kept her awake. After she had touched him, Agatha reclined in Paddy's midnight smell, the fug of uncon-sciousness around him, the manly fetidness, that bouffed out from under the sheets, stale and floppy; it had, she was almost scientifically sure, a soporific effect upon her.

And many times, Agatha had come into the bedroom when she knew Paddy to be asleep, and had looked down upon him. With the door half open and the landing light on, she could see the outline of his face. (Paddy's was the right-hand side of the bed, beside the door; she had to be careful that a beam of light, through the crack in the doorjamb, didn't lay itself ribbonlike over one of his eyes.) When Paddy looked at Agatha, as she slept, he was yearn-ing towards her; when Agatha looked at Paddy, in his sleep, it was in consideration of what it would be never to see him again. Her regard was more judgemental – as if, as was the case, she were trying to work things out about him, about her and him. Her look was not harsh, she felt it to be full of pathos, but the pathos was a magnetic field, returning inwards to herself; it did not reach or electrify Paddy. Once, one night, she did feel great emotion towards him – went down on her knees so as to risk looking right into his face, but this was as Max's wounded father, not as her husband. As that, more often, she imagined him to be dead and was watching her imaginary reactions, calibrating her imaginary emotions. What would it be like, if . . . In her more morbid moments, she did come to check if he was actually still alive: it happened that, now and again, downstairs, she began to believe he wasn't, and had to go and disconfirm this. In the shining doorway, she could no longer tell what it was she hoped for. Paddy's death would offer solutions, of a sort. She felt it to be not good or desirable but powerful and moving; it might take that or something like it to bring her back to life. At other times, she came in to see that Paddy was still breathing in order to reassure herself counterintuitively that Max, miles away in his crib at her mother's, was similarly alive. It didn't mean anything, this connection, but she was shamed to find it almost worked: a case of whether things generally were right with the world, or whether it was all hurt and hell and hurt and, again and again, loss.

Then there were the few hours when they were both asleep and had turned a little towards one another and begun to breathe in sympathy – either exactly together, on the beat of breath, or at opposite ends of a see-saw of inhalation-exhalation; in with out and out with in. This lifted and dumped them, unconsciously; both drew strength from it – the up was more important than the down, and the sympathy was most important of all. Good days tended to follow these good, if brief, together-sleeps.

# CHAPTER 15

I N the security of the breathing house, Agatha tried, systematically, to think herself to the bottom of her thought. She wanted to be inwardly analytical, wished to find a way of figuring her inner self – or selves – for herself; she couldn't, though, was thwarted, almost before beginning and not just cheaply-paradoxically by herself: Freud had vandalized her psyche. There were within her objects-not-objects to which he had appended names and assigned locations and, which was worse, allotted func-tions. It was a vast fairground ride – with this lifting that and that coming across to turn this other this way and that. All of which had made her inaccessible to herself: these names, Ego, Superego, Id, were utter anathema – and just as the word Jesus (unhearable, unsayable) had kept her distanced from Christianity (Jeee-ssusss), so they kept her from what she hated calling but still wanted to call authenticity. She felt a great need to reclaim the parts of herself she had given over into the language of others, the great-grandsons and -daughters of Freud, bubblegum pop psychologists, selfish and helpless writers of self-help manuals; she needed to create almost from nothing her own verbal version of her mind, body and spirit. She believed, started trying to believe, in transformation, becoming grotesque, not self-beautifying. She deliberately tried to make herself remember the violence of the first birth when she breathed purely animal: total breaths, breaths so huge they tore muscles in the chest. At that time, and for a short while afterwards, she had felt in possession of a body capable of living itself to pieces: a machine operating at its resonant frequency, screws falling off. There was too much talk in the common world of madness. Agatha knew that, if she had been capable of going mad, with all that was rending inside her as well as out, she would have then, birthing. Something strange was needed, now, something like what poets have – or used to have; something estranging, as Freud himself must once have been estranging. (She knew, she felt.) He had lost his poetry, expelled it from himself and been therefore exiled by others from it; she demanded the right to misunderstand who she was in her own way. To him she would grant this, the inevitability of self-misunderstanding: that wasn't his insight, merely a strong repetition. It was the teaching of the fathers – know thyself – know thyself, because, at the moment, thou art a stranger to thyself. Analysis would have given her tools, and tools – objects – were the last thing she wanted. (Better to be a stranger to what came along, far better that than to be smugly anticipated by some bastard in a swivel-chair.) Her insides felt chaotic, were completely unfairgroundlike: there were no objects, unless a cloud or a smudge or pathos or debt can be an object. All was unclarity, and she couldn't help but feel it was better, more honest, that way. Around these non-objects was a mist, an acidic mist, which reduced any burst or bloom to a particoloured vapour. Objects were always trying to form inside her, and some of them might even have deserved the name of thoughts or nascent actions. Shoots and trunks of definiteness were reduced to skeleton forms, and then reunited with the smeary mist. How could this be analysed? Erect a scaffold and it was haze before it was half begun; here, there were no structures: clouds, marvellous from the ground or from above, banal when seen from ascending, descending, whited-out planes. Agatha felt herself to be the cloud not of unknowing but of unforming, for the cloud was in a way a form of knowledge. It was gnosis, not reckoning or argument. Projected within the cloud, at times, were discernible penumbrae – these were not made by objects but by different thicknesses of cloud. Mist, and mystery, and the possibility that all this was self-mystification: Agatha wondered whether it wasn't that she didn't want to face hard facts: she was the corrosive one – attempting to prevent anything substantial coming to birth within her. Her dead daughter had been an enactment of this, a dreadful making-physical of what she hadn't wanted: her womb full of acid, dissolving, her baby-cloud, made and unmade, her red flower. In which case, what was Max? Had he survived and stayed solid by virtue of being male? And what Freud had stolen from her inner life, she felt, cinema and television had stolen from her outer. As she grew older, Agatha became aware of the way gestures spread through populations – the embarrassment of seeing white Englishmen, in imitation of Americans in films, giving one another the 'high-five'. She felt this, too, in her own most profound physical acts: even at her most destroyed, weeping beneath the blast of the shower, she had felt herself to be in imitation of scenes she had seen, copying what actresses-pretending-to-be-destroyed had done. This tore her: even putting roses on the grave had seemed to her secondary, or tertiary (actors learning from actors). Probably, she thought, people-before-cinema had based their gestures upon those of people around them. Perhaps in moments of argument they had become melo-dramatic, histrionic, like the actors in stage-plays they had seen. Agatha wasn't in any way sure that something essential, Edenic, had been taken away from humanity –

but she felt lacerated by inauthenticity whenever she tried physically to express, to herself, what she felt she was feeling. At some points in the past – these thoughts weren't entirely new – she had even been desperate enough to consider taking some sort of class to explore movement and dance. But that would have been replacing one set of clichés with another. Hollywood, she had come to feel, was homicidal; it wanted to kill the human element in all behaviour. Perhaps she was idealizing a pre-cinematic world – one where people had kept most emotions unexpressed, because they had not yet been taught the codes of flickering face and body. What were the chances she would ever feel unaffected again? This wasn't self-consciousness, it was style-consciousness – and that was why she hated the problem so intensely. She wanted to get at herself – wanted to feel the breath of her own life upon her face, even if it was bad breath.

Next, she thought, God. Church was one of the places, in imagination, she most often visited outside the house. Once there, she didn't wish to take part in a service, she wished to leave immediately – but to do so knowing she at least had been there, that was what was important; something to do with showing spiritually willing, as if on the church door (it didn't matter which; any denomination, however loopy, would have done – any dusty cavern) God had someone taking names. Agatha's God rated curiosity as a form of worship and physical presence as a participation of the soul. She wasn't able to make Him believe a walk around some cloisters equal to taking communion, but even though He seemed to be blind to some of the things that went on outside His place of worship – *since*, she hadn't any credence left to give to His supposed omniscience (when Rose died before being born, God was only forgivable, only conceivable, if He'd been elsewhere and otherwise engaged) – even though Aggie's God was obviously a bit of a dunderhead where the rest of the world was concerned, inside his little grey boxes of cold, he was attentive to the tiniest of spiritual minutiae. And today Agatha had something, a parcel, she longed to take and deposit – wrapped in the brown paper of anonymity and tied with the white string of convention – beside the for-kneeling-on cushions, between the pews. This she had done before, many times. She never wanted to be around when God, sucker, untied the string and lifted the box free of the paper; and when God opened the box, Agatha always wanted the blastzone to be, somehow, contained entirely within God, within heaven, within where the shrapnel, the shockwaves, wouldn't rip her to splatter. That was for her the purpose of God: to dispose of highly explosive materials by being periodically blown up and seemingly destroyed by them. After the parcel-dumping, Agatha knew she wouldn't think of God and the extraordinary service He offered for several months – but, one day, she would realise that she'd for a while been gathering materials together for her next bomb-box. That, in the past, in the years during and since university, had been Agatha's method of God-dealing – it wasn't worship, although there was always a certain amount of awe as she approached the church, the horrendous parcel in her mental hands, and always a deep gratitude, as she walked away disburdened of it. God had served His purpose and had accepted – for her – His containment, His obliteration. She didn't want more than that; forgiveness, blessing, benediction – the bestowal of grace, if it came from any-where, came out of Agatha and flowed backwards towards the place of her relief, the site she had created, or adapted, for that purpose. Agatha also forgave, which should really have come first but with her came last of all – she forgave God for allowing Himself to be circumscribed and herself for circumscribing Him. And then, like so many others who shared her occult terroristic religion of brown paper packages tied up with string, she went on with her life – lighter, freer, and with a growing sense of doubt that might be debt. Whatever she might persuade herself, it was something external – external to herself, and to the bad cold stone buildings she visited – which had successfully taken away her troubles, Lord. Agatha's box, *since*, was huge; she had wrapped, unwrapped, repacked and re-wrapped it more times than she could have counted – in an instant of regret or annoyance, she had done it twice again; it required immediate delivery, if not it might start to leak, it was leaking, it was leaking faster, it might go off in the house – killing everything. Perhaps she should use God's courier service – perhaps a vicar could be persuaded to carry it away? But she'd never thought of using any other method than a personal delivery service. The great utility of it, the greatest, was that she didn't, at any point, have to speak – not even to herself. There were emotional chemicals and compounds she had put in there which she had never explicitly formulated; all the most explosive things it contained were unworded, inchoate, chaotic.

By the end of the day, Agatha for the first time since they moved in was looking forward to Paddy's return – she wanted to see if she was capable of letting him know what she had been thinking. It wasn't likely, she felt, that she could do more than try to let him in, to know that the effort of forwards-movement was one she was making.

# CHAPTER 16

Paddy phoned around eight, already late back, to say he wasn't coming home that evening: his father was ill, had pneumonia (again), and had been taken into hospital. Agatha asked if Paddy wanted her to do anything – she meant, was he going to try and use this as a way of forcing her out of the house? She wasn't at all sure how she would react to this, whether she was able to go outside, and was very much hoping Paddy wouldn't force that crisis upon her; he didn't, for which she regained just a little love for him. 'Thank you,' said Paddy, allowing Agatha to retain the dignity of the appearance of having meant what she said.

'But shouldn't I come?' Agatha asked – she needed to be absolutely sure he wouldn't attack her for this later.

'I don't think he's in danger,' said Paddy, 'not right now – and he doesn't want a fuss made.'

'If you're sure,' said Agatha.

'There's a hotel near the hospital. I can go and see him in the morning.' Agatha asked about Paddy's father's lungs – they were not in a good state, said Paddy. This, Agatha knew, this or something very like it, was in the end going to kill Paddy's father. If it wasn't this time, this stay in hospital, it would be the next one, or the one after that. His father had said, often, he wanted to be over and done with the whole business as soon as bloody possible. Life in a wheelchair, Agatha knew, hadn't for Paddy's father really been life at all; when younger, he'd been a club-level rugby player and a decent amateur mountain-climber – then, when he could no longer do either of those, a hill-walker – and, finally, a fairly apathetic nine-hole golfer.

Agatha was momentarily distracted by a sound somewhere in the house. Paddy didn't want his father to die, she knew, but also he didn't want his father to live in such a hateful way that he ceased to be recognisably his father. 'I'm going to bring Max to see him, tomorrow,' he said. 'He hasn't asked, but I think he'd like that.' Agatha was immediately worried about the distress this might cause her son; she said nothing. 'The ward isn't too bad,' said Paddy, relaxing into sadness. 'It's just a load of old men coughing all the time. Occasionally they put the curtains around one of them, they cough more and more, then less and less, and then they don't cough at all. Next time you look, it's a different old man – but he's still coughing. My father's just one of the different old men.' Agatha said she was sorry, and Paddy said he was okay. 'I'll call you tomorrow from work, in the morning – let you know how he's getting on.'

'Don't cross any roads,' said Agatha; 'Nor you neither,' said Paddy.

As she put the phone down, it was as if all the rooms were darkening – thunderclouds on the staircase, thunderclouds beneath the ceiling rose. This, Agatha realised, would be her first night alone here. It would be silly to be frightened, what was there to be frightened of? A Victorian house on a Victorian street, people only two or three feet away on either side – a scream would bring them running; streetlights shining in through the front windows; it was hardly the Gothic castle in the Black Forest. And yet – and yet, she knew that she was only reassuring herself because she was in need of reassurance. And that, really, she could these days find the opportunity for terror in the most infinitesimal things. Soon, she thought, I'll be frightened by a speck of dust – just like a kitten might be, that had never known such a thing before.

Agatha followed or tried to follow her usual routine, but she soon realised that it was entirely dependent upon Paddy's being there and her behaving as if he weren't. And so, she let the night start early, pretending that Paddy had just gone to bed and that she wasn't going to join him for three or four hours. She went with her book and sat in the back-to-front room. Her concentration was appalling. She knew enough about reading to know that the eyes don't simply travel along the lines, like cars down a motorway, they cheat — skip ahead to anticipate coming events, double-back to check whether that word really had been that word and not another word. Still, she felt like she was failing the writer; she should have been more disciplined, not so concerned with merely turning pages. It was more important to read the book well than to congratulate oneself for having read it. She was a bad reader, she felt, too scatty, not worth writing for. After half an hour, she put the book aside and listened hard to the breathing; she had been scared of doing this, scared that the unexplained sound of it would begin to scare her. If that were the case, she didn't know what she'd have done — perhaps call Henry and May to see if one of them could come over to stay the night; they'd understand. She wanted to be calmed, to be allowed to return to herself as a better, clearer-headed person. The house had never seemed so quiet nor its breathing so clear and steady. Agatha breathed with it for a couple of long minutes, thinking about Paddy in his hotel room — assuming he too wouldn't be able to sleep. He should have given her the number there, but she always had his mobile if she needed it. She thought for a while about his body, the length of it and the weight of it and the presence of it — all of the qualities that would be absent from their bed that night. Which was when, halfway through this thought, she heard it: a long scraping sound – it wasn't particularly quiet, no quieter than the breathing, perhaps even a little louder; she knew immediately that she'd heard it before, but she couldn't remember when. It was probably, she thought, just one of the accustomed noises of the house. If Paddy had been upstairs, she most likely wouldn't have noticed it: her safety would have deafened her. For five minutes, she listened out for the scrape to come again – but she didn't hear a thing, except the normal nightsounds of outside and inside, and the breathing. Aggie went into the kitchen and made herself one of her midnight expressos, then decided that, as Paddy wasn't there, she didn't necessarily want or need it: she could go to bed at any time. This thought made her guilty, and she had to deal – sitting silently – with the thoughts that followed of why she had been avoiding her husband's bed. It was easier, without him physically around or imminent (all day he was imminent, right from the moment he left – perhaps never more so than in the minutes after he closed the door behind him), to think of him without the sensation of disloyalty, which tended to end thought. Was it really that she no longer loved him? Quickly she dismissed that, then realised this haste was probably the most indicative hint she had. She forced herself back to the question, forced the question back upon herself, talking it through out loud – unafraid of seeming mad; it was worth seeming mad for a marriage, even if marriage to begin with was madness. Agatha knew she wasn't dismissing the idea of not loving Paddy so quickly because she was totally certain she *did* love him. Haste betrayed doubt betrayed her betrayed him. Her first insight, repeating, 'Do I still love Paddy?', and rocking backwards and forwards on the kitchen chair feeling an inner lurch, was that she had been deferring a deep look at this question for so long that her suppression of it had become a quick reflex. If she let it start now, it would burgeon, ramify, unravel – yes, coil out endless (seemingly endless) spools of speculation; the complexity of which suggested not love, no longer love. Love, for her, was rarely baroque like this. She felt she could spend all day exploring with her inner eye the curves and folds, the ivory and gilding, of her love for Max. But Paddy had always been more monolithic: rough, landscape-dominating, weather-worn; profound and profoundly incomprehensible. She had been going out with him for so long that he really did seem, in himself, in his physical presence, the remnant of some long-forgotten religion. This old worship must have been, she now assumed, her first passion for him; and it worried her she could re-create no clear sensation of what and how this had been. Paddy as fresh Paddy: she thought of cowpats, and laughed. Paddy as something that didn't feel exhausted. Not *known* – he wasn't boring to her in that way; it was her incomprehension of him that she had become overfamiliar with, and begun to hate. His work was something she had once wished to understand, and also, she came to realise, compete with him in. When they talked about it, she had often hoped some polished insight of hers, presented casually, almost not mentioned, would be what set him off towards greatness. This, though, wasn't how greatness worked – it probably wasn't how Paddy worked either, great or not. Probably, she thought, *not*; almost certainly. Which could serve to make him more loveable but also more hateable. Early on, Paddy had been an ideal to her – particularly for keeping on with academia when she had pursued income and other, faster rewards. She had respected him almost to the point of agony – and then, again, she heard the scrape-sound. It was louder in the kitchen than it had been in the back-to-front room – no, she couldn't be sure of that. It wasn't quieter, though, and she hadn't been listening with her entire body tensed to receive it. The only thing she could think was that the scrape was coming from somewhere inside the house; that was how it felt: very close, almost upon her. Agatha looked towards the hall, the cellar door, all thought of Paddy and love gone – or maybe transformed into something else. She knew, or felt she knew, that the scrape hadn't simply been a chair being pulled back in either of the next-door houses. That might have been the case for the one she heard in the back-to-front room, but the one in the kitchen just now couldn't have come through an adjoining wall: there wasn't an adjoining wall. She looked again at the cellar door; going down there was of all things the one she least wanted to do, which made her realise it was probably her inevitable task. Deferring the moment of decision, she took herself through the house, every cupboard, every corner, from top to almost-bottom – as she went, she listened, and as she listened, she felt it less and less likely that the scrape would have its source anywhere other than in the cellar. Remembering what it had sounded like, she convinced herself that the sound was surrounded by a slight halo of echo, of room-emptiness. By the time she got down to the hall again, she felt she was ready to put herself to the test: mouse or rat or man or hairy-slimy non-living cellar creature, she knew that now was the time to confront it.

She went back upstairs and got dressed as if for going outside: jumper, jeans, sturdy shoes. These last felt strange on her feet, heavy and unwarranted; she had, she realised, been barefoot for all of the past few weeks. It was like the first day of the school term, after the long summer holidays, exchanging plimsolls for black leather uppers.

She opened the cellar door and for a while stood there looking down into the dark. The torch was now handy, too handy; on a shelf immediately to her right – placed where it had been before, when she made her previous cellar descent. She picked it up with her right hand, which she saw was trembling, and then, almost immediately, without thinking, reached for the lightswitch and flicked it. The bulb flashed, pinged and went black – but only in her anxious imagination, in reality it lit the cellar stairs not brightly but more than adequately. Paddy *had* changed it. The step she'd thought was last was actually two from it – at the very bottom, no rat was in sight, no man, either. Bravely, she took the first downward step. The blood-boom in her ears was so loud she doubted she would hear anything over it. As she went down, she thought of Paddy and of the next time they'd have sex – would they ever, she wondered, have sex again? She was fairly distanced from her descending body, as if lying on the ground looking at the sky and letting a balloon float away. To her left were her and Paddy's Wellington boots, black, and then Max's, white with red spots – he would be missing them; she almost picked them up and carried them to the top of the stairs so as not to forget to do that. She had ceased to feel terror; now she was impatient for all this to be over, for the revelation – whatever it was – to have taken place. Self-conscious, she did not have to lower her head but could stand upright, now she had reached the bottom step. The cellar floor itself, concrete, was a more terrifying thought to her than the stairs: it was, she feared, more likely to have living things upon it – things she might irk or kill by stepping on them. She took a small step forwards and it was now that the scrape happened again. It came as a sound, she knew that, but so sensitized was she that she'd also felt is as a grating within her chest – as if someone were inside there, rubbing two sheets of sandpaper together. She was surprised she hadn't screamed and relieved not to have peed herself – she felt between her legs, confirming she hadn't. Her breathing was too ragged, and she concentrated for a while on slowing it. There were questions to think about: had the scrape been louder down here? She couldn't tell. It had seemed closer, but that might have been because of the dead dirty walls around her. Within herself, she felt very tender – as if she were a hostage, dreaming of a bed whilst tied to a radiator. The scrape hadn't seemed to come from down by her feet, along the edge of the wall, or up above her head, in one of the beams: no bats or rats, then; it had been circumambient (long words were comforting to her) – it had seemed to come from all around her at once: the whole house had scraped. If she wanted to, she knew she could at this point panic: it was there, a button to press, as plain as the rubber button on the black rubber torch with the yellow trim and the black grip-rings around its long shaft. The scrapes were coming at roughly equal intervals (or so she thought) – perhaps she could wait for the next one. She looked systematically around the whole cellar-space. The light from the bulb was yellow and left deep blue shadows where it failed to fall – like rags caught on nails. Because they had moved from a flat to a house, they hadn't needed (yet) all this extra space – they had nothing with which to fill it except, perhaps, their apprehensions. Scared again, she stepped forwards; she would go into the dead centre and turn around on the spot, inspecting everything. This she did, after which – the scrape not having recurred – she felt that perhaps there was nothing more to do than return to the normal, everyday rooms: semi-safe. The air in the cellar was surprisingly warm and dry; all their heat, escaping down through the floorboards. She decided she would wait for the next scrape, after all. Avoided panic became physical discomfort in a very short while – she felt something sweep across her instep. It wasn't hairy or probing or moving – she knew it wasn't a rat high-jumping her foot, its tail leaving an aftertaste of touch across the tongue of her toes: pink and with chicken-leg joints in it all along its length. She knew, but didn't believe. She looked down, and nothing at all was touching her foot; she moved it anyway. Sex with Paddy had been a strange thing to think about when coming down the stairs. This wasn't the best place to indulge in such sad thoughts. Paddy had been wonderful to her, and still tried to be – without pressuring, or even suggesting. A few minutes passed. Despite the warmth of the cellar the adrenaline going stale inside her made her shiver a couple of times. The scrape didn't seem to mean any menace; it was probably just something in the drains below the house, something that moved back and forth when someone next door or down the road flushed their toilet or ran a bath. She knew this was a lie, but was working her way towards accepting it. Otherwise, the breathing and the scrape might, she supposed, be related – she couldn't see how. She turned the torch on and played the light around the beams of the room. Standing directly under the back-to-front room, she imagined the weight of the house pressing down upon her. Reaching up, she put her hands on a couple of the beams and pretended to hold it up. She was becoming playful, and this was enough to prickle her with renewed unease. This time it was almost as if she had anticipated the scrape, was in rhythm with it –

she was able to hear more detail in it: it wasn't just a scrape, it was a number of consecutive sounds. After it had happened, which took less than half a second, she was again aware of the breathing. Wasn't it, too, louder down here? Or could she just all-around hear it?

After a final definitely not panicked look around, Agatha began to ascend. She felt as if she had conquered several aspects of the house, and also of herself. The nape of her neck was especially sensitive to the triumph as she went up the first few steps – it was expecting something, suddenly, to touch it: to render remote all her bravery, false and true; the sharp blade of something. What, now, did she do? Houses make noises: she tried to make herself worried that there was some structural problem with the foundations, but this didn't work. The scrape, like the breathing, came out of the house, was part of it – she knew this. The problem now was Paddy – whether to tell him, how to tell him, what to tell him. She almost wished she hadn't learnt this (learnt what? that their Victorian house made inexplicable noises – for its own amusement, seemingly), so that she wouldn't have to have the conversation about it with Paddy that was now inevitable.

It was only when she got back upstairs into the kitchen that Agatha began to feel truly discomfited, or to recognise the discomfort that had all along been there inside her. The discovery of no cause for the scrape, just as there had been none for the breathing, had been reassuring at first, but now the idea began to reveal its horrors.

If Paddy had been there, she would have felt better; she wouldn't necessarily have told him anything, nor sought protection in him, but his physical presence – his dumb body – would, in itself, have been reassurance enough. But for now, Agatha was alone in the house with – *with what?*

she thought – with the house. The scrape, which she had been trying quite hard not to concretize, could quite easily have been the sound of a knife being sharpened – or even, though she hated herself for the melodrama of the idea, a scythe; long, sharp, curved. She didn't want to die before she had had a chance to see Max again, and to tell Paddy certain important and necessary things regarding Max and how he should be brought up without a mother, or without his birth mother. Agatha began really to panic, and the thing which made her panic most was the memory of her recent bravery in going down into the cellar. How could she have done it? She admired but also blamed herself for being so reckless. She sat down on one of the chairs at the kitchen table, then stood up, then sat down again. What if it *were* the house? What if the house itself was about to fall down? Or what if the house were an evil thing, warning her off? She laughed – relieved to find some ridiculous superstition in herself; it was amusing, and she wasn't going to let herself get away with it. The house was lovely – and felt, if it felt anything towards her, love. The scrape wasn't the house. The scrape came from within or behind-the-reality-of the house. Even in her head, with no-one to speak it to, she didn't want to use the phrase 'from another dimension', the words seemed too science-fiction. It came from *somewhere else*, and she didn't yet know what it meant. The best thing would be to get far away and to have some time to think about it – which would mean going out the front door; which she still, despite her panic, couldn't do. She looked out into the garden and realised that here at least was somewhere she could get to that was outside the house and, hopefully, away from its unnatural sounds. But she hesitated: even the garden was a risk – a crossing beyond what she felt comfortable with. This time the scrape, no louder, seemed more definite, as if it had responded as dialogue to the point her thoughts had reached. Maybe not a scythe, maybe a spade going down into gravelly earth; it was, the thought hit her, her grave being dug and the sound travelling back through time to reach her. Nonsense. But how far back through time? Agatha fetched the key for the French doors from one of the kitchen drawers and trying not to fumble or drop it, to show no sign of terror to herself, she put it clicking into the lock and twisted it twice anticlockwise. The garden was dark and seemed larger than during daylight. Agatha didn't think she could just stand in the kitchen waiting for another scrape, but she was equally afraid of stepping outside the house – part of her believed that it would fall down without her inside it to give it a reason for continuing to stand; would simply cease to be there. She pushed the door open and stepped out onto the lawn – the branches of the appletree already above her head, between her and the cloudy night sky. The air after almost a month indoors felt quite deliciously intricate as it moved over her face, almost as if little fairy feet were dancing on her forehead and cheeks. The garden was nowhere near as scary as she had thought it would be, which almost made her go straight to the front door, out into the street and down to the sea – outside, within the confines of the wooden fence, was a different thing, though, just like another room in the house, only without a roof. Agatha looked up, having already forgotten in the remembered novelty of it the reason she was out there: there were many more stars on the ceiling of the back bedroom than were visible through these halogen-brown clouds. What if she *had* gone out of the house, she thought, would that mean she had left Paddy? The ideas did not follow on, one from the other, but she felt them as connected. As the ground was dry, she sat down with her back against the appletree – immediately wishing for a lit cigarette or perhaps a small joint. She had already got far more out of this night than she had expected. Did I lock the cellar door? She asked herself the question and couldn't answer; it wasn't that she was afraid of something escaping, heaving itself up the steps to sniff the air and track her down. It wasn't that, but in some ways it didn't make a difference whether it was or wasn't – the result was the same: fear. The house, her life, seemed capable of delivering a vast, scything blow. She might just be standing in the hall, but in one moment her head could be sliced off and her existence-for-Max ended. This belief was hard for her to accommodate: she didn't believe that she believed it. She allowed the arguments against it to begin – the *of courses*, the *surelys*, the *you sillys*. They ran in her head a while, and she listened to them being drowned out by a white noise of superstition. It hadn't been this bad since she was little – since creatures climbed out of bedroom corners and made eyes and claws and fangs of the nightdark. It was because Paddy wasn't there – and Max; she needed to be the one doing the protecting, finding her own protection in that. Such a beautiful house! She looked up at the tall wall of it, seeing the stickers on the window of the back bedroom. Easily, a child's face could have appeared there, pale, but it didn't; easily, she could have convinced herself she heard a scream or a scrape. Tonight was going to be bad, the worst, but when it was over she would be fine – and she would do whatever it took to get through to morning. If necessary, she would wait out here all night. The house could be reconquered in the daytime, and strength built up for tomorrow evening and after. Though cold, Agatha felt warmed. There was a scrape – outside, a scrape. And this time Agatha felt as if her body had just become a completely different substance, not stone but sugarcube – with dryness, toughness but also (facing liquid) weakness. The scrape she had just heard, in the garden with the French doors only slightly ajar, was just as definite, just as loud as those in the cellar: the scrape was in her head – it was, probably, madness. Agatha still felt too practical for that, though. 'No, it isn't,' she thought, and the commonsensicality of her own voicing slightly reassured her. The scrape sounded as if it had come from somewhere definitely outside her, but then she supposed, if she were mad, it would. Perhaps she should wait until the voices started before telling Paddy; there would probably be voices. It was some further reassurance to her that she was still, in her semi-terror, thinking of her absent husband. Whether these were reflexes of mind or not didn't really matter. It was sad to think of Paddy as a mere resource, but that was one of the things a husband had to be: a fallback, an at least. Compared to the idea of being entirely without him, beyond him, her reaction to the scrape made his approach necessary – or, at least, useful. She thought of Max, that was her reflex, but then she thought of Paddy; not just as Max's father – she thought of Paddy distinct from the world, then as forming half of it, then as a world in himself. Someone might easily love him again; it was conceivable that someone might be her. The garden seemed less welcoming now – coming out at first had been an escape, but she was trapped just as much here as in the cellar. She waited for another scrape, but didn't hear one – not for a minute or two or five. It was colder and colder, and she didn't want to be scared out of her house as well as her wits: better go mad, if anywhere, in the warm. Agatha went inside and made herself a cup of tea, sat with it on the sofa and continued to wait. She kept her mind very empty, so as to be concentrated for the scrape when it came – but it didn't, not for a long time and then, so it seemed, not at all. Hours passed, and she began for moments to forget exactly what was odd and why she should be afraid of it. She needed to make efforts of thought but was too tired: it was very strange, that was about as far as she progressed. And she knew this wasn't enough. If she were going to tell Paddy then she needed, at least, to have found a way of describing it to herself. She couldn't prove what it was or wasn't – the scrape wasn't demonstrable. If she mentioned it jokily, but she was too exhausted to track logical paths – if she mentioned it at all, right now, in this state, it would be too much to cope with. Instead, she made a deliberate effort to think something else: Max. But she found that he didn't come to her as ideas, rather as memories of sensations. The silkness of his skin, particularly when newborn – that was quite clear; she could wear that like a good cashmere jumper. Then the gloopy stickiness of the messes he left around, recalled by the soles of her feet. Max was always sending her messages via the floor, of impatience or anger. His voice in her head was as vivid as a calling-out from the next room, so she diverted from that, too – imaginary sounds were not what was needed, in this situation. She laughed, and the loud crack of it was a shock. What she felt most physically, like a large block, was just the lack of him – his absence was an awkward, bulky presence. It seemed a lot like pure guilt; it had that lead-like density and dullness – though its edges were sharp enough to lacerate. Acutely, she missed the high sparkle of Max, happy Max, Max most-of-the-time. Around five in the morning, so exhausted, she took herself up to bed and fell asleep almost immediately. The next scrape, when it did come, half woke her – but as she was in the middle of a series of nightmares constructed so as to explain and embody the scrape, she didn't take it for real, or no more real than the others. The rest of her night was undisturbed.

# CHAPTER 17

AGATHA woke up unafraid and felt, as a result, that it would be affected to start working herself towards terror again. The scrape was just another fact about the house she must get used to: the line of rationality had already been crossed with believing in the breathing. Hopefully, Paddy would be back that evening, so she wouldn't be alone with the house – although already she was starting not to care so much. She made breakfast, toast from slightly stale bread; the milk had run out so she had her tea black. There was enough food for a couple of days, were Paddy not to come home, as long as she was prepared to eat tinned. She got the vacuum cleaner out and tried to persuade herself she wasn't doing noisy housework so as to avoid hearing another scrape. Mid-afternoon, Agatha's mother arrived unexpectedly with Max; Agatha was glad she'd spent those hours making the house perfect – almost as if it could be placated by her care of it. As the day was dry and warmish, they went and sat in the garden – it would have seemed strange if they hadn't; and although her mother couldn't know for certain she still hadn't been out of the house, Agatha felt she was proving something by entertaining them here. The question of milk was bound to come up as soon as Agatha's mother said yes to tea. Aggie hoped she would be able to persuade her to go and buy some, leaving her alone with Max. It worked out better than this, though: 'I want to do some shopping, anyway,' said her mother. 'I've hardly been able to get anything done, since I had him.'

'Of course,' said Agatha, 'take as long as you want. We'll be fine, won't we?'

'I don't know what you do all day. We'll have tea when I'm back,' said her mother, and left with a slam of the door.

Agatha's love for Max was atrocious: this time, seeing him in his ignorance of everything that had happened, his surface ignorance of it, she didn't know if she was going to be able to let him go again. She would have to, however; the house, though reassuring to her, couldn't really be said to be *safe* – and neither, if she were going mad, could she. Again the sense of her thought, its practicality, reassured her: Max was grabbing handfuls of grass and throwing them up in the air so that they landed on his head and went down the back of his neck. Agatha didn't want to scare him by becoming distressingly loving, nor did she want to scare herself by giving him any chance to show he didn't know exactly who she was. The front door opened, and it was Paddy who was coming into the kitchen. 'Monster!' he shouted, overjoyed to see his son playing in the garden sunshine, like a vision of how things should have gone all along. Paddy loped out through the French doors and picked Max high off the ground, interrupting the little grass game. With his son in his arms, he felt better. Over Max's shoulder he explained that, kindly, his colleagues had cancelled his classes for the next two days without telling him; they had assumed his father would die, although he didn't say this out loud. After finishing his admin, which took most of the morning, he'd caught the train. 'I'm just so tired,' he said.

'How is your father?'

'Better,' said Paddy, 'as much as he can be. They'll probably send him home again tomorrow. It's ludicrous.'

'Did you manage to sleep at the hotel?' Paddy mumbled a reply that clearly meant he hadn't. He sat on the lawn, bringing Max down with him to ground level – even seated, Paddy was a full head and a half taller than his standing son. Agatha looked at them and smiled; sad.

'Where's your mother?' asked Paddy. Agatha explained, and then they stopped talking and merely watched as Max found his own amusements, including a snail. This was as close to blissful as they'd come, *since*.

Agatha's mother returned, with two department store bags and a very large bottle of milk. She wasn't surprised to see Paddy and asked immediately after his father.

They had tea, and then she said she had to be getting going. 'I can leave him, if you want,' she said. 'I could bring his crib round later.'

'A little longer,' said Agatha, meaning *keep him*, not *let him stay*, 'please.' Agatha's mother gave a grimace and took Max from Paddy; both father and grandmother slumped – one with the burden given, one with that taken.

After her mother went, Agatha became very practical: they needed food for the evening. She didn't like to sound in any way shrill to herself, but Paddy had to be persuaded to go and buy something. He refused to go further than the corner shop, and returned from there ten minutes later, angry, with bread, butter, eggs, bacon, sausages and baked beans. His choice of food annoyed Agatha, as he'd definitely intended it to, but her only response was unvoiced: she knew now she wasn't going to say anything about the house. Today, Paddy was too mule-like and not mule-like enough – if he'd refused to go out at all, she would have respected him more (so she sensed) and might have confided in him. He went to lie on the bed and fell immediately asleep. Agatha kept herself from going in to check on him. The rest of the afternoon and early evening, she sat downstairs and read; she was aware that she was half listening out, anxious, for another scrape but when eventually it came, she found she wasn't at all scared by it. The sound was no more terrifying than the breathing, though it seemed to be coming less regularly than the day before. Paddy woke up still angry and came downstairs aware of trying to control himself and not say the things he wanted to. Agatha cooked them a dinner that was in essence breakfast: Paddy recognized the irony, for her, given the hours she'd recently kept, but did not mention it.

'What does it mean,' Agatha said after they'd finished eating, 'that all the sentences in my head, these days, begin with the words, "Oh, God . . ."'

Paddy swerved into the safety of the philosophical (he often did that when the question was one he didn't feel capable of anwering): 'Do you really mean you have sentences in your head? Not just words or parts of sentences?'

Agatha had not wanted to talk about it either, really; she had said it in the hope that Paddy would ignore it, or rationalize it out of existence, or do what he was doing now – intellectualize, safetyize it. 'I don't think I can really say what the inside of my head is like – it moves too fast, it's too complicated. I'd like to be able to transcribe it, but I can't; I don't think anyone can, no-one has.'

'There is a problem between language, I think, and speed. Faster than the speed of thought is a cliché, but most philosophy crawls – most philosophy is in slow motion.'

'It has to be; it has to pretend it's stupid.'

'No . . .' said Paddy, hoping to be interrupted – he didn't know exactly what he was going to say if he wasn't.

Agatha, for once, obliged. 'Not stupid, then – it has to pretend it's speaking to someone stupid.'

'Again, no. Are you trying to annoy me? Is this one of those arguments where you start saying things that I know there's no way you believe?'

'Oh, God . . .' said Agatha, to make Paddy laugh, and she succeeded, but felt defeated.

'I see,' said Paddy, and stood up. He was carrying his plate to the sink, but not hers. Agatha didn't know what it was that he could see; she supposed that he'd just said something deliberately opaque in order formally to conclude a subject that couldn't actually, honestly, logically be concluded. She was curious to see where this impossible conversation would go, so she pursued it, and Paddy, towards the other side of the kitchen. 'What?' she said, 'What exactly do you see?'

Paddy answered immediately, as if he had been expecting this particular question: 'I see that you are angry.'

'You know I'm angry – that's not an insight, it's a starting point.'

'I know that you are specifically angry.'

'With what?'

'That's your question. Why "Oh God"? Why can't you be sure about what you – and I think, really, about what *we* should direct our anger towards?'

Agatha said, 'Is that it? – do you really think.'

Paddy was resting his bottom on one of the work surfaces – he was tall enough to be able to do that.

'I think that you're asking my permission for you to be angry at a God you stopped believing in a long time ago – before you left school – or maybe you're worried that you didn't stop, and you're looking to me for some reassurance that you did.'

'That could be right,' said Agatha, genuinely startling

Paddy; he had been interpreting this all, he realised, as an argument – a willed, created argument. But her question and the curiosity behind it were genuine, or at least she had chosen to present them to him as such, and as such, he now saw, he should have taken them. 'Are you serious?' he said. 'You would like me to dispose of God for you.'

'Well . . .' Agatha said.

'While I make some peppermint tea, I'll just go over a few of the better known arguments.' Which meant that he had to swerve again, swerve into serious-taking-talking. 'You're doubting your doubt,' he said.

'I'm doubting everything,' replied Agatha. 'I want something solid – as a place to start.' She thought of the breathing, dismissed the thought, then thought of the scrape.

Immediately, she expected to hear it but of course didn't.

'You could start with death,' said Paddy, 'with the fact of death.'

Agatha found she could flow: 'I don't find that solid at all. It's an easy humanist religion-in-disguise, death is. But only because you can't say anything of it, just this and that *about* it and *before* it – just because it's definitely there in some form doesn't make it anything; it certainly doesn't make it a full stop.' Agatha was glad Paddy had been a little cruel, mentioning death; she remembered student conversations like this, in the first few weeks of the first year, when she had found a few people to share her idealism of argument: they could say something about the world worth saying; by speech – impassioned speech – discoveries might be forced. It was not the fault of students that their early earnestness was used as an easy way, later on in life, of discrediting any genuinely searching talk. They might, despite their own awareness of it as student cliché, get somewhere during the intensity of those early nights – somewhere other than in one another's pants.

'I think I agree with you,' said Paddy, cautious as always. 'I was probably wrong, and a bit trivial, to bring death up so quickly and easily. You make me feel like a charlatan. But it is the issue, isn't it? It's what we're really talking about.'

'I'm talking about life,' said Agatha, hating how merely paradoxical it made her sound. 'I'm talking about the difficulty of living – of continuing to live – without know-ing,' she hesitated, 'without knowing which of the many many pricks to kick against.'

'There isn't a possibility of trying to kick against all of them, collectively,' said Paddy, 'under one name – evil or bad luck.'

'No,' Agatha said, 'you want to see that your kicks are doing some damage.'

'Thank you,' said Paddy, hands comically covering his groin, 'for that image.' Even as he made the gesture, he knew how annoying Agatha would find it.

'It's been a long time since I felt so angry, with anything,' said Agatha. 'I feel like painting my room black and listen-ing to the angstiest music I can find – whatever they're listening to these days; God, I'm so old. Has anyone ever written in defence of the moody adolescent world-view, anyone respectable?'

'Not intentionally,' said Paddy, 'and if they were respect-able before, they weren't for very long afterwards. Don't go all Goth on me, please.'

'There's still something stopping me – I don't think a full reversion to adolescence is possible. I have too much money and too many things and too much space –'

'And a child,' said Paddy, again in an attempt, this time deliberate, to anger Agatha into ending the conversation.

'Max *is* what we've been talking about,' said Agatha, 'don't you see that? When I talk about the world I mean the world-for-Max, the world that is going to fall down on his little head as soon as he takes any notice of it.'

'It's fallen already,' said Paddy, 'and I'm fairly sure he's noticed.'

'Why?'

'How could he not? His world has changed – he's living with your mother: that's fairly earth-shattering in anyone's book.'

'What else can we do? He can't be here.'

'You say that.' (And at last they were down to it.)

'No,' said Agatha, 'I *know* that – I know it completely.'

'Then there's your starting fact, your main prick-to-kick: you can't live with your son, at the moment.'

'Our son can't live with us.'

'Or your son can't live with you, one of the two.' They were talking over one another now, not listening before responding.

'I want him here, do you think I don't? – but I'm afraid of destroying him.' At this Paddy went quiet. 'Some accident might happen, when I was distracted.' She remembered how terrified hearing the scrape had made her. How would she have been able to cope with that and Max? And perhaps there were other discoveries, even more disconcerting, to be made about the house. 'I can't cope. Every time he cries, I start crying – and I can't stop. He sees that. He must be trying to find some sort of meaning for it. He must feel how unnatural it is. How different it is from before.'

'He has no idea at all what's natural or not, only what we give him.'

'I don't want him growing up with the insecurity of a mother who can't cope with – who can't even bear it when he winces.'

'Surely it's better to get over this with him around, the routine of it will help.'

'You're not here,' said Agatha. 'It's the routine I'm finding impossible, because nothing's just automatic; I pause before everything; there's a barrier of thought to go through before I can do it – anything.'

'Do you want me to give up work? Do you want to go back to work?' Agatha didn't immediately reply. 'You said that this was the way you wanted it – last time we talked you did, anyway.'

'I do. I need to sort it out with myself,' said Agatha, defeated by Paddy's challenge. She left, to be on her own for a while; upstairs she went, all the way to the attic, where she sat down in the darkness on the bare boards. Recently, since becoming aware of the breathing, she had found herself behaving in a way that was both private (it was important that her actions went unobserved) and demonstrative (her actions must be unmistakable in meaning, had anyone been there to see them). This odd mixture, as much as anything, came closest to being what she could call her mood – a series of almost artful gestures; bad art; they embarrassed her, how could they not? At moments, she realised she needed to *do* something, and she also realised that what she was about to do (not necessarily what she was thinking about doing) wasn't the best thing or the right thing, the most sensible or the most productive;

(she didn't let the scrape interrupt her, this time) it was just the *thing*thing – not unavoidable, because many times before it happened she managed to stop herself, and do something else; but if she were not to do the thing – which presented itself as doable (the thingthing), she was aware then that she was acting in denial of her mood and deliberately avoiding what she would otherwise rightly have done. The relative complexity of this often paralysed her; and again and again she found herself standing after half an hour still on the upstairs landing, still in the middle of a room. It was easier for her to be in a room in which there were fewer not-doable things: an empty room still presented itself as decorated with possibilities; a dark, empty room, slightly less so. She closed her eyes and concentrated herself on the practicality (which was also the unpracticality) of her grief. Paddy, on past form, she knew, would allow her a certain amount of time, about half an hour, before coming to check she was okay – okay, which these days probably just meant that she hadn't attempted suicide.

Whilst he waited out the time before he could safely go up and talk to Aggie, about half an hour, he thought, Paddy did the washing-up. He remembered how, in the hospital, eating crisps, chocolate bars and burgers dispensed from vending machines, he had felt something like nostalgia for the kitchen – he had even anticipated what a pleasure washing-up would be, how normal and reassuring and not to do with grief. The side window of the kitchen, above the sink, looked across towards a dull wooden fence too high for even tall-Paddy to see over. He was glad, particularly now, there would be no inadvertent eye-contact with the next-door neighbours, whom he had no wish at this time to get to know – let them think them strange and stand-offish; as long as they didn't start to come round with offers of sugar, cake, biscuits and friendship.

The idea of that was sickening; it felt like a lurch, side to side. With his hands in the hottest water he could bear, Paddy thought long slow thoughts – about the course of his own and Max's and Agatha's lives. He tried to avoid the practicalities of inference and decision; instead, he was looking for a more trancelike state. In this, he would feel able to divine whether there were still possibilities of distant happiness for all three of them – and, even further off, whether these possibilities could be achieved with them all still together. He became, though shame-faced even in front of himself, visionary; and he did believe, in a semi-mystical way, in them as a family, and by extrapolation, in the family as an abstract. But he knew, equally, that a divorce between Agatha and him would see him intellectually convinced of the ignominy of all families. He was ashamed of his own anticipated inability to maintain a consistency and logic of thought. He wished it weren't so – and so kept himself, as much as possible, on specifics: which hurt, for he couldn't but be aware that his image of Max was wrong, outdated; today's visit had forced that upon him. He was coming not to know his own son and worse, his own son must surely be growing in ignorance of him. If forced to choose between the two states, being known or unknown, he would of course have taken a life gazing at Max, safe, autonomous, through a one-way mirror. There was less of the show-off egotism in Paddy than he sometimes felt was necessary; a more theatrical father would probably have created scenes of separation and recapture. (This was the gaudy of father-hood, something Paddy had never managed to fit to him-self; motley had always been the best he could do.) He put a plate on the draining board and reached for another, and as he did so he thought he heard Aggie shifting and scraping about upstairs. There was no second sound, though. He went back to his thoughts, slightly more annoyed with himself. If he had gone over to Agatha's mother's in the car, she wouldn't have been able to keep Max from him: a polite request, polite but definite even without a lie, would have had Max in the back seat within twenty minutes. Paddy, scrubbing congealed egg-yolk off a plate, felt that he would perhaps have been a better father if he'd been a worse father, or rather one less concerned with immediate cause-and-effect distress. He was proud of his gentleness, but also perceived it, from his own father's point-of-view (projected) as weak. He never made demands; perhaps, he worried, he should make demands – he should demand more of himself, and of the world; he should demand that he stop worrying so much. It wasn't possible: change; personality revision. He thought about deliberately smashing a plate, but then felt shamefacedly emasculated – why not smash up the whole kitchen, if that were sincerely what he felt? Why, he wondered, had he never, not even as a child, destroyed anything of size? Was this simply to do with class – that those who have less are far more likely to deprive themselves of it? Perhaps it was because he had always been so large, and felt so clumsy, that it was the world which needed protection from him and not the other way round. He knocked the plate gently against the side of the plastic bowl, in order to microdramatize (for himself) his humiliation. Did Agatha approach understanding? Did she find herself annoyed by his under-developed capacity for rage or for expressions of it? He didn't think so: he was a modern man, and his masculinity was – to the modern woman she was – hopeless, hapless and comic; comedic, rather. The thought of this sickened him, made him feel unsteady on his feet. He had to put on an act: although he had anticipated enjoying the washing-up and how good doing it would feel, right now (in the middle of this train) it started to feel effeminate and he resented having to do it. They had a dishwasher and he decided then to make more use of it – but he realised immediately the only time for trance this would gain him was the loading and unloading; not enough. He would continue to do the washing-up, gladly, mildly. At this point, he wondered whether he had just genuinely given something up, been humbled in argument with himself, or whether it had just been a camp internal dramatization (apart from the little knock) of a humiliation that had long ago occurred but – what? – he hadn't noticed, been meant to notice? The last mug now on the draining board, he pulled the plug and waited to scoop the pieces of food from the plughole. After all that happened, Paddy had expected Agatha to become depressed – had expected much the same for himself, too. It would be the worst time they had endured, even including the deaths of his mother and her father. He had known this even as it was beginning, in the hospital, after the final scan: it had been a phrase in his head – The Worst. What was beyond his expectation was that some lapse would occur, that Aggie indeed would fail to cope, that she would start to go mad; and that he, though as intimately involved as he had to be, wouldn't at all know what to do. Her non-communication had worried him to begin with; she had never before been a brooder-upon-things – her decisions had always been immediate and instinctive; he had admired this birdlike capacity of hers for changing direction whilst in flight. But he feared she was changed: often her decisions didn't hatch for days and days, and –

was that her moving about again? – when they did they were fully formed, with wings, but flightless; dodo-dos. She had become emotionally mute: he knew there were decisions she was making, inside herself, to which he was no longer privy – decisions which intimately concerned him and Max, but that he no longer had any idea of how they were being taken. Agatha, as each day passed during which they hardly coincided and each night she spent awake and alone, was becoming more and more terrifying to him. He *expected* her to make an announcement, soon – every day, he thought, might bring it out of her. *It's over*: he was anxious this would be it, and that he would have no chance to argue against or to persuade. *It's dead.* He could feel her points of conclusion, when she reached them, but was kept, still, from knowing what they were. It frightened him to see how disconnected from him Aggie could be, whilst in the room with him; her attention seemed all to be elsewhere, as if, in fact, she were in a completely different room. This was no longer a marriage. He remembered points at which they had, despite their intellectual doubts about Nature, felt it Natural to know one another's passing thoughts even when separated the whole day; it had sometimes taken an hour or two in the evening just to talk them through. This, of course, had been before Max. The feeling of separation – he used the word 'divorce' in thinking of it – was nauseating; they might as well have been living at different historical periods, so little communication was passing between them: if this were so, Agatha was the earlier of the two – she left possibilities for emotional palaeology, for excavations; the skeletons of flightless decision-birds; Paddy, for her, could only be some vague idea of the future, *what might be*. He became more and more upset. What if she were really going mad?

Fuck. The floor seemed to lurch like the deck of a ship. What if she were capable of going mad? It might need the live presence of Max to prevent that, but Paddy was afraid he would be abducted into Agatha's abnormal world. Imagine if Agatha were to make or perhaps allow him to keep the same hours as her! A night-two-year-old! He tried to distract himself from this by imagining something worse. Paddy hated to think of Agatha as dead, but at the moment she was undoubtedly and completely dead to him; he had resolved, many times, on confronting her – and had given hours of thought to the most life-penetrating thought-penetrating death-penetrating words he could say. In all of them, he detected the bleat of a husband-about-to-be-left: *Tell me what's going on* or *Let me help you – I love you, you know* or *What's happened to you?* or *I'm scared – scared of losing you – scared I've already lost you*. He had to deal with the possibility that Agatha might already be beyond the point of becoming unbalanced. He felt incredibly lonely in this, as lonely as he could remember; he wanted to call someone, but not a doctor. He did want a second opinion, and the only people he could think of from whom a visit wouldn't be suspicious were Henry and May. He decided to phone Henry from work and to arrange bumping into one another at the railway station. Pretending normality, Paddy would tell Agatha he had invited Henry round for a coffee – Henry would see what he saw, he would leave, and the following day they could talk it through again on the phone.

As he put the washing-up liquid firmly back in its correct place, a couple of soap bubbles boffed up into the air. Completely surprised and delighted by them, Paddy watched as they twirled towards the window-pane. (Again, he heard a sound he assumed was from Agatha – her movements.) He didn't want the bubbles to land and pop but knew they would; they did. He moved across the room, away from the sink, quite as if he'd come to the end of some long decision, a month of pretending he'd been thinking about something else: he didn't really know how he thought any more; he wasn't sure if he ever had. He remembered sequential, philosophical, prosy thought: that was his professional mind, and he could employ it at will, whenever he had no distractions (no Monster). But life-decisions were made in a way far more poetic, now-you-don't-see-it-now-you-do. They were mushrooms of the mind; not there, not there, still not there, then fully formed and going corrupt. Decisions weren't made, they occurred to him – he occurred to them. He wondered if this was how other people's minds worked – then realised that, of course, he'd have to go back to the beginning with the whole idea of other minds. Paddy felt stupid – he needed to be practical: what was he going to say to Agatha? He wanted to tell her the same thing he wanted her to tell him – *It's going to be alright*. For this, he wanted no proof, just strong, warm, irrational insistence. *It's going to be alright*. He and Agatha, though, could no longer convincingly reassure one another; each of them had used the words too many times, and in too many situations which had subsequently proven all wrong. Neither could take the other seriously as a comforter: in fact, they now mistrusted reassurances, were superstitious about them, afraid ever to hear them: *alright* had preceded agony too often to be plausible as anything other than its negatived sense, all wrong, don't worry, it's going to be all wrong. Perhaps in this they had worn one another out – it was hard to see how anything sayable, anything not an event, a good, healthy birth, would fix them for one another.

In five minutes he would take himself upstairs – all the way to the top.

# CHAPTER 18

Coming through the front door, next but one evening, Paddy started speaking a little too early and loudly – careful, however, not to give too much information and be discovered as lying. 'Aggie, I bumped into Henry,' he said, omitting the words *Hey* and *Guess what.*

'Hope it's not too much of a surprise,' said Henry, walking into the front room. Agatha looked at them both for a long moment, distracted; then she became charm, quite tinkled with it. 'Henry,' she said, 'how are you?' He was very well. Just before this, Agatha had found herself on the sofa – she assumed she had fallen asleep there listening to the breathing, but it was only now that she heard the first slow intake. Since noticing it, she had realised that the breathing didn't happen all the time. She had begun to suspect that it was only when she was doing specific things that it was audible, but she hadn't yet worked out which these things were. Certainly, the more routine hours passed without her hearing anything – they weren't memorable, at all. She had no time to pursue this thought now. 'It's lovely to see you. How's May?' She was well, too. 'And Hope?'

'Yes,' said Henry. Paddy immediately became worried that Henry would get to see none of Agatha's torpor, her incipient madness – she would twinkle and charm her way through the whole visit, wittingly deceptive or not. Agatha offered tea or coffee, or something alcoholic. Henry thought a beer, thank you; Paddy with a nod would have the same. Agatha went off to get them. There was a moment of awkwardness: should the two men follow her into the kitchen? In the flat, Paddy felt, they would have – or would at least have kept talking to her (shouting from any room to any other had been unembarrassing, here was different). He looked at Henry, whose eyes had been searching for his: Henry now gave him a definite look, but not a diagnostic one – *this situation is intense* is what it said, not *this is what this situation is.* Paddy wanted to ask, *What do you think so far?* but he could only shrug in a way he hoped was comprehensible. Henry, inexplicitly, shrugged back – and started to talk about his day, would not be drawn just yet. It was only when putting the three glasses on a tray to bring them through that Agatha fully realised they had an unexpected guest and that she was going in some way to have to cope with his visit. This upset her; Henry was not someone with whom she should have to *cope* – she and Paddy were very fond of him; when bad things happened to him, they even allowed themselves to admit they loved him. She picked up the tray and all the way into the front room thought she was going to drop it. 'There you are,' she said almost with triumph as she handed the glass to Henry, who was talking but not rudely and didn't stop for the gift-glass but incorporated a *thank you* into one of his sentences. He was telling an anecdote, which turned out to be quite funny; Agatha found it more amusing than normally she would, because it was such a change to be listening to a different humour: Paddy's was so familiar – and some of what made them laugh had become shamefully (had anyone else known) grotesque; *if* they laughed, *when* they laughed – rarely, and, then, hard; often until crying. Henry talked a while longer about the same funny character at work, less funnily; he drank the first half of his beer very quickly. His was the loudest non-shouting voice the house had heard in months; he enjoyed the theatricality of the large ringing room.

The awkwardness he had initially felt at the major fact he was concealing began to diminish; this, he could do. Paddy had relaxed, somewhat (half-forgetting his and Henry's mission): Agatha's unusual attention and her slightly false responsiveness to anything Henry was saying – surely this wouldn't pass unnoticed. Henry knew her, and how one story of anyone's usually led to one of hers; chain of anecdote. But Henry was probably thinking that nothing much, apart from the big, terrible things, had happened to Agatha recently; she wasn't going to be talking, like him, of confrontations and misunderstandings, annoyances and stupidities. Halfway through Henry's next anecdote, Agatha changed – became slap-serious; she did not interrupt him, though Paddy could tell she wanted to – she waited until he had taken a quiet sip of beer, then until he'd swallowed. 'How many weeks is she?' Agatha asked.

Henry met her immediately; he had, Henry, been blustering, and Agatha had seen the reason: his major fact was discovered. 'Four or five,' said Henry, 'I'm sorry – we were going to wait until the first scan before we told you. It's so ridiculously soon. We shouldn't even –'

'What?' said Paddy, no slower than anyone might be expected to be.

Agatha smiled. 'You're happy, aren't you?'

'I'm anxious,' said Henry, and laughed through the awkwardness. 'I'm happy,' he said, the humour having clearly gone from his laugh.

'I'm happy for you,' said Agatha, blinking. 'I'm delighted – now please go.'

Without hesitating, Henry stood up. Paddy took only this time to quash his instinct to stop him: Henry would have seen enough, from this.

Agatha was radiant as she crossed the room and took Henry by the shoulders and kissed him on the lips. As her face was drawing back, Paddy heard her whisper – but it hadn't been intended as secret: 'Quickly – go quickly.' Henry was leaving a half-full glass of beer but without a glance – he gave little more to either of them. Paddy went with him to the front door, taking his usual shelter in practicality. 'It's great news,' he said as Henry went past him. 'Tell May . . .' he said, and then shut the door when he saw Henry, aghast, obviously, even from the back of his neck, keeping going.

Henry had failed to get through this – and Paddy had put him up to it, unsuccessfully.

He heard Agatha moving about in the other room – he thought she was walking her agitation, but actually she was just sitting down. He went and sat beside her, to be ready. The evenness of her breathing disturbed him hugely: how was she going to get from here to sobbing without some incoherence?

'How did you guess?' Paddy asked.

'I just knew,' Agatha said. 'And I don't want to talk about it.'

'Alright.'

'How was today?'

'Can I just say one thing?'

'What is it?'

'They must have –'

'Yes, it's about as soon as they could have. It happens all the time, though. More than you know. Some people are . . .' Agatha didn't know whether to say lucky or unlucky. 'It happens to some people,' she definitely ended.

Paddy went into the kitchen, shaken, and poured himself a glass of water. For the rest of that evening, he managed not to mention Henry and May, Hope and babies in general. Agatha seemed calm, to him, and felt herself to be astonishingly unaffected by this. After Paddy had gone to bed, she was able to devote some time to thinking it through. She knew that she was jealous, jealous of the pain as well as the delights, but she didn't think she hated May. In all this, she was glad to be accompanied by the breathing.

# CHAPTER 19

THE following afternoon whilst Paddy was out at work May came round, on her own. Agatha had been expecting a visit from her – although there had been no phonecall, *because* there had been no phonecall. When she saw who it was on the doorstep, Agatha wavered for a pulse – did she feel herself capable of this? Just to shut the door, whatever the consequences for future friendship or estrangement, seemed so attractive. Instead, she managed one of the most demanding smiles of her life – one that required emotional pulleys and levers to help it ascend. As May came in, Agatha saw through her belly to what was, at five weeks, likely to be inside her; this did not remain a static thing, though, but ramified nauseatingly into a future, a personality, a giggle and a subject of many many hours of future discussions – if they managed, after this, to remain friends. May stopped in the hall. 'Is this alright?' she asked. 'Are you alright about me coming round?'

'I'm fine, I think,' said Agatha, hoping that saying so would make it so. She had been in the front room just when May knocked, and decided now they should go and sit instead (to protect them both, in some way) in the kitchen. One of Agatha's hands gestured, Agatha hardly knew which, but still May made no decisive move. 'Let's try,' said Agatha, 'at least.' Which brought May to her own surface, and Aggie could see her eyes going glassy as she stepped past her. By the time they had reached the back of the kitchen, wordlessly, Aggie had breathed herself back into composure – deep and two and out and deep and two.

A scrape that moment did nothing to disturb her. May, too, had somehow calmed herself. 'Just a glass of water, please,' she replied to Agatha's next question.

'You can have whatever you like,' Agatha said, and realised the question had phrased itself as if to a child.

'Just water, please,' repeated May. 'I'm off caffeine – and you know I hate all that herbal tea-stuff.'

Agatha poured them out a couple of large glasses, straight from the tap; they had a water filter, but she felt it was at this moment an affectation: she didn't want to wait for a fresh load supposedly to purify.

'I came to apologise,' said May.

'You don't have to,' Agatha said quickly, trying to interrupt the prepared speech; she was very concerned she might detect traces of pity in it, something she knew *would* make her hate May – and Henry, too.

'No, I'm sorry you guessed. But I'm more sorry that we didn't tell you. We'd decided not to tell anyone until –'

'Henry said. I understand.'

'We didn't know, last time we came round. I was so embarrassed, when I found out. I thought I'd stay away until I could see you safely – I mean, you wouldn't have had to guess, because I'd have told you.'

'I realised that, after Henry said.'

'We feel really bad,' May said.

'Do you?' asked Agatha – she was trying not to remember five weeks in, and all the feelings of world-importance and nauseous physical glee; of being definitely blessed and other people being so sorry-seeming and unfulfilled.

'Oh, Agatha, it's such crappy timing. It makes it look like we did it deliberately to taunt you.'

'No, it doesn't,' she said. 'Don't make it a tragedy when

it's not. It looks like an accident. I don't mind about that.'

'But you do mind about us not telling you.'

'No – a little; I don't like to think of you staying away.'

'Then tell me what it is.'

'I'm annoyed we can't be honest any more, with each other.'

'Do you mean Henry and –'

'No, I just mean you and me.'

'We can.'

'We're not being honest now.' Agatha was amazed at her own tranquillity, almost proud of her clear, direct-stating voice. Although she had not said it, both of them had heard *You're not being honest now.*

'I'm trying to be honest,' said May.

'Then tell me how happy you are.'

May overcame the impulse to look away. 'I'm so happy,' she said. 'It's the wrong time, and –'

'No, that's the lie-part,' said Agatha. 'Tell me about the being happy – I know it's what you're ashamed of. That's why we can't be honest, otherwise.'

'It feels different to the first pregnancy,' said May. 'I feel more certain about it – not because I know what's coming, anything could happen, I know that; but I think I've stopped being so rational about it. I'll listen to the doctors, but really I know everything is going to be fine. I feel fantastic. Not sick at all.'

'Thank you,' said Agatha, breathless.

'Are you sure you wanted me to say that?'

'Don't apologize,' said Agatha, very definitely. 'Don't make it seem as if you were just saying the right thing for me.'

'No. When I came round, I didn't want to talk about being happy at all.'

'You wanted to tell me, on and on, how miserable you were.'

'Oh yes – I am.'

'But only on the top – the rest is joy.'

'It's not as simple as that.'

'I think it is – there's terror-joy and worry-joy and I-don't-know-what-else-joy. They feel different from being happy, and they are, but they're just part of joy – which is a difficult thing to feel. It has no gravity, no morality; it feels evil. I remember.'

May felt she should be silent. 'I know you do,' was what she wanted to say.

'I am happy for you,' said Agatha, and it felt as if something were unclenching or perhaps unravelling inside her. 'I'm able to protect that from all the rest. But, really, you could have chosen a better time.'

'We –' said May, then realised Agatha was joking and that the conversation had been moved on. 'Oops,' she said.

Agatha closed her eyes and listened to the breathing for a few moments. She felt May taking the opportunity to look closely at her face. Agatha had been missing the companionship of the breathing and even of the scrape. She hadn't heard it whilst alone in the house that morning. It seemed, this past few days, only to be with her when she was in company. Which was strange, as to start with she hadn't been able to hear it except when on her own. Perhaps, she thought, the house was getting bored with her. Her memories of the morning were very indistinct, almost non-existent – perhaps she had fallen asleep on the sofa.

May left, and Agatha didn't hear the breathing again until that evening, when she was in the bedroom with Paddy, watching him get ready for bed.

# CHAPTER 20

IT wasn't any longer the breathing or the scrape which scared Agatha, it was the periods of self-absence – during the day, she seemed no longer to exist; occasionally, she could remember coming to a dim sort of consciousness, hearing a single intake of breath. Most of the time, most of her time, seemed to pass without feature. At first she assumed that, after so many late nights, she had been falling asleep to catch up. Now, though, she feared that her memory was failing. She would look through the left half of her book, sure she had been reading it for the past few hours, but couldn't remember any of the incidents her eyes moved back through; then, when she started again from the point where her memory bleached out, the words seemed oddly familiar and she became convinced she had after all read them already. So, when Paddy's getting up woke her this particular morning and she felt herself to be fully there, she wanted to tell him what had been happening. He was finding clothes to wear, by touch. After a minute attempting to phrase the opening statement, she gave up and made another sort of confession.

'May came round,' she said, out of the darkness and out of what Paddy had been assuming was sleep.

'Good morning,' he said, then, 'When did she?'

'I don't know,' said Agatha. 'I think it might have been yesterday.'

'Why didn't you tell me, then?' was what Paddy almost said, in an annoyed voice; instead, he let a gap occur – into which came a second unsayable: 'Why are you telling me now?'

'She seemed fine,' and now Paddy remembered why this would have been so important; he hadn't immediately thought of May as pregnant.

'That's good,' he said.

'She wanted to apologize.'

'For what?' said Paddy. 'For being pregnant?'

'Yes, I suppose she did – to begin with, anyway. But, no, she came round to say sorry that we'd found out as we did.'

Paddy looked at the bed. 'That was –'

Agatha interrupted him and explained how the conversation had gone, in a softly distorted manner – underemphasizing her own nearness to cruelty. 'I think we need to do something to show them we've forgiven them.'

'What?'

'Invite them round,' she said.

'For dinner?'

'I'd – yes.'

'On their own or with other people?'

'On their own – then we can talk about it, a bit. If the subject comes up.'

'Fine,' said Paddy, relieved it hadn't been something much worse. This detail of one of Agatha's days reminded him how little he knew, how little she told him, about any of them. He hated to think of it this way, but it seemed like progress – relaxation; though, sooner or later, he would have found out that May had been here and would have been mildly peeved not to have been told.

'Come here,' said Agatha.

Paddy went over to the bed, bending with long fingers to feel its edge and not stub his toe.

'Here,' said Agatha, meaning somewhere beside her in the sheets. On all fours on the bed, Paddy moved his face closer and closer to hers. When she was able to put one hand behind his head and feel one of his ears against her wrist, she pulled him in for a single, gentle kiss. 'You're a good man,' she said. 'Thank you.'

Paddy instantly knew that, at some point, later in the day, he would have to lock the door of his office and spend a short while crying. It would be fine, he would be fine, on the walk to the station, and on the train – routine could keep off the emotion; but he mustn't allow himself between now and the locking of the door any gap of inactivity or unfocussed thought: not until he'd organized a place for his sad joy. He pulled back from the bed, smiled at her though he knew it was too dark for her to see, and went off to finish getting dressed. This, he felt, was what Agatha wanted. She for her part wasn't quite sure why she had just done that. Her first untrue explanation to herself was that she had been grateful for Paddy's lack of reaction to what she'd said about May. But then she realised it was more to do with how close she was to leaving him. He must surely know about this – it wasn't something she felt she had been able to disguise. And she had wanted to apologize to him for forcing him to live in such horrible limbo. There was the risk, of course, that the apology would reveal to Paddy the limbo which he somehow had failed to notice before. As he pulled away from her, she had been dismayed to feel the heat of his hope – his face was blazing with it; she was directly responsible for this flow of fresh blood. She thought of the weight of Paddy's head, the responsibility she had always felt for it when it was lying on her shoulder – and through this of her responsibility towards his whole life. She remembered the feelings of her shoulder, in moments after his head had been lifted away; its shape still being acknowledged ·by nerve-prickles, the muscles and bones not quite certain it had gone. Strength was what the kiss had been meant to give him – not hope; hope was atrocious. Agatha could hear Paddy pulling through the laces of his shoes (it reminded her of him putting on Max's first pair of impractical lace-ups); and she could hear or imagined she could hear his changed mood in all his sounds. The extent of his love scared her; the power she had over him, through this love, was something she wanted to get rid of, to return to whomever she'd first taken it from – but that, of course, had not been Paddy; the power had been latent: she had merely spent year after year drawing it together and making it acute. What had seen itself over that time as a process of loving, now seemed the construction and refinement of an instrument of elaborate torture. That was their relation, and her part in it, her part in it at this present time. She wanted to call Paddy back and to explain exactly where she was; how close he was to losing her, how close he should be to losing hope. But anything she did now would make it worse; self-paralysis was the only solution. Let him go – deal with the day. Do not kiss or thank him again, not for a long time. Let his ardour, that's what it old-fashionedly was, diminish over the next week. If she did this they would return, eventually, so long as she hadn't ruined him, and he didn't as a result ruin things, to where they had been only a few minutes ago. She heard Paddy going downstairs, then the quiet noises of his breakfast: each of them was treasurable – around each of them she put a mental frame. They were here, they were for the moment present; this might not always be the case, this probably would not be the case. Again she thought how the most perfect solution would have been his death, and again she was dismayed that the last time she killed this thought she hadn't killed it properly. At some stage, she was going to have to mourn Paddy; hope in him, not merely life but life-with-hope, that was what made such mourning an impossibility. The day was already wrecked-wretched; she wouldn't be able to do anything with it. Agatha hated herself for her compassion and her stupidity.

The hours that followed were a gloom of equal density. The breathing was intermittently present, and this perhaps prompted her. She remembered what had happened in hospital, with Rose – not fragmentarily, as usual, but telling herself the story of it, hour by hour. She didn't know why she had suddenly become brave enough to do this; it was hard to believe her emotions were so intimately connected with the lives of Henry and May. Perhaps she merely, after the disastrous conversation with Paddy, needed to test herself – to see whether she was capable of going through the worst of it alone. All was a horror for her: specifics of it made it difficult for her to believe in or continue living in her own body. She had felt herself to be absolutely monstrous, couldn't think of any disfigurement – goitre, hump, cancer, elephantiasis – which could have been worse. Hers – her growth – was worst because it meant she could pass for normal; men would give her their seats on the Underground (when she still thought she could go out), and some women who were strangers would even touch her belly and ask how many months. Agatha had become, as she saw it, the most grotesque parody of motherhood – and it had felt like being strapped to a tragedy. One of the things for which she most hated herself was the stupid persistence of her hope. At the birth, after Rose eventually emerged, Agatha had still thought there was a possibility she might be alive. To believe this was, shamefully, to believe in the miraculous – that Rose had a silent and invisible heartbeat. But she was born as she was, and would never move or take a breath or make a noise. Wrapped in a blanket and handed gently to her (she could not fault their tact), the face Agatha looked down on she couldn't help but see as perfect – if nothing else, perfected; already at its best and most and last. The weight then in her arms (4lbs 7oz) had never really left her. *Since*, her brain had assembled a collection of images of women with dead infants: refugees carrying little corpses through border crossings in hopes of medicine or magic; westerners making dashes to hospitals with floppy blue bodies in their arms. There was no solidarity in this; she couldn't wish her complicity or her compassion upon any other woman – and the thought of their emotions made her own move turbidly around within her, as the gurgling of Paddy's stomach had often made her own go glug. Whatever would happen to her, with Paddy and with Max, with Paddy's father and her own mother, the worst had already happened; but this made her feel no better. That her life had already managed to accommodate the worst thing she could have imagined, and that she hadn't been utterly destroyed by it – this was a torture rather than a consolation. At moments, with the sounds within the rooms, she thought she might be going mad (although in an exaggerated, literary way), and while the prospect terrified her, it also gave her a little more moral respect for herself. If she could bear her life, then it wasn't unbearable; she wanted to feel it was irresistible – she wasn't a freak of suffering, able to prosper by it. She hated, on television, to see the murder-victim parents and the freak-accident lobbyists who had found a vocation in their grief. Was that unfair? She wanted nothing to do with the partisans of tragedy, the paysans of the tragic. Much better to move, alone, to somewhere no-one knew her, and never speak again of what had happened – spend one day a year shut up in tears and collapse. But that, too, was a glamorous and literary idea: to get on a witness-protection programme for those who had seen the worst. It annoyed her that she had been permanently changed and it annoyed her, also, that there were people incapable of seeing anything different about her; not friends, these had all been able to see the change, the minor wrecking of face and aura – not friends, but street-strangers, shop assistants, even call-centre workers. Agatha wanted respect as well as anonymity: inside seemed the only place for this. She got no expressed respect here, but had been able to maintain a horizon of dignity (meaningless dignity, perhaps), and anonymity was a given, though it had been apart from rather than among, and that was a different definition. The crowd wouldn't have confronted-comforted her, and it might very well have ignorantly injured her, but she would have felt something small had been achieved merely by being for a while part of it.

What should she do when Paddy got back home that evening? She didn't know, had not been able to decide on any better course than a slight withdrawal of herself from him – another slight withdrawal, in the long series. He would react, detecting this, with a darkening of mood, but this was only routine: he would see it as pattern and cycle, whereas she feared it had reached decisive, final. Emotionally, she felt she recognized, she had been moving towards an end of them; and she had done this, horrifically, by mimicking what would have been the first gesture in the opposite direction. This had been perverse but definitely *alive*, and the pain it was going to cause Paddy was part of the energy it had already given her. If he tried to kiss her, she would have to let him, and then take a different course, away-away-away. She would maintain a greater physical distance between them, her replies would have to be given even more slowly, after an even longer pause. It terrified her (as so much terrified her these days) that something so infinitesimal as a wrong kiss, mistimed, could make the epoch, could bring about the end of their marriage.

At first Paddy was late, then he was very late, then he called from the hospital: his father had collapsed, been rushed straight into intensive care. 'He's going to die, this time,' said Paddy.

'You said that before,' said Agatha, meaning it to come out more kindly-sounding than it had (all the day's plans for the behaviour of evening were being scrapped).

'He doesn't have any strength left – you can see it. I think he wants this to be the last time. It's too much palaver, going back and forth between here and home.'

'I'm sorry,' said Agatha, thinking of the day just gone; apologizing, in disguise, for that. She felt like apologizing for everything she had become but had to make do with expressing sympathy for everything Paddy was suffering, and conventionally at that.

'Don't be sorry,' said Paddy, 'you know I'll be glad when he's not suffering this any more. I want him to die, too.'

'You don't have to say that.'

'I do. Or it's like – I don't want him to have to go through the pain and process of dying. But I do want him to be dead, already – so that all the process is over. I'm sorry, I've been storing up things to say. I want my old dad back. I don't know the man in the bed upstairs. My dad wouldn't know him, either. He certainly wouldn't like him.'

'Do you want me to come?'

'No. Thank you for offering. If he were properly conscious, I'd want you to bring Max, but that isn't going to
happen. His brain isn't all working any more – it isn't
getting enough oxygen. Sometimes he says really stupid
things, really quite offensive. He says things to the black
nurses that I'm surprised they don't hit him for. He calls
them big black mammas. It's ugly.'

'Are you alright?'

'I'm going to go back – I've got to go back. I don't want
him dying when I'm not there. All of it just makes me
think of my mother, and how he was then and after that.'

'Are you sure you don't want me to come?'

'Yes. The only thing I can take is knowing I'm looking
after you – your interests – oh I'm fluffing what I mean to
say. I want to say I want to protect you but I don't want
you to react by saying I'm being patronizing.'

At another time, perhaps any other time, Agatha knew,
this is exactly what she would have done. Now, she said:
'It's the right thing – I want to be protected. Give him my
love. Kiss him for me.'

'I tried to do that a while ago. He'd been quite still. I
thought it was the end, but the nurses weren't all that
interested. I went to kiss him on the forehead and suddenly,
clunk, he tries to sit up and splits my bottom lip. I look
like I've been in a fight.'

'You have,' said Agatha, then added, 'you are.'

'I fucking hate it,' said Paddy. 'I fucking hate death. I'll
call later.' They said goodbye, Paddy telling her he loved
her. She said, 'I love you,' and she said it again a second
time and a third time; so that he would know it wasn't
conventional or avoiding-something: he did, she sensed,
he understood; he put the phone down.

# CHAPTER 21

AGATHA called her mother to let her know what was happening – and the question immediately came up: 'Do you want me to bring Max round?' Again, Agatha tried to explain – without saying anything too direct – why this wasn't a good idea. Her mother refused to understand, but was not cruel enough to force Max upon her. There was a possibility, Agatha sensed her mother felt, that he might be neglected. Although the idea that she would be such a failed mother that she might damage Max worked to her advantage, in keeping her mother off, Agatha knew the resentment was likely to last years – on both sides.

When finally she was able to put the phone down, the house felt like pure relief. Although it was early, for her, Agatha went and lay on top of the bed – where she fell asleep until morning.

What woke her was another call from Paddy: his father was still alive. He had not regained consciousness but had become threateningly stable.

'It was being awake that was killing him,' Paddy said. 'He was trying his hardest to die. And now he can't do that any more, he's doing better. He could go on for, I don't know, a month.'

'Come home, then,' said Agatha, who felt slightly changed by her own night of unconsciousness but hadn't had time to work out how.

'No,' said Paddy. 'I have to stay here.' Agatha knew there was no point asking why – this, waiting it out, had become Paddy's task. He was stubborn, particularly when caring; she had her own memories of this, and her own pride in it.

'Can I bring you anything?'

'No,' he said. 'Don't come.'

'I could . . .'

'Look after yourself,' he said, then became embarrassed. 'It's not really my father any more. But he's still my responsibility. How's Max?'

They talked for a while about the latest Agatha had heard, which was nothing, really.

'My father thought he was great,' said Paddy. 'It was good he was able to know him. I have to get back.'

They said goodbye without saying the word love – both of them knew that last time had been an extreme point, and so would the conversation after the death, but for now they would be a little moderate.

Afterwards, Agatha began to feel very glad that the last time she'd seen Paddy she had kissed him and told him what a good man he was. Even if her reason for doing this had been completely confused, it had – given what had happened since – been exactly what she would wish to have done. All she hoped was that Paddy hadn't started to interpret it as it had been attempting, for her, to mean; that he had it as love rather than imminent departure.

During the day that followed, her mother phoned again and again, to ask what was going on – eventually Agatha lied, telling her she was about to leave for the hospital so that she could be with Paddy; that cut down on the calls but did not stop them completely. When Paddy phoned again, mid-afternoon, Agatha told him about the lie. He said he'd deal with her mother if she left messages wanting to speak to her. 'My phone's off, anyway – most of the time.' Paddy explained, in return, that he'd called Henry and told him what the situation was. 'He said if there's anything . . .' Agatha said she'd be fine but was glad she had an explanation of how May had found out – for she, too, had begun calling often, imploring Agatha to pick up, then leaving emotional messages.

Late in the afternoon, May came round, knocked and then shouted through the letterbox. Agatha had been making coffee in the kitchen so wasn't embarrassingly in view when May walked past the front window. 'Aggie,' May called. 'Come on, Aggie – it's not good! You shouldn't hide yourself away like this.' Agatha hoped almost to the point of actual prayer that the next-door neighbours were out, wouldn't hear this mad implied version of her. May slammed the letterbox a few times as hard and loudly as she could, shouted, 'I'm really annoyed with you. You have our number. We want to help.' Then, just in case, she wrote a short note and shoved it through the door. Agatha waited half an hour at the back of the kitchen; the note might be a trap for her shadow behind the glass. When eventually she dared the hall, she didn't want whatever May had written to make her cry so picked the folded piece of paper up and stuck it one of the cookery books.

Paddy phoned again, that evening, to say that his father's condition was unchanged. 'So it's another night in that lovely hotel,' he said.

Agatha was worried he would have heard something about May's attempted visit, but if he had he was tactful enough not to mention it.

After her full sleep of the night before, Agatha stayed up until three or four. She sat on the sofa, thinking. She tried to think about how she should think about her life, how judge it if she couldn't escape from it or even take a step back, not abstractly or wankily (she thought this word), but as a practical way of deciding what to do with it next: leave Paddy or not leave Paddy;

(she was reassured by the sound of a scrape – a rarity recently) have Paddy move out or move out herself; take Max or not take Max. How would it be, this new life of hers, without the features they had so constantly for the last years given it? It might, she was afraid, be a little like being alone in a house with nothing to do; her present was her possible future. Only of course, as she knew, it wasn't. A split from Paddy would mean ground-floor flats in puke-ridden streets; distance between herself and Max would mean a different self, one capable of maintaining that distance indefinitely. Even as she kept her son off now, she knew it was a perversion: partly she was afraid if she had him back she would never let him escape the circumference of her arms – not even at night. Suffocation was possible, definitely, metaphorically and not.

Whilst she was going through all this her eyes were sometimes open, sometimes closed. Occasionally, the lights gave a flicker – or perhaps it was more that the room seemed to change, slightly. Agatha wasn't at all able to perceive how. She knew how easy it would be for her to add seeing things to her probably-mad capacity for hearing them. But she didn't just doubt her senses, she doubted her doubt of them – and, yes, now and again, she felt that there was a quick difference about the room. It was too quick, at least to begin with, for her to be able to tell what it was – which was why she'd firstly put it down to a flaky electricity supply. An hour or so after midnight, she lit a candle and turned off the overhead. The room still, occasionally, seemed to alter. It was unnerving, particularly as it did not coincide with the scrapes; these she still, very rarely, noticed – only one or two. The breathing was present, but not as a constant – sometimes there were long gaps between breaths, and when they did come they seemed slowed-down. No longer could she have mistaken them for wave-crashes. Agatha's growing anxiety began to exhaust her, until eventually she gave in and took herself up to bed. Before she fell asleep she had time to notice that this room, too, once or twice, even in the dark, seemed to flicker with difference.

The next day was quiet, interrupted only by calls from Paddy, which she took, and messages from May, which she tried to ignore. Apart from the garden visits of cats, climbing the flowery appletree, and the ignored knocks of a meter man (she presumed), she was left quite alone. This made for practical problems: food, mainly. Everything fresh had already gone, there was a very little milk, almost no coffee, and basics such as rice and pasta were only enough for a tasteless meal or two more. From what was left in the cupboard, experimentally bought packet soups, stale biscuits, pickled onions, she improvised lunch. There was a large packet of porridge oats, and she had a bowl of them for dinner, milklessly glutinous. What she ate, though, wasn't particularly interesting to her; during the day, it – whatever it had been before – had been getting worse. She had begun, in half-moments, when she wasn't really occupying herself, was just present in the body but a couple of steps back from the threshold – she was beginning to catch glimpses; no idea what these were of, none at all: they replaced the flashing sense of the rooms changing: her eyes were getting better at catching these moments. Only very gradually, over the next few hours, did she begin to work out their rules. One of the later realisations was that *it* wasn't an *it* but a *they* or even a *him* or a *her*. This had inevitably been preceded by a connection: the breathing and it; its breathing. The glimpses, though, to begin with, really were only that; things, forms, seen through a gap in the trees from a between-towns train. At first, when it was still an it and didn't breathe, she perceived it as a cloud – and so this was the first of their rules she worked out: they floated. Also, when glimpse after glimpse added up to what, with some effort of synthesis, could be taken as an impression, she realised that they did not always float the same height off the floor: at times they seemed almost and in some flashes tantalizingly upon it, wavering a few fingerwidths above; at others, they were in the air by two or three feet. This perception led to another, glimpse-gained: that their shape changed in accordance with their distance off the floor. There was a very basic rule: the further up, the wider. From the start, Agatha had thought she was seeing heads in the shapes; this, she didn't allow herself to trust: faces had always troubled her – she saw her father's in fires, wallpaper patterns, leaves of trees, behind-eyelid shadows, sometimes she saw it in apparently complete blankness, the brown carpet of their flat, its whitewashed walls. But she realised after a while that it was in fact, though fact wasn't exactly how it felt, heads and not faces that she saw. This fine distinction enabled her to approach belief: heads were more factual, less sentimental; she would have wanted faces not heads. The glimpses seemed to be without colour and even without light or dark; when she began to make them out, it was more as a weight become visible – as if the molecules of the air by sagging slightly had revealed some presence between or within them: what little was there wasn't where it would have been had nothing been there. The heads, without (to begin with) faces, had a greater density than the rest of the glimpses – theirs was a darker weight. Though she doubted everything she was seeing and at times dismissed it with relief, she somehow felt the heads as more massively present and so doubted them less. Once she had determined the rule which related distance off the floor to width, she began to notice that the heads disposed themselves as they would have done on human bodies: when the body reclined, the head was at one end – perhaps slightly raised; when the body stood, the head topped it off. There was an in-between state, too, which she realised was the commonest, where the body seemed truncated, not at the length of either standing or lying. This was sitting, and in this position, once she had recognized it, the bodies were slightly easier to discern: she sensed the angles, shoulders and knees. She wanted to see hands, a hand – for some reason, over and above heads, or even faces, this would have been a confirmation of if not the humanity then the human form of the them, whatever they were. As gradually she worked out their rules, she began to get more and more from each glimpse: it felt, because of this, that the moments the glimpses were there were lengthening, although really she was increasingly aware of what she was looking for, what *this time* she needed to check. Another of their rules, if they could be called that, was that they weren't at all fussy about where they appeared or when; they seemed to have no preference as to rooms, conditions of light, time of day. For Agatha went through a second and a third and a fourth night without Paddy, and endured also the days in between. The food had almost completely run out, even the porridge – which she now hated. There were tiny apples on the tree, but when she tried eating one it bitterly corrected her. And, in truth, she hardly noticed the hunger – and, if she did, it seemed a fitting accompaniment to all the other sorts of emptiness she was feeling. Throughout this long time, Agatha stood in the breakers of a rough sea of dread: mostly, only her ankles were cold-scalded; sometimes – a freak wave – her mouth and nose went under. In a way, she was glad at last to have something to ascribe the scrapes and breathing to; it was better thus than completely without cause, though perhaps no less mad. The breathing, however, before it altered, slowed, had seemed constant, characteristic, as if it came from one person always; the glimpses, although she knew them far less well, seemed more variable. She wasn't completely sure they were always the same entity; she wasn't, most importantly, sure whether the heads contained male thoughts or female. (The thought of their thoughts terrified her for several hours.) What reassured her most of all was that the glimpse-figures seemed to be completely unaware of her. Once or twice she tried stepping towards them, though the moment of their presence lasted long enough for her only to begin to move; they did not react, their heads did not lift. When this failed, Agatha tried saying boo (it helped to keep the sound comic – a scream would likely have affected her more than them) – this they ignored or were unable to hear. As far as she was able to tell, the figures lay, sat and stood completely separate from her – a different universe, at the very least. Something in this, after a while, was a disappointment to her; it meant they weren't there *for* her – this was the vanity of her grief: of course the house was centred and dependent upon her, so why shouldn't everything in it be, too? She had by now become accustomed to her earlier terrors; both the breathing and the scrapes were as sympathetic elements of the house as the floorboards which she knew to creak and the ceiling-corner spiders' webs she had not bothered to dust away. Part of her believed that, with an act of will, she could make it all go back to what she had previously thought of as normal; another part that if she ever tried to exercise her will, the entire network of weird relations that had been established would evaporate – the house itself would cease to exist, and she would be left either buried beneath a pile of rubble, splinters and shards or standing on an oblong patch of brown earth between the neighbouring intact houses. The continued reappearance of the glimpse-forms, by resisting the destructive possibility of her will, became another of her terrible reassurances. And she began, perhaps partly as a result of this, to change her interpretation of them – after all, they were appearing to her and her alone. The absence of anyone else in the house wasn't allowed to obstruct her particular logic – she *had* had, she was now becoming aware, slight glimpses even whilst Paddy had been around; he had never mentioned seeing anything unusual here – and the flaw in this, that she and he hadn't been anywhere near confidentiality ever since they moved in, was also explained away: had Paddy been sufficiently unnerved, their estrangement would have ended – he would have spoken, maybe not deliberately or articulately, maybe it would have been a whimper or a yell, but he could not have suppressed such flashing and repeated fear. As she looked at them harder, whenever during the third and fourth hungry nights they appeared, another perception came upon Agatha: although the attention of the glimpse-person wasn't concentrated directly upon her, it *was* upon something. There was not exactly an object but a part of them she could sometimes see which wasn't a part of them; it had even less of a definite form than they did – was sensed as an area opposite in substance to what they were; buoyant to their weight. She made guesses as to what it was, a thing they carried and which held their gaze away from her – it was a mirror, a hole in space, a skull, a book. There was no reason, she knew, why their focal point should have a name she would have been able to guess or give. With annoyance, she was unable to dismiss the possibility it was some kind of crystal ball in which they tried to see the future. Falsely or not, Agatha began to suspect that their focus was, after all, upon her – and the more intensely and intimately for being indirect. It began to be an argument that the glimpsed never did look directly at her, or at anything else around them; she was being, she came to sense, ignored – ignored, though, only to be all the more intensely focused upon *through* the not-object. For several hours, the fourth night, she went down the path towards believing that what they had and held was, in true fact, her soul – which was why she was unable to see it and also why she felt inspected and known within it. They became for this brief epoch of thought her definite guardians; in their hands (she now assumed hands for them) she was both held and beheld. Taking this as her truth, she found it more difficult, when they made their one or two next flash-visits, to see them from the point in the room where she was physically standing or sitting. Instead, she felt herself to be in their hands looking *not* up at their head, their face, which with its possible gain in insight was what she would have wanted, but out towards where she – Agatha – bodily was. This happened in instants, and she experienced it not as mirror or television but as a real being-outside-herself. And this, which might have been expected to terrify her most of all, horrify with ideas of madness again, was a timeslice of sensation that made her cry afterwards for long minutes out of transcendent relief: at last, she was away from what she was – she was held by someone else and held *as* something else – not daughter, wife, mother. It gave her the oddest following feeling, that she had all the release and guilt of having slept with someone other than Paddy without ever actually having done so. It was an instant of total unfaithfulness – not just to him but to herself as herself. The transformation of being loved for different reasons, in a different way – the new sense of existence that she imagined an affair might have given her – this came upon her all at once. And such an extraordinary moment could not but change her when she returned to Agatha, hardly having left. She wept hugely, with sobs like axe-blows – weeping for how much she loved Paddy and how estranged from her he must feel. Although she wished it, she knew she would never be able to deceive herself into thinking that the glimpsed were Paddy or Paddy-outside-himself. They, or he or she, cared for her and loved her, as she had felt, in a completely different way – and it was this otherness of affection from what she knew so much better as Paddy's which made her mourn that so overwhelmingly. It *was* mourning, she realised – it, his love, had been allowed to die; she had not necessarily killed it but she had held it still so that it might cease to live, so that Paddy might help her put it to death. Yet what destroyed her most of all was the possibility that she was mistaken – that this love lived, and she had succeeded only in paralysing it, causing it to suffer, yes, and weaken and begin suffocating, but not finally to die. Paddy did not exist in a glimpse: it was his triumph and his tedium that he was always there. And, she realised, he was constant if not in his love – she had assisted in making that an impossibility – then in his attempt at love. Suddenly, she could not believe her own stupidity and ingratitude and lack of grace, and all towards him. In the next glimpse, which turned out to be the final, climactic one, she felt herself looking out from the caring hands at an Agatha who was as alone and guilty as she had ever been – a woman who had quite possibly succeeded in turning the best of everything into the worst. This devastated her. She panicked, phoned his hotel, only to have the man who answered refuse to put her through. Later, she realised this man had been perfectly reasonable – the time must have been around four in the morning, her voice would have sounded to him as an insane female warble of distress. He said he would pass on a message, and she, out of frustration, said no, not to say she had rung. She called Paddy's mobile but he had turned it off for the night; she left no message. A minute later, she called Paddy's mobile again and said over and over that she loved him – when she was cut off, she called back and said it again. She apologized for everything she had been and done, *since*. A while later, she called back and apologized for sounding so mad. She wanted to tell him to ignore how distressed she had been, she was better now, but she knew her best honesty had been in her first, uncontrolled message. Then she sat back to wait for his call and to worry her way towards a way of dealing with it. After an hour, the one between five and six, she became aware that she hadn't during that long time had a single glimpse. She felt completely and deservedly abandoned.

# CHAPTER 22

A ROUND nine the next morning Paddy phoned to say his father was definitely dying and then, after a few hours more, an unexpectedly long time, phoned again to say he had died. Even between these two calls, Paddy – Paddy's voice – sounded changed, as if he had been carrying a monstrous burden which had now blessedly been removed, and replaced by another even more monstrous one. It was only when she put the phone down after the first call that Agatha remembered her after-midnight messages to Paddy and realised that he hadn't mentioned or given any hinted acknowledgement of them. This, she thought, was partly because what was happening to him was so much more important, so overwhelming, and partly because what she had said fitted, in every way, with that happening: she had given her reaction in advance, so Paddy no longer had any need to thank her for it. During the second call, Agatha heard the beginnings of his suppression of the resentment that she hadn't been present when his father could have shown his vulnerability and his final love. It wasn't clear – it wasn't yet possible for her to tell what longer term effect this might have on relations between them. In a strange way, Agatha wasn't exactly sure how seriously Paddy was going to take the death of his father. On the phone, she tried her best – told Paddy he'd done all he could, that his father knew he loved him.

There was, Agatha felt, a moment during grief when an illusion of choice appeared; she had felt this very much with her own father. And how she had grieved subsequently was directly related to how she had reacted to the illusory possibility of choosing either to be stoic or succumb. The choice, definitely, was an illusion: Father-grief, for her, had been a bad, long beating-up – she could try to cover her head, so her skull wasn't smashed and her spine wasn't snapped but any idea of being in control departed from her with the first blows. From all that she had known of him and from what she could tell about him now, down the phone, Paddy saw two options: one was to abandon himself, to fail to deal with the situation and to do this partly in the belief that it would force her back from her own internal exile; the other was to stay Paddy, be heroically solid, accept his own conditions and cope.

As she put the phone down, again with the words *I love you*, Agatha wasn't sure whether her tone had nudged Paddy one way or the other: she had tried to be neutral, but how can one be neutral comforting, or trying to comfort, a husband for his father's death? Agatha became aware, as she took herself through to the front room, that she was trying very hard not to judge Paddy. How would he react to this new death? It was terrible to feel that their future together might depend on this. But what worried her more was that she couldn't tell which of his reactions would be most likely to bring them back together: she couldn't guide him towards one or the other, and she knew herself to be perverse enough that if she caught him meekly following her guidance, that might be the signal of the end. Flagged up, it certainly wasn't. What she had always wanted, one of the things, was a resistance – an equal and opposite force so that she might know she had some kind of surface against which to build the lean-to of her life; no buildings – they were vanity; some wall or cliff against which to press, rest, beat and break her fists. Paddy was solid; solidity was the function of the father she had

made him into and had made of him. He had called her
(both times) from just outside the main entrance, standing
in rain – she had been able to hear other hospital visitors,
dropping one another off, picking up what was left of one
another. 'You can leave me a message,' Paddy had said, 'if
you want me to get in touch. I have to stay here a little
while – there are – there's stuff to be done. I want to stay
here a little while. I better get back, or they'll move him:
I got the man in the next bed to promise . . .' He rambled,
a little; full of love. After that all she could hear from him
were sobs, *I love* and *you soon*. Stranded now on the sofa,
she knew she was a long way away from where she was
meant to be – from where the pride of her life should have
been centred. She turned on the television, hoping for
something completely irrelevant – and slammed into a
talkshow discussion of euthanasia: a woman in a wheelchair pleading for the right to die. Off. She thought of
Paddy, walking along corridors in the hospital, and
irrationally she feared for him: another pulse of the old
morbidity – he might die there, never come back. Probably, he was dead already – heart-attack, brain tumour.
She closed her eyes and looked at the institutional art
upon the walls of Paddy's corridor; she did not know this
hospital, but she knew hospitals. He turned into a ward,
and she imagined she saw the curtains drawn around the
bed of his father – another coughing man who had coughed
more then less then stopped. The coughing man in the
next bed along gave a nod – he had defended the body
from the nurses: perhaps someone would do the same for
his son or daughter, if he was lucky enough to have one.
Now should be the time to collect Max, to recollect her
life; whatever happened in the future with Paddy, she
wasn't going to leave him now, not for the next six months,

at least. They were becoming more married, with every minute that had passed since his father's death.

Agatha almost decided to call a taxi and take it to her mother's, fetch Max, then take another taxi – or ask her mother to drive her – to the hospital. This was, she felt, what Paddy probably wanted her to do: although the most sensible thing would be to let Max for the moment stay where he was. If they had been going to hospital, just for a visit, they might quite easily have left Max, for ease of everything, with his grandmother. What decided Agatha against leaving the house was the feeling of not wanting to make Paddy's experience of his father's death a divided one: What if she arrived just as they were wheeling his father's body to the morgue? It would botch the whole day – Paddy would, as things were, remember it purely, as purely awful – father dead, Agatha not there, Max not home. She could help him most by showing him she had changed, or was trying to change, when he got back. There were other reasons Agatha had for not going, ones which she didn't want to have to confront. Still, she was afraid of leaving the house; she felt she could, though, and that was a change, an improvement. There would be a funeral – she would be expected to go. She would, in herself, work towards the knowledge that, on that day, she would cross the threshold: it would be an occasion. Right now, as another reason, she didn't want to see Paddy at his worst and find herself unable to cope. Better for him slightly to recover, at least enough to drive home.

And then, later, Paddy returned – carried Max through the front door, still sleepy from the drive; in Paddy's hand, a bag full of food: bread and butter and more basics. Agatha could tell even from the front room there was something different about this entrance, the atmosphere as well as the sound of it; she came out into the hall and gave a little yelp when she saw her living son. She took him from Paddy's arms and immediately began to wake him up with soft talk and little shakes: she didn't want him coming to consciousness in a half-strange house – she must show him around it and let it have a good look at him, too. The terror implicit in this second thought she put definitely to one side. Paddy, who had been expecting an argument in the hall, went placidly back to the car to get the rest of Max's accoutrements; it took him four trips to bring it all inside: pushchair, foldaway cot. He felt almost contented, merely being Dad, toiling out of sight to make things function. Because it had been a while since he'd dealt with Max's stuff, he resented it. He thought of African tribes-women, infants tied to their backs with a single piece of cloth. Why this array of apparatus? What was the necessity of it all – mortal fear of faeces? It was a good, distracting thought; he had too many other things he could be thinking about. He could hear Agatha upstairs bouncing Max on her hip and sing-talking to him; they were in Max's room, now for the first time really Max's room with Max in it, still unredecorated, still pink. Paddy waited to hear his son react to this, scared by the newness and strangeness of it all – but he didn't; he was probably too sleepy. Paddy carried the cot folded-flattish upstairs. Agatha, when he brought it in, was showing Max the insides of all the cupboards and reassuring him they were empty so he wouldn't worry about what might be lurking in them. Max was quite capable of falling asleep again, if only he'd been allowed. Paddy, phoning ahead of himself, had made Agatha's mother promise not to hype him up on sugar. Under any other circumstances, she would probably have made her resentment known. He remembered her look of relief as she handed Max over.

'Everything alright?' he now asked, forking the question between the two of them – wife and child.

'He loves it,' Agatha said, in a tone that conveyed her own acceptance. Paddy felt wise, as if he really *had* learnt something in the years which were meant to bring maturity. Listen very closely to what people say they want and give them the exact opposite. Agatha saw this mood in Paddy, felt it might become a dangerous smugness, but decided not to crush it; Max needed as much confidence around him as could be manufactured. Paddy brought up more of Max's stuff from the hall (the whole reason for their moving here – car to hall to bedroom, easy); Agatha made some noises about where it should go, pointing with her free hand – Max drooling and now, yes, asleep on her shoulder. Paddy obeyed; they were sensible choices, and he saw no reason to challenge them. The cot went where they'd seen it when they viewed the house; he unfolded the zigzag shape, admiring once again its succinct design. The world of babyhood had been completely revolutionized, or at least made-over, since he and Agatha had passed through. Agatha thought about putting Max straight down as he seemed so groggy from the journey – and she wasn't sure if he was properly taking anything in. (Max did feel a very basic delight in being in a small room again with both Mummy and Daddy, and it wasn't so hot there.) But she decided it was better he become familiar with some of the rest of the house, upstairs at least, even if it was only in a dreamlike state. She carried him past Paddy, along the hall and into the big bedroom. It was very important Max knew how close they slept to him (if not, in some ways, to one another). Part of Agatha stepped away from her explanation and looked back upon herself: she had been consumed, again, by motherhood – not wholly, there was an aftertaste of self-consciousness. But being this absorbed in something, something human, not a book, felt exquisite, extraordinary: Max might be saving her, saving them, them together, and by doing that saving the world. He was never meant to be glue, but they were never meant to be shattered and scattered. Max, she thought, seemed to like their bedroom – he clearly wasn't picking up any bad vibes from it. Not wanting to push things, she decided to complete his tour of the house tomorrow, the attic (he was still nodding off whenever she stopped jiggling him up and down) – the attic could wait. She carried Max into his bedroom and began carefully to undress him: he needed changing; he needed a wash.

Paddy, sitting in the front room, had decided to leave Agatha to put him down alone. It had been frustrating, dealing with the practicality of bringing Max away from his grandmother, then getting settled in the car; there had been no chance for intimacy, though Paddy took some small soul-nourishment from Max's mere presence. He was comforted, too, by the way things had gone with Agatha. He had come away from the hospital with several conversations worked out in his mind; he knew what he must begin by stating, and what he must say if Agatha refused to reply, or replied this way, or that, or even that: screaming. Max *must* come home; Agatha *must* prove that she did, as he'd been overwhelmed to hear her say on the phone, both in her messages and when they spoke, love him – she *must* make their marriage a real marriage again, from both sides. He had had a wide selection of ultimatums ready, and then he'd junked all of them. Instead, he would forget about being sensible, diplomatic; he would drive over to Agatha's mother's and fetch his son home. It would be, he had felt, worth whatever argument might ensue –

their argument would be different, from Max's being there with them. His thoughts were interrupted by a familiar screaming: Max didn't like the bathroom; he had started wailing almost as soon as they were through the door. 'What is it?' Agatha asked. 'What's wrong?'

All Max would say was, 'No!'

Paddy decided not to go and ask what was happening. It would leave something for Agatha to tell him, or for him to ask her if she didn't.

Max fell asleep as soon as he was in his cot. Agatha turned the knob on the radiator, to make the room a little cooler – defying the memory of her mother. She drew the curtains and tucked him unnecessarily in again. Now for Paddy, who was waiting in the front room, calm-seeming.

'Yes,' she said, and he could see how changed she was – his father's death, he thought, it must be that. 'I agree: we have to have Max with us again. We have to try to be a family. And I have to deal with my problems, I know. But we can't move.' Paddy saw she was holding him off, until she had completed. He realised, too, what had happened: they had both been going through multiple variants of the conversation they *might* have if he came back with Max, and this was the outcome of all of them: Agatha was stating the conclusions, their conclusions, for the both of them – and it was both of them, he also realised, himself as much as her, who had decided she would be the one to state them; Paddy required some capitulation; Agatha needed to begin controlling things again. What she had said, and the fact of it being her who said it, was an elegant solution. 'I'm so sorry about your father.' Aggie stepped forwards into Paddy's open arms and for a long while they disappeared into each other – even if you'd been there, you wouldn't have been able to see them.

# CHAPTER 23

Tʜᴇʏ went to bed – spontaneously, and with less trepidation perhaps than they should have felt. But even as they were beginning gently to kiss and tenderly to touch, both were convinced it was going to be worse for the other. There had not been, *since*, a complete lack of physical intimacy between them; they had hugged, fairly often but usually in the kitchen, and almost never within sight of the bed. This hugging had sometimes begun as a more necessary and urgent holding, calming. Occasionally, in their urgency, they had kissed, but to all this there had been a definite limit. Sex was impossible, and both of them were wordlessly agreed upon that. Their motives were slightly different: Agatha's came out of aversion, Paddy's out of respect and, if he had been able to admit it, aversion. There had been, as with any birth, six weeks afterwards of a medically imposed No; this was the zone of stitches – but it had already been clear that their own shared private No was louder, harder and would resonate longer, if not for ever. Sex towards a second child had been purposeful as well as fun, a recreation; sex now, they both in their different ways thought, would be sex in the void – sex thrown off a cliff and falling. Paddy knew he was not prepared in his heart – what he thought of as his heart – for a return to such agony; Agatha tried to convince herself of her indifference, the importance of other, practical concerns. She wanted to reassemble herself, to put the pieces back in order if not have stuck them together, before.

In the weeks since they'd moved into the house, and

since she'd taken to the nights, Paddy had been at his most reassuring when asleep. She had wished, in a way, that he had been properly comatose, then she could have rolled him from side to side, biffed him up a little, chuffed his cheeks and ruffled his hair; she could have dandled his hand in her lap, run her tongue along the inside of his lower lip – and all without his ever knowing of it. She had wanted to romp around him on their bed, frollicking like a lamb – yes, she wanted to frolic, a frolic out of grief. These impulses had been incomprehensible to her; she realised they had something to do with being childlike, with a tragic seriousness of play – she definitely had not wanted to have sex. Instead, she wished she could toy with his penis as if it had had nothing, in any conceivable way, to do with the death and birth of Rose. If she could do this, she felt, she might be able to resurrect something of what she believed she should feel about Paddy's body and therefore, hopefully, perhaps, Paddy, too. She had also been aware of something necrophiliac in her feelings: why should she want an unresponsive body? She certainly didn't want him to be hard, be useable. It was distressing to her – extremely distressing, to feel that Paddy being Paddy, Paddy being intellectually, consciously Paddy as well as physical, smell-and-texture-giving Paddy, was somehow a failed thing for her.

This time, they rolled around for a while, play-fighting. Agatha had wanted play, Paddy was managing to respond – perhaps they were both aware of Max close by in his room and how he had already changed what they were prepared to do. For the moment, though, even as Agatha held Paddy down and gently bit his lower lip, then less gently, there was no abandonment, or only hints of the future possibility of it – but none of the hints could reveal

how fardistant that future might be. They had lost any
confidence they might once have had in the potentialities
of this act: union was a there – not a word they either of
them thought, but an area of concept towards which they
felt they were meant to be heading: coming together.
Agatha could not help thinking of a woman from her
antenatal classes who had so wanted to avoid tearing
that she rubbed wheatgerm below her vagina for all nine
months of pregnancy, to soften it, make it more stretchable;
and then, when the birth came, the split had gone upwards,
ripping her clitoris completely in two. After this intrusion,
Aggie's head became full of graphic gynaecological illus-
trations of exactly what would soon be taking place and
the possible consequences of that having taken place.
Difficulty. Deformity. She might have to stop, which she
really didn't want to do – part of her was gleeful at
returning to physical communication with the man who
was her husband: he felt and smelled and even sounded
*good*. Aggie became nervous, nauseous: she tried hard to
forget about her body, what it had once been and what it
now was; the wrecked, the repaired – forget it in one way,
in others remember it.

When they lay together, Paddy always instantly forgot
that he was so much taller, standing, than Aggie; she was
and had always been a bigger, more dominant sexual
presence than he – as a persona, more existent, confident
in that existence. She had been, he knew, a great deal more
sexually experienced than him, beginning their relationship. He had early on felt the usual male insecurities
and she had used the usual words and means of tender
reassurance. But it hadn't merely been inexperience, it
had been intensity of presence: Paddy had never been able
fully to participate in his body – sports at school had been

awful and even now running was a humiliation: his knees were besotted with one another, couldn't pass without kissing. He had always known that whatever swiftness he possessed was mental. But now, Paddy revelled in being close to Aggie's face, skin, hair. His old familiarities came back to him; he had, each instant, a thousand tiny recognitions and remembered above all, and this full-consciously, that he knew this woman *well* – better than anyone. It was never predictable where her pleasures were going to hide, but Paddy was confident now that he'd find them, just as he'd found them many so many times before. He was all for her – alive to her sensations, wishing them exquisite; crafting her experience, worried that it might be a wrong one.

They were turbulent, together; lips crushed against teeth; elbows found their way into ribs; his fingers snagged on knots in her days-uncombed hair – Ow! she said; sorry, he said; it's okay, she said, just be careful. He knew that to say, I *am* being careful would turn sex into argument – sex as that wasn't a bad thing, sometimes necessary, but now they very badly needed sex as agreement; agreement, at least, to have sex. But perhaps it was going to be both that and argument, anyway; the debate and conclusion their bodies were having and reaching was about time and timelessness – could they still look forward, after all that had happened? Could they remember their future? Close up and gentle, rough and fragrant, their faces caressed one another, they caressed one another's faces – Paddy was stubbly, Aggie worried her skin might be too dry, papery. Their bodies were winning the argument, overcoming time; they were gently, stupidly, physically wise. Wisdom wasn't necessary, but only to keep going and doing in the hope that the right would occur and the wrong be avoided or, if not, then only be momentary – and it wasn't bad, the doing, it was fine, and then it got better. It was fuck and sex and yes it was good right now especially if, yes that was it, that was it, keep going, keep going, like that, just like that. Try not to think, thought Paddy. He was afraid of his clumsiness, all his possible mistakes – they would not do. It would not do; Aggie wanted to break away, to save them from some approaching disaster; but just then, Paddy came – wept within her – his eyes opening, grabbing, and she felt the full tenderness of his achieved vulnerability. Something comic in her had always wanted to slap him round the face, at this precise moment; she doubted he'd even really notice, or mind. She was glad to remember this impulse, it was a definite retrieval from the person she'd been – it reconnected. The feeling was a little like being coked; curiosity as to what was next took over from any code of behaviour. She remembered drugnights and felt a body-nostalgia to be back in the middle of one of them – sitting round in a circle of friends, talking shit; she had always felt cosier taking drugs like this, in private: then, if someone insisted, go out to a club (usually they just wanted to talk more shit – Paddy, now touching her, had been there for one of these evenings but had felt and looked and behaved like an incomer). Agatha, the racing driver of her own big-engined motormouth: neaaaow! – negotiating the hairpin bends of her childhood, zipping past the pile-ups of later life. From this, her audience would *learn* something; cocaine gave her this certainty – it made her a little schoolmarmish, prim – when coked, she liked to organize people – even get them to play organized games; truth games, of course. She also liked to be outraged and, on more than one occasion, violated. That had been before Paddy. She remembered going down the stairs into the cellar; how she had thought about sex with Paddy. That memory was enough – Aggie was surprised by her orgasm, mugged by it; she came, hugely, with a heave. And almost as soon as she did, she began to cry – the heavings of her chest continuing the same but now ending in sobs. It too had mugged her, this sorrow; she hadn't spotted it, round the corner: it wanted things from her, possessions, griefs she had held precious and carried around with her. Paddy knew this, saw it as he looked across at her and felt better for seeing it – some release had been achieved, at least.

Afterwards, after she had gone to the loo, Aggie went down into the kitchen – what was there to eat? She was *very* hungry – she hadn't felt this hungry since being pregnant. With delight, she found Paddy's shopping bag. Through the ceiling she blew him a kiss. There was bread, butter, marmalade – to start with she would have some toast with butter and marmalade. She got a knife from the drawer and cut the white loaf into thick slices – a little thick for the toaster, but she shoved them in anyway. Too hungry to wait for them to do, she grabbed an apple, took a bite, then reached into the bag for some Brazil nuts. Boiled eggs, she then decided, would go very well with the toast. Unsalted butter, and Marmite instead of marmalade; soldiers to dip. Paddy, who was still in bed and had been expecting Aggie to rejoin him put on his dressing gown and came to find her: he had started again to think about his father, and this time he wanted to turn these thoughts into conversation. Aggie had already changed her mind about the boiled eggs and was now boiling some vinegared water in a pan to do them poached. After a few moments, when this seemed to be taking too long, she put a full kettle on to boil. The toast had started to burn but she didn't notice until too late. She pulled the black oblongs out of the toaster, burning her fingertips – carried them across to the bin, dropped them. 'Hello,' said Paddy. 'What's going on here?' It was half-past nine at night. 'I'm hungry,' said Agatha. As she said this, she was slicing some more bread for toast, if anything, thicker than before. Bacon would be just great – fried, not grilled. Do this properly. Aggie set the toaster, fetched a frying pan, put it on the fiercest gas ring so that the blue flames reached all the way up its sides. Paddy asked, 'You're having breakfast?' 'Egg and bacon,' she said. She went over to the vegetable tray: 'With grilled tomatoes – if you'd like some.' (She had now decided to fry the eggs as well.) 'No, thanks,' said Paddy. He would have liked to give Agatha a proper kiss, but she was moving too fast, too erratically. He thought of their joke, when they saw Max, or any child, playing over-violently, becoming fractious: T-minus fifteen and counting; T being Tears. This would come crashing, but it was good to see Agatha so energized – about food, though? She had fretted over her weight for months, *since*. The water was now boiling in the pan (the kettle, unnoticed, had clicked several moments before): Agatha added some salt and some more vinegar (she had changed her mind back to poached eggs, more healthy), then – unable to persuade Paddy – cracked in three eggs. The bacon, she put under the unpreheated grill, soon to be joined by the sliced tomatoes. In the meanwhile, she poured herself a glass of milk and after putting the bottle away drank it in one, got the bottle back out of the fridge and poured herself another one. Paddy tried not to smile at her milk moustache. She was making him forget his dead father. 'Are you sure you don't want anything?' she asked, biting the corner off one of the even more burnt pieces of the second round of toast. Paddy wanted to join in but felt he would be being dishonest if he did and Aggie would sense this and hate him for it. He just wasn't hungry. 'I'm alright,' he said. The tomatoes, halved, went under the grill, and Aggie buttered the toast – taking another couple of bites as she did so; after which she cut another slice of bread and put it in the toaster, to replace the one she had almost finished. 'Come on, come on,' she said, squinting at the slowly grilling bacon. Paddy watched. Agatha took a step back. 'How long have the eggs been on?' she asked. 'About a minute and a half,' he replied. Agatha looked at the buttered toast on her plate. 'They'll be done now, won't they?' Paddy didn't want to be caught criticizing Agatha's cooking. 'Well . . .' he said. She looked down into the saucepan, across the top of which a white foaming scum had formed. They had a piece of kitchen equipment especially designed for plucking poached eggs out of water – Agatha reached for it now, unhooking it from the rack, and dug into the foam: the egg rose out semi-translucent, undone, and then the yolk split and spilled onto the hob. Agatha shrieked in disappointment – and carried the remains of the egg across the kitchen, dripping yellow and translucent through her fingers all the way. She thumped the metal thing against the side of the sink, splatting what little was left of the egg down the plughole. Paddy did nothing. Agatha walked back over to the cooker, through the eggy mess on the floor, and immediately dug around in the saucepan for another egg. It, too, wasn't done – gelatinous and sloppy. She got this one halfway to the plate before it slipped through one of the gaps in the spiral spoon and fell right down between the oven and the kitchen unit; it broke as it hit the floor, and yellow splatted out at Agatha's toes. 'Why aren't they done yet?' said Agatha, very petulant. Again Paddy held himself back from suggesting she leave the remaining egg a little longer. This time, Agatha picked the plate of toast up from the side and held it just over the edge of the saucepan. A smell of meaty burning was coming from somewhere. The third egg was lifted from the water and dropped immediately onto the toast – where it slopped around, still translucent and, even to Agatha, clearly inedible. She put the plate down on the hob, where it couldn't sit straight, tipped slightly – sliding the egg off and down the other side of the oven. Crying now, but angrily, Agatha yanked the tray out from under the grill – too violently – some of the boiling fat that had been on top of the now part-charred bacon leapt onto her feet and she dropped the grill tray in shock. It clattered to the floor, spraying more hot oil on her ankles and spilling the tomato halves – still hard and uncooked – in all directions. In a final gesture of despair, Agatha pulled the plate of wet toast off the hob and onto her lap as she let herself slip onto the floor. And now it would be alright, Paddy judged, to say something: a moment before, and Agatha would have snapped at him to go away. He knelt down and put his arms around her; he decided not to speak, though. Aggie sobbed and asked him why everything always went wrong? He didn't answer. He thought of carrying her through into the front room, but didn't want to risk getting oil on their sofa. He lifted her up onto the sink, he was big enough, she light enough, and put her feet under the cold tap. Upstairs, Max started to wail as if in sympathetic distress.

# CHAPTER 24

MAX did not wake up the next morning until almost half-nine; clearly, Agatha's mother had made him fit in with her hours, and at least this made Agatha's adjustment from night-wakefulness to day slightly less abrupt. Paddy was able to see him for half an hour, but then he had to get on the phone and make arrangements for the funeral, deal with his father's solicitors, tell people. This was how it would be for the next two or three days.

After the first relief of having him back, Paddy realised how estranged he felt from his son: all the time he had put in, over the past two years, of evenings, weekends, of being a *present* father – and still Max would only be comforted, ultimately, by his mother. There were some terrible looks Max gave him: *Who the fucking hell are you?* Even the *fucking* seemed to be unmistakably in place. It would take months of redoubled effort; and Agatha's paralleled efforts, which he could already see, and which he fully believed in and supported, would only make it harder for him. Perhaps it would be a good idea to take a fortnight off, spend it at home; it was still several weeks until the Easter holidays – perhaps by then, he thought at his worst moments, the damage would be irreparable; perhaps it already was. Paddy envied the nonchalance, the unanxiety of previous generations in their parenting. He was sure, on some levels, that this preoccupation with a child's happiness – constant, perpetual – was decaying for both the child and the parents: it was, to steal an idea given by Agatha's mother, a mouth perpetually full of sweets – that these were Max's milkteeth did not matter, the taste was inculcated, the whole life was guiltily being set. One of the maxims of child-rearing that Agatha and he had always been agreed upon was that a child should, fairly early in its life, become aware that it was not the only thing in its parents' lives – this was a main reason for their wanting a second. A knowledge of lack of centrality was something that seemed to have benefited the children of their exemplary friends. The better balanced among these were the ones with a mix of care and really-don't-care. Parents had to be able to maintain the illusion at least that the child was independent of them, and that they were independent of it. This wasn't easy; and the people Paddy could think of who had gone one way or the other, and the extremes of clinginess and destructiveness to which their children had swung in reaction, were a pretty grotesque crowd. One mother they knew had a three-year-old who refused to have his hair cut; she had to do it whilst he was asleep. Yet now, what was left but Max? He was on his way to being an only child, with all the attendant problems; this was something that they had never wanted, in fact had been explicitly, statedly, to each other and to others against – two or three was the number they had been aiming at.

They made the house safe. Paddy went out and bought three stair gates, something they'd never needed in their flat. He felt a sad pride as he screwed them one by one into place (this, at least, was something he *could* do – not that it was beyond the skill of Aggie) – at the bottom of the main stairs, the top, and the bottom of the attic stairs. This was as he'd envisaged – it made him feel adequately fatherly; it was a holy chore. Paddy knew Max was quite old to be developing a technique for the stairs; luckily, they were carpeted with thick, non-abrasive wool.

Max back in Agatha's life brought with him love, shit, noise and a thousand distractions. She remembered why they had once called him the Monster. The weeks with his grandmother had not been well spent. Change, decline, had been inevitable, but it was no less devastating for that – its inevitability was its ultimate devastation. Max had regressed, and it would take Agatha a hard week even to get him to acknowledge the potty. Her mother preferred nappies; they made her feel in charge of the whole process. She was a demon changer and had always offered to do nappy duty whenever she came round. This, inevitably, was accompanied by a short speech on improvements in diaper design. She had become an aficionado of brands, and Max had been spoilt – getting used to the plumpest, most environmentally destructive ones. When her mother spoke on this subject, Agatha felt she could remember the safety pin sticking into her chubby infant thighs – what kind of memory was this? A wanted and needed one, confirming and opposing what her mother said. Max had become more babyish in other ways, too. His grandmother had, it seemed, talked to him, all the time, in goo-goo-goo language; he was burbling quite happily, every trace of undissolved words gone. There was a lot of recuperative work to be done, and Agatha became furious with her mother for having necessitated this. She hated the idea that Max, so young, had *forgotten* things. (Often in the past she'd had to prevent herself treating him like a project, a work project, with goals to be set, targets to be achieved, a defensible outcome.) He was far more excitable – Agatha blamed her mother's sweet tooth – and more implacable when angry. Max, too, was far less distractable than he'd been before; his distractions required planning; for which there was no time – she being occupied, most of the time, with failing fully to distract him. Perhaps this was inevitable, she thought; perhaps it would have happened anyway, whatever had or hadn't taken place outside him. But it gave her another set of guilts, these ones far more specific than those she had replaced.

Max made it feel a very different house: when he was awake, there were very few moments of pause. Aggie, the first full day, tried to get him to take his afternoon nap, to allow her to catch up, but he seemed quite out of the carefully inculcated habit.

Almost instantly, Aggie had became nostalgic for the previous time – her time of time; being indulgent of it, frivolous with it, investigative through it. It was lost; and the other time Aggie now became concerned with was the time stretching forwards, and wondering how long she would have to wait before she had some more of this velvety-rich, self-indulgent, bath-advertisement, woman-imagination time. With Max there in the house, there was no time as such, merely a succession of actions, improvised to stave off his boredom. Of course, Agatha resented Max for taking her away from herself, again; as he had done when newborn. What surprised her most, and dismayed her entirely, was exactly how *much* she resented him for this. It wasn't just anger – she was honest enough to admit that; at points it became, though she felt nauseous with the implications – at points it became straightforward hate. Aggie needed distraction from these thoughts of Max and, perversely, she tried to find this in other thoughts of Max. She looked at him perhaps as closely as at any object that had ever held her attention. How had he been affected, on the most profound levels, by all that had happened to them? It was almost impossible to tell – and she was afraid she would only find out years and years later, when any linking of cause to effect would be a stupid act, probably one of despair. If Max went bad, they would inevitably blame what had happened to him in his third year.

Whilst she had been pregnant, Max had liked to put his hand on her growing tummy; nowadays, he still demanded this, to touch her ungrowing (and sadly unshrinking, too) tummy, and she still – meaninglessly – let him. She was glad he hadn't been old enough fully to take in her pre-paratory introductions of the idea of a lovely little sister, a Rose. Still, she thought Max was a much more melancholy child; deep blue was there, as well as his usual green, crimson and yellow. She admired and was terrified by his capacity for passion; she wished it for herself (had she had it and lost it, or allowed it to be mothered-embarrassed out of her?), and she tried to mother it out of him.

Aggie had a terror of overprotecting Max, but even more of resenting his happiness, his ignorance of what had happened. There were huge fears inside her, as to what she might not be able to prevent herself taking out on him. She formulated it: 'Because Rose died, part of me wants Max to die, too. It would tidy the world up, if he were gone; if he were gone, I could be done with the whole thing.' Sometimes she felt it was as if Max had acquired, through no fault of his own, entirely through their doing, a second shadow: whenever he did something for the first time, a handstand, spoke a sentence with a sub-clause, picked up a book and read it for himself, said he was tired and wanted to go to bed, imitated a chicken – every time, there was another darkchild behind him who was never going to do these things.

It was hard not to wish him away so that his deathly little twin would go, too. He was polluted with pathos, and Agatha felt furious at herself, for not being able to forget, and at Max, for not allowing her to forget. At times, though of course he wasn't, she seemed to catch him being deliberately tragic in order, it followed, to be cruel. There was a possibility that he'd learnt this sort of emotional manipulation from his grandmother, but the idea that he'd been corrupted so completely was almost unbearable: to have given birth to a male version of her mother – better never to have given birth at all. And this was another set of thoughts about Max which other, more presentable thoughts had to be brought out to replace. He was very handsome. He was very healthy.

Max also, and inevitably, brought joybursts with him; to be his parent was to become, at moments, the sky on fireworks night. He could not help but make Aggie feel again the old ecstatic wonder of being a mother and Paddy the deep rich ache of felt fatherhood. It was the recovery from these moments that made Agatha resent both them and, though she hated the idea, Max, too.

Arrangements for the funeral had become more compli-cated – Paddy hadn't been aware of how exacting his father's will would be; still, he supposed, the dying man had had five or six years to draft and redraft it. A particular church was specified, particular readings and particular hymns – all of which would require Paddy to travel halfway across the country, have meetings, make arrangements. It would be easier, he told Aggie, if he stayed overnight. 'That's fine,' she said, trying to stop Max banging his head into the corner of the kitchen table.

'Are you sure?' Paddy asked. He had worries which he knew there was no way he could express: Agatha; Max.

'It needs to be done,' said Aggie. 'That's all there is to it.'

But it wasn't – Paddy knew it wasn't. He was afraid of leaving Agatha alone with Max. Somehow, he thought, she would absorb him into her depression, her dark world. He couldn't be sure if she thought she amounted to an actual danger to Max: she was his mother, she spent her life keeping him from small harms.

'I'll be home as soon as I can,' he said.

'We'll be fine,' Agatha said, and Paddy felt as terrified as he could remember. This was irrational, he told himself; the telling did not work.

Before Paddy went, Agatha felt vaguely worried that without him there she wouldn't be able to cope with Max. This was nothing to do with practicalities; the mechanics of it were already returning as reflexes. She was more anxious about becoming distracted, by the house, by some new manifestation of its feelings towards her. But within a couple of hours, Agatha's worries flipped around and everything − Max − life − life alone − seemed all too horrifically copeable with; Agatha felt like a nurse in Accident and Emergency, experienced beyond com-passion. Her emotions had been professionalized, cau-terized, the scar tissue made into hard, useful shapes: hooks. Paddy's coping, she took as read − it was what he did, who he was. And she feared, now, that between them they could cope with anything − even Max's death; and this thought, of course, made her fear Max's death more than ever, because she knew that − after the loss they had already suffered − life would then no longer even be a case of coping; it would be, as recent weeks had felt, mere survival for their separate selves. The delineations agreed between them, of time, of doing, would evaporate. There would be waste, emptiness, rooms, time, and the cliff face to climb of one another. It was agonizing, this thought, so, to begin with at least, she did not let herself near it; it left her in imaginary confrontation with the tall wall of the damaged other. Max, for the moment, stood between them – if either of them saw something they did not wish to see, a neglected wound, a stretch of ugliness, they could always pretend (to themselves most of all) that Max's latest movement, dodge, had covered their view, that they were no longer sure they'd seen what they'd seen. Gashes there were, too big to ignore, where the cliff – along with a measure of self-esteem, or intellectual interest, or political engagement – had collapsed. There were slumps in one another that they had glimpsed, areas of slag and slurry – Max, in reaction, must be held higher up, closer to the eyes – he must come to obscure the whole view of the other; and the risk here was that they would each bring him up so close that they would begin to see flaws in him, too. He could not remain undamaged – how could he? This compassionate boy they had been trying to raise – alien to dismissal and cruelty and the weaponry of other little bleeders. How could he not notice? She desired more than almost anything not to come to hate him for this, his seeming ignorance and insensitivity. But her concentration upon this started, during the afternoon they were alone together, to make her think that she probably already had – had come to hate him. It was atrocious, to feel this; Agatha was wary of exaggerating to herself, but knew she wasn't. There were conscious decisions she had made, about how to deal with Max when he returned. She had been determined that, by their own actions, melancholies, they would not demand of him any exaggerated response, they would not warp his universe with the gravity of her grief. He would know of his sister's existence, her manner of existence, in their hearts and before their lives, and he would know, later, he would be told of her momentous continuance in their hearts and therefore their lives, but for the moment his jolliness, his callousness were to be taken as gifts – *had* to be taken as gifts – from their wrapped appearances; he might hold out to them a box of earth, a worm in greaseproof paper, an applecore found beneath the carseat. Or all he might disgorge upon them might be an indifferent vomit, a puke that he himself was surprised by and hardly, really, noticed. These would be, she insisted, had to insist, boon and blessing and – if they needed to take further their insistence, in order to continue – these would be purpose and confirmation of purpose. Max went beyond being a reason for living, he was a lived life. It was hard, without him, to see how there might be life at all. And his death, his glorious variety of possible deaths, preoccupied her more even than it had done immediately following his birth. Agatha thought up ways and ways he might just. And as the afternoon turned darker, Agatha began to think of killing Max. Her momentary revulsion was only that – momentary, and revulsion could be overcome, by focus, by hate. It was a possibility, and the only illusion before had been that it wasn't: she had often thought about killing Max, but always by terrible accident. Never before, not so far as she could remember, had the idea of deliberately ending his life come to her. And now, as he was in his cot taking his afternoon nap, all the accidents turned themselves into murders.

She felt dreadfully released – as if friction had disappeared entirely from the world of the house. Tidying up after Max's morning was a long, slow hallucination in which movement required no effort at all: her hands sliced through unresisting air, finding themselves at their destinations a moment before she expected. She *could*, kill him – she could, because there was nothing and no-one to stop her. For a giddy half-hour, she tried to find where her guilt had gone. It was necessary to force herself into Max's room, to look down upon his sleeping-breathing body. He was fine. In the strangest dislocated way, she felt he wouldn't be harmed by being killed – the harm was all in him continuing to live. His breathing was a little annoying, so fast, so grabbed. Wouldn't it be better, she thought, wouldn't it *solve* everything for all of them? Paddy would know what to do. She would have her choices made for her – would never have to go outside again. Max wouldn't have his wronged life. She wished his breathing would stop, so that she could return to hearing the house. He was still unknowingly asleep when she left his room; it annoyed her, in a minor additional way, that they hadn't managed to redecorate it before he moved in.

Agatha continued to tidy downstairs, aware that really she was doing something preparatory – to what? She was no longer sure. Max would need a bath, and that was all she began to think about. In detail, she considered how deeply it would be filled – how long she would have to leave the taps running. She was, she found, able to picture the bathroom in its every detail – down to the toothbrushes in the glass. She remembered how, once upon a time, she hadn't been content, setting off for work, unless she knew she'd made their toothbrushes, hers and Paddy's, kiss; forcing their bristles into one another. It seemed such a disgustingly cutesy thing to do, like calling Max 'the Monster'. The person she had become wouldn't be capable of doing something so twee; she didn't yet know what other capacities, in their stead, this new person had acquired.

Without letting herself think about it at all, she went to the phone and dialled May's number. Luckily, but not completely surprisingly, she was in. 'Can you come round?' Aggie asked, after the hellos.

'Why?' asked May. 'Is everything alright?'

'I think I'm going mad,' Aggie said. 'I think I've already gone mad – I'm thinking so many things.'

'Of course you're not mad,' May said. 'I'll be round in ten minutes, maybe fifteen. I'll have to bring Hope. Is that okay?'

Agatha almost used this as an excuse to say no, she was alright, she'd just had a panic. 'Come,' Aggie said, 'come quickly.'

Max woke up the moment she put the phone down, crying in a way she knew meant a full nappy. It was a plaintive wail, as if he'd been insulted by his own body and was fully aware of the indignity. With fear, Aggie went upstairs – she almost didn't want to allow herself to touch him. After the phonecall, there was now no difficulty with guilt; she hadn't had to find it, it had come looking for her. Lifting him from the cot, Max felt twice as heavy as usual – and it was an adult weight, though not in any way she could explain. She took him into the bathroom, where he immediately began screaming; the place still terrified him, for some reason. The automatism of nappy-changing did not happen: everything was clumsy – her movements, Max's kicks. There was so much shit, and he seemed determined to get it on her trousers. May would be there, with Hope, in five minutes; there was no time to change. 'Stop it, Max,' Agatha said, and in imagination hit him. Then she hit him – a straight slap across the face. For a second she thought he hadn't noticed. Perhaps she had done it gently enough for him to think it a game. But he started to cry, a big cry with a terrifying amount of momentum; this wouldn't stop before May arrived. She fought him clean, then into the nappy, before picking him up for a hug. For a pulse or two, she thought she'd have to be sick in the toilet bowl. 'Shh,' she said, 'shh, my baby boy.' What would May think if he were distraught like this, when she arrived? Aggie pulled his hands down and assured herself there wasn't yet a red mark on his face. Standing up, she looked down into the bath – perhaps this had been enough; no need for more. Just then, the doorbell rang. It was only when she opened it to May, Hope and the winter air that Aggie realised she had tears on her face right down to her chin.

May gave her a long, hard hug in the open door. 'Oh dear,' she said. 'What's wrong?' This was not a question Aggie could answer either immediately or honestly. She could feel Max holding onto one of her legs, slightly afraid of these new people.

They went inside, Hope carried through in her plastic basket; she was asleep, and May wanted her to stay that way so they could talk. Max, though, had recovered from his fear and was becoming playful. He very much wanted to grab hold of part of Hope, arm or leg, and shake her into life. For one terrible moment, Aggie – as she told him to stop! – thought he might be aiming to give her a slap. 'Come and sit here,' she said, and had Max imprisoned in her arms.

May continued asking what was wrong; if Aggie didn't want to talk about it, she thought, why had she phoned up? May would understand her not wanting to talk at all. She knew already about Paddy's father's death – Paddy had called Henry with the news. 'Everything's wrong,' said Aggie, exaggerating to deflect.

'The house isn't wrong,' May said, ignorantly. 'Max isn't.' She smiled at him and he, overcoming some of his adult-shyness, smiled back.

'I'm so alone,' Aggie said. 'I'm in so much trouble.' She

had wanted to say pain but had swerved off from the self-pity. In doing so, she'd said something appallingly close to the truth. May understood her to mean in trouble emotionally and took the slight melodramatic tone as a good sign: it wasn't humorous but it had a little of the old Aggie in it. 'With Paddy?' she asked, seeing no way of avoiding the name, even in front of Max.

'With myself,' Aggie replied.

'You're definitely not mad,' May said, aware that in a very short time, months, they wouldn't be able to talk this way with comprehending children around – even now it felt transgressive.

'How can I know?' Aggie said. 'It might be too late. I might be unsafe already.'

'Unsafe?' May couldn't understand.

'To Max,' Aggie said, 'to me.'

'How could you be a danger to Max?' May knew, vaguely, about Aggie's suicide attempts – they were long ago and could be filed under glamour.

'By being me.'

'You're his mother,' said May.

'I see,' said Aggie, in danger, she herself felt, of becoming very distant and allowing her mouth to say things she really didn't want said. 'You mean I'm inevitably a danger to him.'

'I mean you're not. You're a good mother.' Perhaps, Aggie thought, that was what was upsetting her most: after the slap, she couldn't help but see herself as a bad mother.

'I'm not,' she said.

'Look at him,' May said. 'Look how well he is.' Aggie looked at his cheek, checking again for a red mark – and this time thought she saw one, or rather two: shadow fingers. She wanted to take this as an opportunity of evidence, and confess to May, but couldn't: she was becoming annoyed at her friend – that she couldn't see through the situation any better.

'That's my mother's doing,' said Aggie. May didn't know where to go, though a change of subject would be wrong. She felt now that Aggie had had something specific to tell her, but that in her way of asking she had muffed it – persuaded Aggie not to. In doing so, she had harmed her friend. This was as far as she could understand: it was too late to take Aggie literally: mad. Agatha, too, had given up on the visit – and, a little, given up on May *as* a friend. Max got free of her but had lost interest in sleeping Hope. Instead, he went and started opening and closing the door to the back room. Whenever he slammed it, Agatha told him to be gentler – which he would be, for a bang or two. They talked for half an hour more but were never again likely to achieve much. Only right at the end, as Aggie apologised for not offering May anything to drink, did they come close: if this little neglect had taken place, both of them thought, what other ones were possible? But for May it appeared as neglect of society whereas Aggie felt it as neglect of love. 'It doesn't matter,' said May, very much wanting to insist that it did.

'Next time,' said Agatha, already thinking of ways she might put this off for as long as possible.

They were in the hall when, as a final attempt, Aggie asked May, 'Do you remember when we met?'

And May said, 'Yes – of course. We were at a –'

'I don't,' said Agatha. She smiled sadly at her friend. 'Do you see?'

May knew she had been left no way of answering and so left already thinking of her next, more successful visit.

But the remark had given her a sense of true dangers, and her final glance was towards Max.

With May safely gone, Agatha decided to give Max his bath straight away – there was no point putting it off. She carried him upstairs, screaming, into the bathroom and turned both taps on full. She couldn't yet tell whether this was routine or final – whether Max would soon be clean or not be. She began to try to undress him, which was difficult because he kept his elbows down and in, his knees touching. Another Agatha would have been able to flirt him out of his clothes; distractions would have been offered, a smooth flow of achieving talk. Now, it was resistance facing resistance, each with a clearer idea of what the other was about than what they were selfishly trying to do. Max wasn't consciously surviving but was passionate in his delaying of the future; Agatha, resisting his resistance, wondered whether the way Max was behaving – his brave little worst – would decide matters.

By the time the bath was full enough, Max was wild-seeming, red-faced and naked. Agatha, however, let the taps flow some more and then some more. This in itself wasn't an act but it could, if it so chose, become one. Max didn't seem to be any more scared of the unusually deep water than he had been of the bathroom as a whole: his forebodings of the place, Agatha saw, were probably about to come true – which made her wonder what exactly they had been, and disappointed that, even if Max were to survive, she would never properly find out.

The water had almost reached the overflow, so she turned the taps off and, by reflex, stuck her fingers in to test the temperature. It was colder than tepid – the hot had run out; Max wouldn't like it. And then she realised, quite horribly, that this might no longer matter: scald or shiver, his comfort was in the past – if.

She lifted Max into the water; he squealed as his feet touched the surface, then went quiet as the cold climbed his body. When he was fully in, he started squealing again – but this was no longer resistance, it was horrible pleading and Agatha wanted it to stop. Her son was a greater force than this – capable, if he wanted, of destroying the world. She was ashamed of how easily he had given in to her, to death if she was death. This weakness of his made her, for an instant, entirely despise him – and then she rebounded into compassion; not as if he was her child, as if he were anybody's that she had been entrusted with bathing. But again she changed into hate: he should be more to her than just anybody's – he should be sacred with life. She put her hand on the crown of his head, thinking at that moment that it had been the very first part of him to enter the world. Push him under or pull him out? She held herself there for longer than was in any way usual. Max would know – Max would sense something about to happen; it would be mad if he didn't. The sense of freedom was hard to distinguish from the sense of all this already having happened. She wanted Max to convince her of the worth of living, and in himself, by being himself, he just couldn't do that any more. This was so terrible, this one hopeless thought. Oh, she wanted Paddy to come through the front door and stop her stupid experiment – and this was exactly what happened. Now he was coming through the door, not the front door but the bathroom door, and she hadn't heard him in the hall, or on the stairs. She had no time to pull Max from the cruelly cold bath, to calm him and normalize him. Now he was close beside her and now, together, they were lifting Max from the water, up in their arms, water going everywhere, not mattering. He knew – he must know. She helped him carry Max into their bedroom, where they wrapped him in one of their huge white towels. It was strange: Max wasn't shivering or crying, he was laughing – and Paddy, perhaps, was magically turning the whole thing into a fun game. They weren't tickling Max but he was laughing as if they were: laughing with a tensed stomach, laughing against. 'You came back early,' said Aggie. 'Why?' But Paddy didn't answer because Paddy wasn't there, and the hands which had saved Max seemed to have been hers alone.

# CHAPTER 25

W HEN Paddy really came back, Aggie didn't confess – not because she felt nothing had happened; she knew it had, and that it had been defining. But because she also knew, as certainly as she'd ever known anything, that it was conclusive. Max was saved; Max was safe. Her attitude to him had in a moment changed. With some guilt, she realised the sense of release she now felt was similar to that after her failed suicide attempts. They, looking back, had become cyclical, addictive. What happened with Max could only be a single occurrence: she had gone through it and now she was purged of it, permanently. One of the most important things was not to spend time doubting this. She had been changed both by what happened and what almost happened – most of all, by how close that almost had been. But in a nearly miraculous way, she felt, she had been changed *back*. Something inside her felt reset; what she had been so long lacking had become possible again: the sense of a start. There had nearly been an end – a really final one. With that danger gone, all was potential.

She welcomed Paddy home with restraint – euphoria would panic him, she knew. It was better, gently, to have the realisation come that there were things he need no longer worry about, or fear. Not only was Max safe, she was safe, too.

Despite being tired from the journey and emotionally exhausted by all the arrangements he'd had to make, Paddy was almost immediately aware that Aggie was better. She looked better, for a start – she looked as if health were not exactly hers but a thing that could be hers. There was a new clarity about her; not just her skin, her eyes. His insight didn't go far enough to see this as a renewal, although he knew she'd got it back from somewhere. Right but wrong at the same time, he attributed the change to Max. It worried him he had had to be away himself for this to happen, but he was too generous not to be glad. 'How are you?' – he was careful to ask this before asking about Max, who he assumed was asleep upstairs.

'I'm fine,' Aggie said. Then she asked him about his trip. She found she was almost desperate to hear, not just to hear his news but to hear him speak – but she knew he wanted to go and see his son, so she took him by the hand and led him all the way to the crib.

On the stairs, Paddy thought they might be going to bed, and he was so tired, but the turn into Max's room felt right as well as a relief. They stood for quite a while, silently looking.

Afterwards, they came downstairs and ate the food Aggie had made.

It was time for them to have the conversation. Neither of them had planned it, but it was happening in sync with both their thoughts: Aggie anxious it was coming too early, Paddy relieved it was happening at all.

'We've had a rough time,' Paddy said, not intending the start, and achieving it all the more efficiently.

'Oh God,' Aggie replied. They were now sitting at opposite ends of the sofa but facing in towards one another. On the floor were finished glasses of red wine – a quarter-full bottle; Max had been checked on and was safely asleep: nothing was there to restrain. 'God-God-God, yes.'

'Are you still thinking about Him – about God?'

'Less and less.'

'I suppose I should say "good".'

'I'll say it for you. It's just, now I have to live with all of everything – I can't parcel any of it off.'

'To put it in a box and address it.' Aggie was mildly astonished Paddy had come this close to her imagery; then, all at once, she remembered how common this had once been for them – how coincidence was what they were. This had been one of their jokes: without consulting, they would both come back at the end of the day with bags of identical food – even when they'd been anticipating this possibility, and trying to buy something the other wouldn't ever think of, something disgusting: curry pizza, tinned oysters.

'That's exactly how I always thought of it,' she confessed, with a smile of deep encouragement. 'Which is why I knew I was cheating.'

'Have you given up on it?'

'On God?'

'On the box.'

'You are my box – and don't pretend you're not, or that you don't know it.' The modulation into flirting didn't completely surprise Paddy, as it would have done even a few hours before. 'That's not an easy job,' he said.

'But in return you get me as your box.' On this, they each took a quick eye-journey inside the other's head – couldn't not.

'Yes, I do,' said Paddy, but still in hope. 'That can't be an easy job, either.'

'You don't use me enough,' she said.

'And you, the past few months, you've hardly used me at all.'

'Well,' she said, 'I thought you were full.'

'This is a bit silly,' Paddy said. 'Boxes.'

'But they're true: I thought I'd break you if I put any more in – split your sides.'

'We've both been trying to protect the other . . .'

'When they didn't need it.' Aggie managed to make this both a question and a conclusive statement. Paddy wasn't prepared to seem sure. 'Perhaps I did – it was so bad, so fucking awful.'

Aggie was glad Paddy had started to swear: it would make the rest of their talk freer – she could be more sloppy in what she said and hit her accuracies with greater sting. 'Was it worse than now, your father?'

'That's different. I have to deal with the guilt of wanting that – and the fact that part of me is almost celebrating it. I knew my father, and I knew what he felt about it.' Aggie was prepared to let Paddy speak at any length – the rest of the evening, if he wanted. 'But how can you mourn something that hasn't lived? You can't, logically. You haven't known it – and so you're mourning a possibility, or you're mourning all the possibilities it could have contained, which are infinite, as far as you can see them. That was why it was such a relief to know she had been a girl; because some, not 50 per cent, but some of those possibilities died. It's very hard mourning an infinite being – and it's very hard,' he wanted to drop his level, one he'd never reached before, 'to say these sorts of things. They seem to come out the wrong shape, as if I'm trying to make us into something special – and we both know, now, how many –' He stopped.

'They can't speak like you,' Aggie said. 'You said that so well.' She could cry, she knew, but it was delightful – part of the conversation, and to show him his effect. He didn't move towards her; his instinct was right. 'I think,' she said, 'it was like that for me, too. But also more specific. Not just that she was inside me, and I wanted to feel and so get to know her – I felt I did, and I'll never know if I was right.'

'Oh, that's so sad,' Paddy said, stating his heart.

'I know.'

It could have ended there, the conversation; they were reconciled enough, at least for the time being. But Aggie still felt she had to say, 'I hated you so much.' Paddy had known but hadn't expected this. He didn't reply. 'And it was impossible you didn't hate me, too. I treated you despicably.'

He allowed himself, 'No . . .'

'But you didn't seem worth treating with respect.'

'That's pretty harsh.'

'I know – I'm sorry. You didn't. I thought somehow you should have been able to intervene directly – to force me to feel differently. When you couldn't, I hated you even more: you were weak. I needed you to do it for Max. I blamed you for the way I was treating him – which was unbelievable.'

'Which,' said Paddy, 'was why I came close to hating you.'

'It's good to have him here.'

'At last.'

'If that's the most you're going to say.'

'He *has* changed,' Paddy said, 'and I don't think for the better. Whatever he is, it's our fault, yours *and* mine; we have to cope.'

'Coping's not enough; we have to redeem.'

The truth of this was hardest for Paddy to accept, not its excessiveness – though it was far beyond the comfort of usual conversation.

'I think I've been trying to do that from the start,' he said, 'right from when he was born.'

'And only now we realise we didn't need to.'

'Not *he* was redeeming *us*?'

'No. He didn't care. And now we're going to be corrupted by our own good motives – because we can't not care, and he's become too important. We don't have to redeem for him, that again is too much. It's for ourselves, and then it will be for him.'

'Do we start by forgiving?' he asked.

'I suppose so. It's obvious, but we'll probably have to get used to that again – the shopping, normal days: I've been so perverse – not having him here when . . .'

'It wouldn't have been better. Not until now.'

'We might have learnt something,' she said.

'Or broken it.'

'He's strong, as long as we don't keep working at making him weak. We have to accept all the possibilities. Yes, he could die. So could we. We live with that but we live outside it, too. He lives outside it all the time, and we have to let him. I'm starting to think I can. It's not exactly a trick, because I have to believe in it so deeply – both that he's safe and that he's unprotectable. His heart has to beat without my help. As much as I want to be inside him, checking it's all working. And it's the same with the rest.'

'We won't interfere with each other, you don't think?'

'No,' she said. 'The opposite. If we know, we can help – help *not* to, most of the time.'

'You'll be annoyed with me.'

'I will, but not for long. I never am – not for more than half a year.'

He laughed at the acknowledged pain.

# CHAPTER 26

A BRIEF discussion on the phone had made the whole
funeral morning, in advance.

'We can come round and pick you up,' said May, 'from
your house – right from the front door. In the car.'

'No,' said Aggie. 'We'll walk over to you. We'd like to
walk.' She, changed, was aware Paddy was listening at her
end, and that Henry at the other would very soon hear.

'Are you sure?' asked May. 'We don't mind. You don't
have to carry Max all that way.'

'It isn't far, is it?' Aggie asked both Paddy and May.

'No,' said May. 'Well . . .' said Paddy.

'We'll be round in about an hour,' Aggie said, definitely
and definite in her wish to avoid pathos.

Half an hour later, the three of them were standing in the
hall – although Paddy wasn't sure he was ready, and Aggie's
doubts had begun before she said goodbye to May. About
other things, she was certain. Paddy must know – Paddy
must be told if he did not know already: about what had
happened, and how she had come to explain it to herself;
about the house, the breathing, the scrapes, the object. This
was necessary, both for their future together and for its basis
in a past during part of which she had been so separate from
him. Oversimplification was a pleasure, now, as well as a
danger; true complexity would be one of her ambitions,
telling. She thought he *did* know – *must* know something.
When they got back from the funeral, when Max was
asleep, when the others had gone, when the anticipated
moment arrived – as she relied upon it doing, with the
house's help – they would talk, again. But this time, she

would try her best to exhaust the truth. If a whole night were necessary, Paddy would listen a whole night; listen, in a way, just as she had listened. This, Aggie knew; in this, she found the whole of her security – Paddy had always been patient.

'Ready?' he asked. Max was excited at the prospect of outside. He made familiar noises and bounced in a very Maxlike way.

'I think so,' said Aggie, trying to strengthen herself by admitting vulnerability.

'You don't have to,' Paddy said, and he saw how dutiful and pitiful he was; this didn't displease him.

'No,' she said, 'I do.' She nodded, and he understood – going and opening the door for her.

She picked up Max and took Paddy's hand, although he would have to let go when he locked the house behind them.

Aggie stepped forwards onto the doorstep, which she was aware had always been there as simply as this, and would always have been as physically simple to cross. She sensed Paddy's patience behind her – how he would be prepared to arrive late at the funeral, perhaps even miss it, if that was what was necessary to bring her back to life. Paddy sensed what Aggie must be feeling; it was a similar panic to his the first time he took newborn Max outside. Then, he had begun to understand the instinct behind right-wing thought: all of this outsideness needed to be repressed – it was unspeakable it should be allowed to continue, wildly; discipline was required. Make it safe; make it completely incapable of harming the important things, most important of which was Max; make it Switzerland. He didn't want to infantilize Aggie, but he now felt a similar protectiveness towards her. Why did everything have to be as it was? Why did it have to be so aggressive? The world, the moment they were out of the front door, would be upon them – it would be all they could do to hold together. Aggie was very aware of the sky. She had lived for what seemed like so long with ceilings instead; apart from those brief and relatively recent times in the garden with Max, and even then they had been canopied by the branches of the appletree. The street, she knew, was certainly going to be bizarre to her – bizarrely exposed (not just her to it but it to her). She stood there on the threshold, feeling how much space would soon be around her, and also how the surfaces there – dirty, gritty, detailed – would press in upon her eyes. But Paddy remembered what he had realised, the first time out with Max: all this terror on his son's behalf was his own shame, nothing to do with Max-in-the-world. Happily, happily, the little boy would lick back at the tongues of strange dogs, run to embrace oncoming cars, become deranged with excitement when a shop window showed him himself and his father, in the world. And Aggie, too, felt for the first in a long time, exhilarated by the possible dangers of the world, and of her dangerous presence in it. The world would remain with her, would not protect her, might harm her, *would* harm her, but she would express herself – from now on – by joyous resistance and if not that by stubborn participation.

Agatha stepped onto the garden path, carrying Max; Paddy followed after, hand almost touching her shoulder. They were a family, vulnerable but also a world in themselves; not cohesive in any way apart from love: damaged, repaired, continuing.

With which at last I give them all three entirely to you – they will need your protection, now, and even more, your imagination; without it, they are strong but stuck, can exist but lack: let them live a while longer, forget them slowly.